D0296205

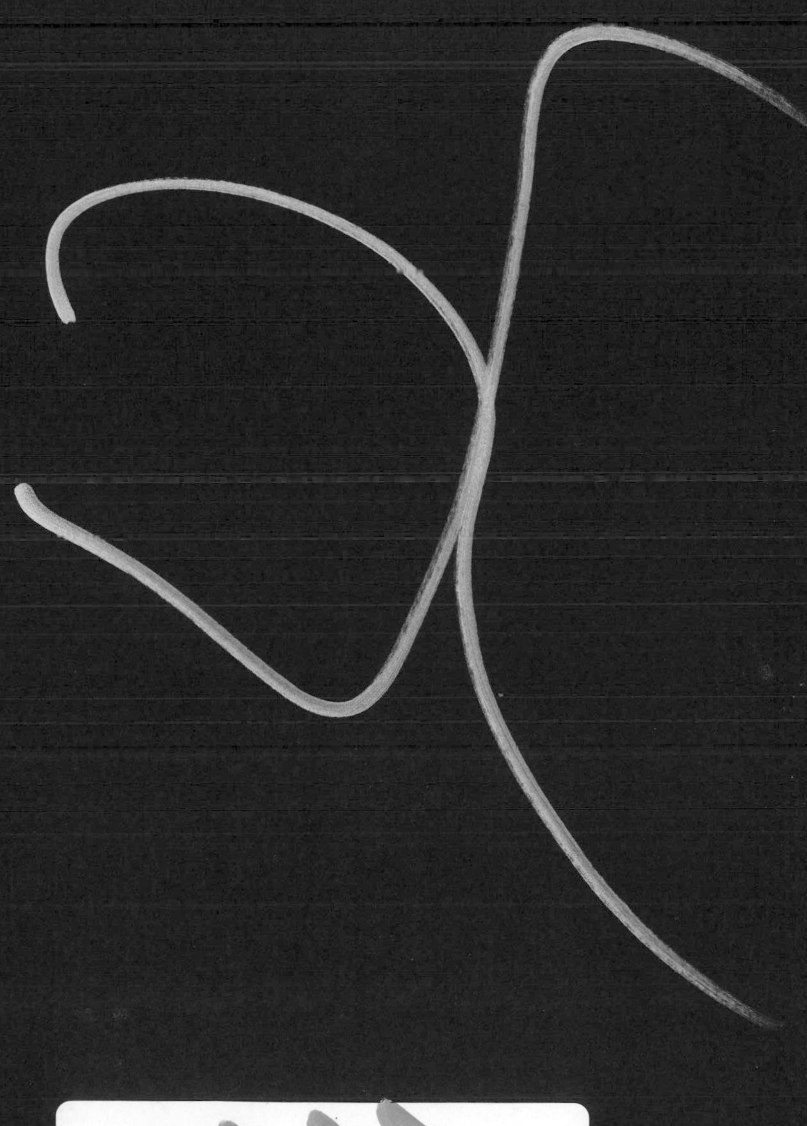

04139234

A BIT OF DIFFERENCE

A BIT OF DIFFERENCE

SEFI ATTA

FOURTH ESTATE · *London*

FOURTH ESTATE
An imprint of HarperCollins*Publishers*
77–85 Fulham Palace Road,
Hammersmith, London W6 8JB
www.4thestate.co.uk

First published in Great Britain by Fourth Estate 2014
First published in the US by Interlink Books 2013

1

A catalogue record for this book is available from the British Library.

ISBN 978-0-00-753103-5

Typeset in Quadraat OT by Palimpsest Book Production Limited,
Falkirk, Stirlingshire

Printed and bound in Great Britain by Clays Ltd, St Ives plc

For my father Abdul-Aziz Atta,
forty years in memoriam

A Bit of Difference

Reorientation

The great ones capture you. This one is illuminated and magnified. It is a photograph of an African woman with desert terrain behind her. She might be Sudanese or Ethiopian. It is hard to tell. Her hair is covered with a yellow scarf and underneath her image is a caption: 'I Am Powerful.'

An arriving passenger at the Atlanta airport momentarily obscures the photograph. She has an Afro, silver hoops the size of bangles in her ears and wears a black pin-striped trouser suit. She misses the name of the charity the photograph advertises and considers going back to get another look, but her legs are resistant after her flight from London and her shoulder is numb from the weight of her handbag and laptop.

She was on the plane for nine hours and someone behind her suffered from flatulence. The Ghanaian she sat next to fell silent once she mentioned she was Nigerian. At Immigration, they photographed her face and took prints of her left and right index fingers. She reminded herself of the good reasons why as she waited in the line for visitors, until an Irish man in front of her turned around and said, 'This is a load of bollocks.' She only smiled. They might have been on camera and it was safe for him, despite the skull tattoos on his arm.

I am powerful, she thinks. What does that mean? Powerful enough to grab the attention of a passerby, no doubt. She hopes the woman in the photograph was paid more than enough and imagines posters with the prime minister at Number Ten and the president in the Oval Office with the same caption underneath, 'I Am Powerful.' The thought makes her wince as she steps off the walkway.

She has heard that America is a racist country. She does not understand why people rarely say this about England. On her previous trips to other cities like New York, DC and LA, she hasn't found Americans especially culpable, only more inclined to talk about the state of their race relations. She has also heard Atlanta is a black city, but so far she hasn't got that impression.

At the carousel, a woman to her right wears cowry shell earrings. The woman's braids are thick and grey and her dashiki is made of mud cloth. On her other side is a man who is definitely a Chip or a Chuck. He has the khakis and Braves cap to prove it, and the manners. He helps an elderly man who struggles with his luggage, while a Latina, who looks like a college student, refuses to budge and tosses her hair back as if she expects others to admire her. There is a couple with an Asian baby. The baby sticks a finger up her nostril while sucking on her thumb.

It takes her a while to get her luggage and she ends up behind a Nigerian woman whose luggage is singled out for an X-ray before hers is.

'Any *garri* or *egusi*?' a customs official asks the woman playfully.

'No,' the woman replies, tucking her chin in, as if she is impressed by his pronunciation.

'*Odabo*,' the customs official says and waves after he inspects her luggage.

The woman waves back. The camaraderie between them is tantamount to exchanging high fives. Before 9/11 he might have hauled her in for a stomach X-ray.

'Will you step this way, ma'am?' he asks, beckoning.

Walking into the crowd at the arrival lobby makes her eyes sting. She always has this reaction to crowds. It is like watching a bright light, but she has learned to stem the flow of tears before it begins, the same way she slips into a neutral mood when she sees Anne Hirsch holding that piece of paper with her surname, Bello. She approaches Anne and can tell by Anne's involuntary 'Oh', that she is not quite the person Anne is expecting.

'It's nice to meet you,' Anne says, shaking her hand.

Anne is wearing contact lenses. Her grey hairs are visible in her side part and the skin on her neck is flushed. She looks concerned, as if she is meeting a terminally ill patient.

'You, too.'

'Now, is it . . . Dee- or Day-ola?'

'Day.'

Anne may well begin to curse and kick and Deola would merely take a step back. It surprises her how naturally this habit of detaching herself from her colleagues comes. They walk outdoors and into the humidity and racket of the ground transportation zone, two women in sensible suits and pumps. Anne waddles – she is pigeon-toed – and Deola strides as if she has been prompted to stand up straight.

'How was your flight?' Anne asks.

'Not bad,' Deola says.

Lying like this is also instinctive. She wouldn't want to

come across as a whiner. A bus roars past, the heat from its exhaust pipes enveloping them.

'Did you get enough sleep?' Anne asks.

'I did, thanks.'

Anne regards her sideways. 'I'm sure a few more hours won't hurt.'

Deola's face has revealed more than she would like. They head towards the loading bay as Anne suggests she go to her hotel and start her review the next morning.

'If that's all right with you,' she says.

'Of course,' Anne says.

'Thanks,' Deola says.

She has been working at LINK for three months, following a lacklustre stint in a consultancy that specialized in not-for-profit organizations. LINK, an international charity foundation, has a hierarchy, but not one that encourages rivalry as the accountancy firm she trained in did. LINK's money comes from well-meaning sources and goes out to well-deserving causes. She is the director of internal audit at the London office and Anne is the director of international affairs at the Atlanta office.

Anne leaves her at the loading bay and returns with her car, a cream-coloured Toyota Camry. The mat on Deola's side of the car is clean compared to Anne's, which is covered with sand. Anne has changed into sandals and her feet are pale, even though it is summer.

'So how is Kate doing?' she asks, as she drives off.

'Kate's very well,' Deola says. 'She's back at work this week.'

Kate Meade is Anne's counterpart in the London office. She is pregnant with her second child and was sick with toxoplasmosis.

'It must be catching,' Anne says.

'Toxoplasmosis?'

'No, pregnancy, I mean. When last we spoke she said someone else in London has been on maternity leave. Pamela?'

'Pam Collins.'

'It must have been hard, with all the absences.'

'Pam will be back soon.'

'Yes?'

'Yes. She's just had her baby.'

Deola could be more forthcoming, but she prefers not to talk about her colleagues. Pam is on maternity leave until the end of the summer. The administrative department has been in a state of backlog. There was some talk about hiring a temp, but Kate decided not to. They had a temp from New Zealand once before and he took too many cigarette breaks.

'Ali and I would like to have one,' Anne says. 'What did Pam have?'

'Um . . . a boy, I believe.'

'Ah, a boy. That's what I would like. Ali wants a girl.'

Deola assumes Anne is married to a Muslim man, which makes her regret her moment of anxiety when, on her way to the bathroom on the plane, she saw a man who looked Arab reading an Arabic-to-English translation dictionary. He was dressed in military khakis. She was not the only passenger giving him furtive looks. Now she wonders if he was working for the US government.

She has reservations about the orange alert the US is on. She has referred to the alerts in general as Banana Republic scare tactics, like Idi Amin or Papa Doc trying to keep people in check with rumours of juju and voodoo, and has compared the Iraq war casualties to Mobutu sacrificing human blood to the gods to ensure his longevity in office. She is in the US to learn how the Atlanta office managed their launch of Africa Beat, an HIV awareness campaign. She and Anne talk about the UK launch, which is a few months away. Her colleagues in Atlanta have not been able to send all their financial records by e-mail or to explain figures via the phone.

Stewart 'Stone' Riley is the US spokesman for Africa Beat. His biography reads like a rocker's creed: born in a small town, formed a group in high school, suffered under commercialization, was crucified by the press, rumoured to be dead, rose again in the charts and the rest of it. He claims he is influenced by rhythm and blues. Deola has heard his music and it sounds nothing like the R&B she listened to in the eighties, music with a beat she can dance to. In London, the spokesperson for Africa Beat is Dára, a hip-hop singer. He is Nigerian, but because of the accent over his name and his tendency to drop his H's, Anne mistakes him for French West African. Deola tells Anne he is Yoruba.

'Dára?' Anne says, stressing the first syllable of his name instead of the last. 'Really?'

'His name means "beautiful". It is short for "beautiful child".'

'That's appropriate,' Anne says. 'He is very beautiful.'

Deola does not know one Nigerian who thinks Dára is beautiful. They say he looks like a bush boy, not to mention his questionable English. It is almost as if they are angry he is accepted overseas for the very traits that embarrass them.

'Do you speak the language, then?' Anne asks, hesitantly.

'Yes.'

'I thought you were British.'

'Me? No.'

She tells Anne she was born in Nigeria and grew up there. She went to school in England in her teens, got her degree from the London School of Economics and has since lived and worked in London. She doesn't say she has a British passport, that she swore allegiance to the Queen to get one and would probably have got down on her knees at the Home Office and begged had her application been denied.

'You see yourself as Nigerian, then,' Anne says.

'Absolutely,' Deola says.

She has never had any doubts about her identity, though other people have. She has yet to encounter an adequate description of her status overseas. Resident alien is the closest. She definitely does not see herself as British. Perhaps she is a Nigerian expatriate in London.

'Atlanta doesn't have any programs in Nigeria,' Anne says.

'London doesn't either.'

'I suppose that's because you haven't been approached.'

'Actually.' This slips out with a laugh. 'The management team doesn't trust Nigerians.'

Anne frowns. 'Oh, I'm not so sure about that. It's the government they don't trust, but it's a shame to hold NGOs responsible for that. I mean, they are just trying to raise funds for . . . for these people, who really don't need to be punished any more than they have been already.'

Deola tells herself she must not say the word 'actually' again on this trip. 'Actually' will only lead to another moment of frankness, one that might end in antagonism. Nor will she say the words 'these people' so long as she works for LINK or ever in her life.

She tells Anne that Kate Meade is considering a couple of programs in Nigeria. One is to prevent malaria in children and the other is for women whose husbands have died from AIDS. The London office funds programmes in Kenya, South Africa and other African countries that have a record for being what they call 'fiscally reliable'.

'Do you like living in London?' Anne asks.

'I do,' Deola says, after a pause.

'It's very European these days.'

'It is also very American.'

'How?'

'You know, with hip-hop and the obsession with celebrities.'

Anne shuts her eyes. 'Ugh!'

Sincerity like this is safe. As a Nigerian, Deola, too, is given to unnecessary displays of humiliation.

'Do you think you will ever go back to Nigeria?' Anne asks.

Deola finds the question intrusive, but she has asked herself this whenever she can't decide if what she really needs is a change in location, rather than a new job.

'Eventually,' she says.

Atlanta is more traditional and landlocked than she imagined it to be, with its concrete flyovers, greenery and red-brick churches. She had envisaged a modern, aquatic city because of the name, which sounds similar to that futuristic series that was on television in the seventies, *Man from Atlantis*. Downtown, she counts three people who are mentally ill. The common signs are there: unkempt hair, layers of clothing and that irresolute demeanour whether they are crossing the median, rolling a pushcart up Ponce de Leon or standing by a dusty windowpane. It is like London of the Thatcher years.

Her hotel is on Peachtree, some ten minutes away from the Atlanta office. Anne will shuttle her there and back tomorrow. She thanks Anne for giving her a lift from the airport and arranges to meet her in the lobby the next morning. At the reception area, she joins the line and checks into a single room with a queen-sized bed. She inspects the room after putting her suitcase down. She prods and rubs the furniture and unclasps her bra. She needs to buy new underwear. She knows a Nigerian couple in Atlanta she could call, but she finds them enamoured with consumerism – cars, houses, shops and credit cards. They brag about living in America, as if they need to make Nigerians elsewhere feel they have lost out.

She turns on the television and switches from one cable station to another. She clicks on one called the Lifetime Movie Network. The film showing is *She Woke Up Pregnant* and the subtitle reads: 'A pregnancy for which she cannot account tears a woman's family apart.' She turns to another station. Surprisingly, a Nigerian Pentecostal pastor is preaching. He is dressed in a white three-piece suit and his shoes are also white. His hair is gelled back and his skin is bleached.

'Stay with me,' he says, coaxing his congregation. 'Stay with me, now. I'm getting there. I'm getting there. Oh, y'all thought I was already there? Y'all thought I was through delivering my message this morning? I haven't even got started! I haven't even got started with y'all yet!'

He ends with a wail and his congregation erupts in cheers. A man waves his Bible and a woman bends over and trembles.

Deola smiles. Nigerians are everywhere.

Tonight, she dreams she has accidentally murdered Dára and deliberately buried his remains in her backyard and she alone knows the secret. The police are searching for him and the newspaper headlines are about his mysterious disappearance. The newspapers spin around as they do in 1950s black-and-white films until their headlines blur. She wakes up and tosses for hours.

The next morning, she is still sleepy when she meets Anne in the lobby, but she tells Anne she is well rested. Anne grumbles about the price of her Starbucks latte on the way to the office and sips at intervals.

'The problem is, I'm hooked on the stuff. And it's not as if you can go cold turkey, because the temptation is everywhere.'

'London has been taken over by Starbucks,' Deola says.

She has heard some requests for a latte that are worth recording: 'Grand-day capu-chin-know.'

'That's a shame,' Anne says. 'I'll be there next month and I know I won't be able to help myself.'

'Isn't Rio having their launch next month?'

'Yes. I'll be there for that.'

'Do they have Starbucks over there?'

'I hope not.'

The Atlanta office is also on Peachtree. People in the elevator glare at them as they hurry towards it – the usual disdain inhabitants of cramped spaces have, followed by a general shyness. They all look downward.

The reception wall has the logo of the foundation's network, two linked forefingers. The office is mostly open-plan space with workstations. Deola meets Susan and Linda, who are also auditors. Susan is a CPA who trained with an accountancy firm and Linda has a banking background.

'Don't you think she sounds British?' Anne asks them.

'Well,' Susan says, 'there's some Nigerian there.'

There is some Chinese in Susan's voice. Her thick-rimmed glasses are stylish. Her jacket is too big for her and her slender fingers poke out of her sleeves.

'I think she sounds British,' Anne says.

'She sounds like herself,' Linda says.

Her braids are thin and arranged into a neat doughnut shape on her crown.

There is a Linda in every office, Deola thinks, who will not waste time showing a newcomer how much her boss annoys her. Why she remains with her boss is understandable. How she thinks she can get away with terrorizing her boss is another matter.

'I should say English,' Anne says. 'What does British mean anyway? It could be Irish or Welsh.'

'I don't think Ireland is part of Great Britain,' Susan says, blinking with each word.

'Scottish, I mean,' Anne says.

'I can't understand the Glaswegian accent,' Deola says.

'I couldn't understand a word anyone said to me in Scotland,' Anne says.

'They probably wouldn't understand a word we say over here,' Linda says.

Deola notices leaflets on 'commercial sex workers' and is conscious of being between generations. Old enough to have witnessed some change in what is considered appropriate. Her colleagues walk her through their system and she reverts to her usual formality. They show her invoices, vouchers and printouts. It is not relevant that they are in the business of humanitarianism. There are debits and credits, checks and balances. Someone has to make sure they work and identify fraud risks, then make recommendations to the executive team.

As an audit trainee, she was indifferent to numbers, even after she followed their paper trails to assets and verified their existence. How connected could anyone be to bricks, sticks, vats and plastic parts? Her firm had a client who did PR for the Cannes Film Festival and it was the same experience working for them. With Africa Beat, the statistics on HIV ought to have an impact on her and they do, but only marginally. The numbers in the brochure are in decimals. They represent millions. The fractions are based on national populations. Deola knows the virus afflicts Africa more than any other continent, women more than men and the young more than the old. Her examination of the brochure is cursory. She has seen it before and it is the same whenever she watches the news. Expecting more would be like asking her to bury her head into a pile of dirt and willingly take a deep breath in.

Ali is a woman – or a Southern girl, as Anne refers to her. Her name is Alison. Deola doesn't find out until later in the evening when Anne treats her to dinner at a Brazilian restaurant. Ali is from Biloxi, Mississippi, and she is a florist. Anne is from Buffalo, New York, and she used to be a teacher there. They don't watch television.

'We haven't had one for . . . let's see . . . five, six years now,' Anne says. 'We read the newspapers and listen to NPR to keep up with what's going on.'

'I watch too much television,' Deola says.

She chides herself for finding belated clues in Anne's stubby fingernails as Anne gesticulates, so she brings up the title of the Lifetime Movie Network film.

'I thought, this has got be a joke. She woke up pregnant?'

'The networks in general don't credit women with any intelligence,' Anne says. 'Mothers especially.'

'I can well imagine,' Deola says.

Their table is under what looks like mosquito netting dotted with lights. Behind them is a fire with meat rotating on spits. The waiters wear red scarves around their necks and walk over once in a while with a leg of lamb, pork roast, filet mignon, scallops, shrimp and chicken wrapped in bacon. The bacon is more fatty than Deola is used to.

'But we can't decide who gets pregnant,' Anne says. 'So wouldn't that be perfect if one of us wakes up and boom?'

Deola has finished eating her salad, but she picks at the remnants of her grilled peppers and mushrooms as the thought of artificial insemination diminishes her appetite. Or perhaps it is the realization that she might one day have to consider the procedure, if she remains single for much longer.

This is an unexpected connection to Anne, but she won't talk about her own urge to nest, which has preoccupied her lately. Anne might regard what she has to say with anthropological curiosity: the African woman's perspective.

'There's always adoption,' she says, wondering if this is appropriate.

'I did think of that,' Anne says. 'You get on a plane and go to a country that is war-torn or struggling with an epidemic and see so many orphans, so many of them. But at the end of the day, you have to have the humility to say to yourself, "Maybe I am not the person to raise this kid. Maybe America is not the place to raise him or her." You have to ask yourself these questions.'

'You must,' Deola says, crossing her arms, as if to brace herself for more of Anne's rectitude.

'It's that mindset,' Anne says. 'Our way is best, everyone else be damned, the world revolves around us. But I think when you travel widely enough, you quickly begin to realize it *don't*, don't you think?'

Deola reaches for her wine glass and almost says the word 'actually', but she stops herself this time. 'Actually', the tongue jolt. 'Actually', the herald of assertions. She could insist that America is torn apart by the war and she could easily challenge Anne's assumption that the rest of the world is incapable of transgressions.

'I expect people in England are more open-minded,' Anne says.

'England? I'm not so sure.'

'I guess it would be more obvious to you living there. But that's why we are in such a mess over here, and it's a question of being able to reorient yourself. That's all it takes.'

'A little reorientation,' Deola says, the rim of her glass between her lips.

'You know?' Anne says. 'If there is one thing this job teaches you, it's that. You can't get caught up in your own . . . whatever it is. Not in a world where people starve.'

'No,' Deola murmurs.

It is just as well she hesitated. She finishes her wine; so

does Anne. A waiter approaches their table with dessert menus. Anne says she really shouldn't and opts for a black coffee. Deola has the passion fruit crème brûlée and asks for fresh raspberries on top.

Actually

An incident on her flight back to London reminds her of something that happened a month ago during her first trip for LINK.

She was in Delhi to audit a charity for children. She stayed at the Crowne Plaza hotel and had enough time on her last day to ride in a rickshaw and visit Janpath Market with the programme director, who later drove her to the airport. She had just joined the departure line when she saw an American ahead of her, who was wearing – of all garbs – a cream linen suit and a panama. The American grabbed an Indian man, who was edging his way to the line, by the shoulders and steered him away. 'No-oo,' he said, as if he were speaking to his son. The Indian man went to the back of the line without saying a word. A moment later, a couple of Americans walked up. One was complaining, loud enough for everyone to hear, that he was going to miss his flight, and the man in the panama stepped back so they could get ahead of him.

What happens on her way to London is that she is again standing in line, this time to board her plane out of Atlanta, when a man cuts ahead of her. He is tanned with grey sideburns and is dressed in a navy jacket and striped shirt – executive-looking and clutching a John Grisham novel. She is three passengers from the flight attendant, a black American woman, who is checking boarding passes. When it is her turn, the flight attendant looks at her, looks at the man, who is still not in line, and takes his boarding pass first.

She is tempted to snatch her stub from the flight attendant, but she doesn't. She eyes the man once she gets on the plane, but he is too busy pushing his hand luggage into an overhead compartment to notice. She brushes past him before he sits. She is loath to say an incident so trivial amounted to discrimination – it wasn't that straightforward, was it? – but she thinks it anyway.

Only after the plane takes off and levels out is she able to reason that it might have been an innocent oversight. Then she remembers her conversation with Anne the previous night, which remained one-sided. Anne paid attention whenever she spoke and seemed eager to hear her opinions. Why couldn't she be more responsive to her? Was it that learned lack of trust? That resistance to being misinterpreted and diminished? Hardly, she decides. She was merely being expedient.

She sleeps most of the flight to London. It is Saturday morning when she arrives and the rain is a light spray. On the Gatwick Express she shuts her eyes while enjoying the motion and identifies the languages that people on mobile phones are speaking. There's French, Igbo and Portuguese. London is like the Tower of Babel these days. Still, she prefers it to the London she moved to in the eighties, despite the latent resentment she observes when people quicken their pace past a group of rowdy Pakistani teenagers or the Romanian mothers who beg.

She also detects some guilt, that aftertaste of the sumptuous meal that was empire. England is overrun with immigrants: African and Eastern European children they granted asylum are leading gangs, Islamic clerics are bragging about their rights and the English can barely open their mouths to talk.

Nigerians can never be that sorry for their transgressions, so sorry that they can't say to immigrants, 'Carry your trouble and go.' Nigerians made beggars out of child refugees from Niger and impregnated their mothers. Nigerians kicked out Ghanaians when Ghanaians became too efficient, taking over jobs Nigerians couldn't do, and named a laundry bag after the mass exodus: the Ghana Must Go bag. Nigerians aren't even sorry about the civil war. They are still blaming that on the British.

She takes a taxi from Victoria Station. Her flat in Willesden Green is walking distance from the tube. The Jubilee line is partly why she bought here. Initially, Willesden Green did not appeal to her, coming from her parents' flat in Westminster. The pavements were filthy with litter, cigarette butts, spit and dust. But there was a black hair salon and a cosmetics shop that sold products for black hair, containing ingredients like hemp and placenta. There were also a few Halal butchers and a West Indian shop where she could buy yams, plantains and cherry peppers. On Saturdays, she would walk to the library centre to study for her exams and take breaks at Café Gigi. Now, the centre has Belle Vue Cinema and the pavements are cleaner. Occasionally, she sees other Nigerians at the minicab office and the African textile shops, which can be comforting.

The woman she bought the flat from had a cat. She didn't find out until she moved in that there were cat hairs embedded in the carpet. At night, they tickled her nose. She was so besotted with her new property that she got on her knees and scrubbed the hairs away with a brush. She loves her bathroom the most because it is the warmest room. Nothing is more depressing to her than a cold bathroom, especially in the winter. Her bedroom has a draft; so does her kitchen. She will only walk on the linoleum floor in her fluffy slippers, and the sink tap drools. Her yellow Formica worktop is stained. The fanciest feature in the flat is the staircase that descends into the sitting room. She made the mistake of buying IKEA furniture, which is beginning to fall apart, but her mortgage is almost paid and her flat has more than doubled in value.

Her walls welcome her. She sits on her sofa, facing her window. There are no messages on her phone. Later in the afternoon, she warms up her Peugeot 205 and drives to Somerfield to stock up on food. The car park is full. She thought Somerfield was huge until she saw American superstores like Wal-Mart, but the quality is better at Somerfield, she thinks, picking up a packet of bacon. That unbeatable English quality, even when it comes to the correct proportion of pork meat to streak of fat.

On Monday morning she wakes up with menstrual cramps. They have worsened since she went off the pill a year ago. Her stomach is bloated and the bacon she eats doesn't help. She takes a couple of Panadols with her orange juice, knowing that she shouldn't, and goes to work by tube. Her stop is Wembley Park Station. She crosses Bridge Road and begins her long walk past Wembley Stadium and Mama Calabar, a Nigerian restaurant. Sometimes she hops on buses instead of walking and on cold wet days she drives in. The weather is warm for a change. LINK is on the second floor of an office block, which Kate Meade once described as a rabbit warren. This morning Kate is lamenting about dust in the ducts. They worsen her allergies during the summer and she is also trying to cope with nausea.

'Even the smell of my deodorant makes my stomach turn,' she says.

'Gosh,' Deola says.

'I blame Pam,' Kate says, with an air of spite. 'The last time *she* was pregnant, I got pregnant. Now, *she's* away on maternity leave and I'm pregnant again. Keep away from Pam, I tell you.'

Deola shakes her head in sympathy. Kate is in that crazy hormonal phase.

'What did you think of Atlanta?' she asks, sitting behind her desk.

Kate's fringe has grown so long it covers her brows. Her glasses are steel-rimmed and round. Forlorn is the only way to describe her. Behind her is a grey filing cabinet, on top of which are piles of yellow clasp envelopes and a framed close-up photograph of her daughter cuddling the cat that gave her toxoplasmosis.

'It wasn't bad,' she says.

'It's a funny city, isn't it?'

'A little.'

'It's Southern, yet it's not. I don't expect you had much time to see it.'

'Not much.'

Kate grew up in Liverpool, which is noticeable whenever she says a word like 'much'.

'Everything is enormous there,' Kate says. 'The buildings, the roads.'

'Wal-Mart.'

'Their cars! Did you see the size of the trucks they drive over there?'

'I did.'

Kate spreads her arms. 'It's incredible. You have these huge trucks and there's always a little woman at the wheel.'

'Always little women,' Deola says.

A wave of tiredness threatens her. At work, she plays up her English accent – speaking phonetics, as Nigerians call it – so that people might not assume she lacks intelligence. Speaking phonetics is instinctive now, but only performers enjoy mimicking. Performers and apes.

'Everything is enormous in America,' Kate says. 'Everything except, of course . . .'

Kate taps her temple. She has a master's degree in international relations and prides herself on being knowledgeable about what goes on in the Hague. She has never named her university, calls herself a grammar school girl, but she is quick to point out her husband went to Bedales and studied physics at Cambridge. He has a Ph.D. and has received grants for his research. He is an inventor. Kate is the second most frequent traveller in the office. Her trips are fieldwork related. Graham, the overall executive director, is more the photo-op guy. He attends conferences and summits and deals with the trustees. Kate stands in during his prolonged absences.

'I'm sorry,' Kate says. 'I shouldn't have said that, but they can be a little thick across the pond.'

'No need to apologize,' Deola says.

She is amused whenever the English denigrate Americans. She attributes it to inverted admiration. In America, she was astonished to see how many of them were on television, teeth fixed and playing up their Englishness or speaking with American accents, acting so colonized.

'I can't bear to listen to their views on this stupid war and I hate the way they keep saying "I rack" and "I ran". At least try and get the name right if you're going to bomb another country to smithereens'.

At the beginning of the Falklands War Deola thought the word was 'Forklands'. She was in her A-level year in England and was of the impression that only members of the Green Party and Save the Whales got upset about wars. Weirdos, basically.

This war is different. Everyone she knows in London is outraged. Everyone wants to win the debate, which has become a separate war. Strangers are co-opting her as an ally, including a drunken man who was seated next to her on the tube. He tapped a headline and said, stinking of beer, '*We* have no business being over there.' Lines must also have been drawn because she has not met a person who is for the war. Not one. They might not even exist. They might be on CNN to rile up viewers and raise ratings for all she knows. But she is sometimes convinced, watching the dissenters, that this is their chance to make like rebels, now that the backlash is not as severe as it was when their opposition could perhaps have had some effect.

Kate slaps the table. 'Anyway, your trip to Nigeria.'

'Yes?'

'Think you'll be ready in a couple of weeks?'

'Sure.'

The Nigerian programmes are not pressing enough to warrant Kate's change to a brisk tone, but Deola plays along.

The timing was her idea. She asked to go in the week of her father's memorial, without revealing why.

Her father died five years ago. She was the last in her family to find out. He was playing golf when he became dizzy. His friends rushed him to hospital. They didn't know he had high blood pressure. Her mother called to say he'd suffered a stroke. She got on the next flight to Lagos, but her father died before her plane arrived. She would have liked to have a sign that he had died, a white dove, anything as she flew over the Atlantic and the Sahara. Nothing. Not even an intuitive feeling, unless she could count the unrelenting pain in her stomach, which she couldn't suppress by repeating prayers.

'So where are we?' Kate asks. 'How long do you think you might need over there?'

'A week at most.'

'Is that all?'

Deola nods. She intends to finish her work in a couple of days and spend the rest of the time with her family.

'Good,' Kate says. 'So here is their correspondence, lit and stats. Their presentation is not very polished, but I understand printing is a problem over there. Plus, it's not about their presentation, really. I'm more interested in their accounts and the rest of it.'

Kate is brilliant with statistics, but she has no clue about accounting. Debit this, credit that, as she calls it.

'Would you like me to visit their sites?' Deola asks.

'No. We're just at the preliminary phase. I will have to go there at some point, but that'll be much later, after I'm over this.' Kate pats her belly.

'It's best you don't travel until then,' Deola says.

'I don't mind the travelling. I just don't need to be falling sick again.'

'Malaria is the one to watch out for in Nigeria.'

'So I've heard. I've also heard the pills make you psychotic. I think I would rather have malaria.'

'You wouldn't,' Deola says.

She has had malaria many times. The new strains are resistant to treatment.

'Mind you,' Kate says. 'Toxoplasmosis was no picnic. Here, take a look.'

'I'll come round,' Deola says getting up.

Kate pushes the papers towards her. 'No need.'

'It's okay,' Deola insists.

She assumes Kate is being decent as usual. Kate is hands-on about being decent. Kate dug out her Nigerian NGO files when Dára agreed to be the spokesperson of Africa Beat. Graham was against violating their policy of giving priority to countries with a history of fiscal dependability. Kate had to persuade him.

Deola walks to Kate's side of the desk to look at the correspondence.

Kate covers her mouth and mumbles, 'Hell.'

'Are you all right?' Deola asks.

Kate stands up, face contorted, and rushes out of the office.

Now, Deola feels foolish as she sniffs her shirt for perfume. Kate's office smells vaguely of snacks with Asian spices that will linger on her all day. She waits for Kate to return, wondering if she would be better off leaving. Kate walks in wiping her mouth with the back of her hand.

'Sorry about that,' she says.

'Was it my perfume?'

Kate shakes her head. 'Not to worry. Anything sets me off. It's awful. I can't wait until this is over. I'm going mad. I had a huge tantrum this morning and upset everyone at home. You know why?'

'Why?'

'Toothpaste.'

'Toothpaste?'

'Yes! Toothpaste! Someone left the cap off!'

'I should leave you alone,' Deola says.

'I'll be fine,' Kate says, sitting down.

'No, no. I'd better go. Can I take those with me?' She points at the papers. 'I'll bring them back when I'm through.'

'Yeth, pleathe,' Kate says, attempting to smile.

Kate has a habit of lapsing into a lisp whenever she asks for favours.

Deola takes the correspondence to her office, which is next door to Kate's. The carpet is the same throughout the office, greyish blue. Her window is clouded on the outside and there is dust permanently stuck on her white blinds. She has 'in' and 'out' trays on her desk and a matching organizer for her pens and pencils. There is no other indication that she intends to remain here. She doesn't even have a calendar yet.

She leafs through the brochure of the NGO that supports widows, WIN – Widows In Need. It was established in 1992. The print is blotchy and uneven in parts. The tabulation lines in the appendix are shaky and she comes across a statistic at the bottom: the average age of the widows is thirty-nine, her age.

Great, she thinks, pulling a face.

—

For the rest of the morning, she revises her report on the Delhi trip and drafts an audit programme for Africa Beat. Then she makes notes about her pending trip to Nigeria, listing the information she needs to request, contacts she has to make and when. She reads the literature on WIN, which is somewhat unfocused and suggests that women of childbearing age have the highest risk of HIV infection. The director, Rita Nwachukwu, is a former midwife.

Graham comes to work looking quite pink. He is back from Guatemala. His bald patch is shinier. Deola only remarks on the weight he has lost. He offers doughnuts to everyone in the office in his usual defiant manner.

''Ere,' he says to her.

There is sugar in his beard. Deola takes a doughnut and is careful to bite gently so the strawberry jam won't leak on her shirt. They are in that section of the corridor between his office, hers and Kate's. Kate walks out of her office and Graham presents the doughnuts to her.

Kate flops her wrists. 'Get those away from me.'

Kate is a vegetarian and she practises yoga. She worries about gaining weight.

'Go on,' Graham growls.

'You slob,' Kate says, brushing the sugar out of his beard with her fingers.

Kate and Graham flirt incessantly. In private, Kate tells him off for eating junk food and he calls Kate an 'eejit' if she mislays reports. Today, Kate barely taps his arm after she cleans up his beard and he cries out, 'Ow! Did you see that, Delia?'

'I saw nothing,' Deola says, stepping back into her office.

He sometimes slips up and calls her Delia. He also talks

about his morning commutes in present tense, saying, 'I'm driving down the street,' while she is thinking, *No, you're not. You're standing right here talking to me.*

She overhears Kate saying, 'Graham, don't!'

This is another workplace symbiosis that amuses her, married employees seeking attention from each other, even when they are ill-matched. She has encountered other prototypes at LINK. They have their smiling woman who takes collections for birthdays and their peculiar man who looks bemused at every request, as if he alone in the world makes sense. There must be others like herself, walking around wondering if all their years of education should end in a dreary office, but they must be equally as skilled at putting on façades.

Later in the day, Graham tells her he is flying off to Paris for a conference. Deola hasn't been to Paris in years. The last time she was there, she was in university. It was during the Easter holidays and she stayed with her cousin, Ndidi, whose mother worked for UNESCO. She travelled overnight from Dover to Calais by Hoverspeed. It was freezing and there were drunken passengers on board singing football songs. Ndidi met her at Gare du Nord and took her to her aunt's house in Neuilly. Ndidi had a Mohican haircut and had just bought herself a black leather jacket; Deola was in a red miniskirt, fishnet tights and thigh-high boots. How stylish they thought they were, kissing each other twice, and they laughed so hard that holiday that she peed in a chair at a crêperie.

Why hasn't she been back to Paris, she asks herself as she leaves the office in the evening. At first, the Schengen visa put her off. For a Nigerian it was a byzantine application process if ever there was one. She got her British passport, then the Eurostar train began to run, then the terrorists started with their threats. She waited until she was sure they wouldn't blow up the Channel Tunnel. Now she has no one to travel with. No one who is enough fun. Ndidi lives in Rome and works for a UN agency. She is married to an Italian guy and they have twin girls. Ndidi doesn't even have time to talk on the phone any more.

This week feels especially long and Deola is relieved when the weekend starts. She is lying on her sofa in her pyjamas on Saturday morning, watching a programme on BBC2 with hosts who are as animated as cartoon characters. They talk about the latest hip-hop dance and after a while she changes to Channel 4, which is showing a reality experiment on beauty. Her TV remote is on the carpet by a glass with orange juice sediment and a side plate with the remnants of her bacon sandwich. She is relishing the taste of acid and salt in her mouth when her doorbell rings. The ding is loud, but the dong is broken and drops like a thud.

There is no intercom system in her block. From her window she can see pollarded trees, green rubbish bins and dwarf gates. A high hedge separates her block from the next, which has a collection of gnomes in its front garden. Across the road is a white Audi A3 parked by a postbox.

It is Subu, who lives in Maida Vale. She and Subu trained in the same accountancy firm. Subu started off in management consultancy while she was in audit. Now Subu is a vice president of an investment bank and travels to places like Silicon Valley and Shanghai. Subu's job has something to do with derivatives. Deola, for all her accountancy training and business experience, still doesn't understand what derivatives are, and she cannot imagine how Subu, who is a born-again

Christian, copes as an investment banker. Subu won't swear or go out for a drink. She believes that angels have wings and Heaven and Hell are physical locations. She tells her colleagues they will end up in Hell if they don't accept Christ as their lord and saviour. Her colleagues seem to accept her as she is, though. They call her 'Shoe Boo', as if she were a puppy or computer game.

Deola toys with the idea of not answering her door as she goes downstairs. Just before she travelled to Atlanta, she and Subu got into such a heated exchange over the bombing of Baghdad she swore she wouldn't speak to Subu until Subu was willing to admit the war couldn't be justified on religious grounds.

'You're back?' Subu asks.

'I am,' Deola says.

'Since when?'

'Last Saturday. One minute.'

Deola checks the mail on the ledge in the hallway. There is no mail for her, mostly junk and bills for her neighbours, a group of young women who live on the ground floor. They might be South African or Australian. She hasn't been able to identify their accents and has not bothered to ask where they are from. They say hello whenever she sees them in the hallway.

'Why didn't you call?' Subu asks.

Since she gave her life to Christ Subu has had an authoritative air. It is almost as if she became Christ's wife on that day. She no longer wears makeup because she is born-again, but she won't be seen without a hair weave.

'I had too much to do,' Deola says.

She reaches her landing before Subu makes a move, so she

waits as Subu lugs her tote bag up the stairs. It is the size of a Ghana Must Go bag. Subu spends thousands of pounds on designer accessories. Her wardrobe is a shrine to Gucci and Prada.

'I hope I'm not disturbing you,' Subu says.

Subu's voice is thick and slow. She will not alter the pace of her voice or her accent for anyone, not even at work, which is commendable. She will keep repeating herself until she is understood and businesspeople are quick to catch on whenever big money is involved. As she once said, 'They don't try their "Pardon? Pardon?" with the Japanese.'

'It's all right,' Deola says. 'I was just watching television.'

She reminds herself to be patient as Subu catches up with her. They easily get into rows about abortion, homosexuality, Darwin and Harry Potter.

Subu sits on her couch. 'You're enjoying travelling around the globe like this.'

'Please,' Deola says. 'I was only there for two days.'

'What were you doing?'

Deola shortens her answer so as not to be boring. LINK wants to standardize their audits internationally. She had to study the Atlanta office's programme and write one. It will be incorporated in a manual and translated into other languages.

'To keep things uniform,' Subu says, forming a circle with her fingers.

'Otherwise, they would normally send me somewhere remote.'

'Like Burundi.'

Deola nods. She need not pretend her job is as glamorous as Subu's. She admires Subu's business savvy. She was not as motivated as Subu was during their accountancy training. Subu was promoted to manager after she was made redundant. Subu was first to buy a flat.

'What's going on, Shoe Boo?' she asks.

'I thought I should check up on you.'

'Have you decided on the flat?'

'I've left it in God's hands.'

God? Deola thinks. Doesn't He have more important things to worry about than a speculative property investment in Shanghai? She was raised around Christian and Muslim relatives and celebrated Easter, Christmas and Eid ul-Fitr. In university, she dabbled in transcendental meditation and Quaker prayer meetings. She would have joined the Church of Scientology just to see what they had to offer if they hadn't asked her to fill out a questionnaire. Subu was brought up in the Celestial Church of Christ. As a child, she wore white gowns and buried curses in the ground. Subu is now a member of an American Pentecostal church in London. It is democratic in the sense that anyone can be a pastor, and capitalistic in the sense that her pastor encourages his congregation to be prosperous. She attends single-women fellowships and prays that God will use her as a conduit. Deola finds it hard to take Subu's church seriously, particularly as she grew up with Subu's pastor and remembers him with a Jheri curl, dancing to the Gap Band's 'Oops Upside Your Head'. But she has seen how well Subu has done in her career and once in a while is tempted to join. Most of the time, it seems like a moral obligation to avoid churches like that, but perhaps God doesn't give a hoot about hypocrisy or squandering of tithes. Perhaps all He really does care about is that He is loved, honoured and obeyed.

'What are you doing this weekend?' she asks.

Subu hisses. 'I don't know, but there is this car show.'

Subu's ideal weekend outing is to the electronic shops on Tottenham Court Road. She gets excited about gadgets and machinery like digital cameras and surround-sound systems.

'I was even at a funeral yesterday,' she says.

'Whose?'

'One man in our church.'

'What happened to him?'

'They say it was his liver.'

'Hah? Any kids?'

'Three.'

'Three.'

'All under the age of ten.'

'Please tell me his wife was working.'

'I heard she was catering. I don't know them very well.'

There is a Nigerian crowd in London that Deola is not part of. People who came in the nineties when the naira-to-pound exchange rate plunged. They came to work, not to study or to get professional training. They settled in Lewisham, Peckham, Balham and any other '-ham' they could transform into a mini-Lagos. Through her church family, Subu gets invited to their *owambe* functions, where they dress up in *aso ebi*, play juju music, spray money and eat jollof rice and fried goat meat.

Deola finds it odd that Nigerians go to funerals as if they are social occasions that anyone can gate-crash – they just show up, look sad and leave. She has been to three funerals, all three in Nigeria. The first was her grandfather's. Her mother had to pin her head tie in place. She was that young. The second was for a governor of her secondary school, Queen's College. Her headmistress asked for class representatives and she put her hand up. The funeral was at Ikoyi Cemetery and she attended it in her Sunday uniform and beret. It was terribly hot and people arrived by the bus-load. The third was her father's funeral at Victoria Court Cemetery and his was just as crowded. Her relatives forced her to dance at the reception following his funeral, but she didn't think that at sixty-seven he was old enough for her to celebrate his life.

'I'm going home soon,' she says.

'Anything?' Subu asks.

'I'm going for work. They want me to look at a couple of NGOs.'

'Thank God,' Subu says.

God again, Deola thinks. Is this a habit, an affectation or a fear of life? Whatever it is, it releases a puerile desire in her to upstage Subu by declaring she is a nonbeliever.

'In Lagos?' Subu asks.

'One is in Lagos, the other is in Abuja. Nothing special, but my father's five-year memorial will coincide and at least I can be with my family for that.'

'How are they?' Subu asks.

'Fine.'

'Still with the bank?'

'Still with the bank.'

Deola's mother lives in Lagos, as do her brother, Lanre, and sister, Jaiye. Her father was a founder and chairman of Trust Bank, Nigeria. Her mother owns shares in the bank. Lanre is deputy managing director of the bank. Jaiye is a doctor and her practice has a retainership with the bank. Her family has survived without her father, but it might not have without the bank.

She asks about Subu's mother, who is also widowed and lives in Lagos.

'My mother is well,' Subu says. 'Harassing me as usual.'

'Still?'

The pressure to marry is relentless. Being single is like trying to convince a heckling audience your act is worth seeing. Subu could be the chairman of her bank and her mother would say, 'But she could be married with children.' Subu could be the prime minister of England and her mother would still say, 'But she could be married with children.'

Deola worked as an account officer for Trust Bank after she graduated from LSE, during her national service year and the year after. Her mother tells her to come home for good, to work for the bank, by which she means Deola ought to find a man to settle down with. She drops hints like, 'I saw this fellow and his wife. She's expecting again,' or 'I saw so-and-so. They have another one on the way.'

'My family wants me to come home for Christmas,' Subu says.

'Will you?'

'Naija? Naija is too tough. No water, no light. Armed robbers all over the place and people demanding money. I told my mother to come here instead. I will send her money for a ticket. Let her come here and relax.'

Subu, too, has a British passport. She refers to Nigeria as home, but she never goes back. She sends money home to her family and her mother stays with her whenever she is in London, sometimes for months. Nigeria, for her, is a place to escape from.

'Are you going home for Africa Beat?' she asks.

'Africa Beat is based in South Africa.'

'Why? When you have a Naija spokesman?'

'They have a high rate of infection there.'

'More than us?'

'We're getting there, small by small.'

Subu shakes her head. 'People should just abstain.'

Deola resists raising her eyes. She suspects Subu has had more lovers in her church family than she has ever had dates in her secular circles. Subu's ex-boyfriend was a deacon and Deola was curious to know what he'd done wrong, since he was so Christianly. All Subu would say about that was that she'd reported him to God, after which Subu decided she was going to be a virgin all over again, declaring, 'My body is my temple,' with a smile, as if she were not quite taking her abstinence seriously.

'As for Dára,' Subu says, 'they practically worship him in this place.'

'He's done well for himself,' Deola says.

'He has, but please, what streets of Lagos is he singing about? His parents are lecturers.'

'They are?'

'At Lagos State University. He was going there before he found his way here. He was not an area boy.'

'He wasn't?'

'At least that is what I heard. I'm glad he's made it, but he should stop telling lies about his background, and these *oyinbos* don't seem to be able to see through him.'

'Maybe they don't want to,' Deola says.

She never bothered to question Dára's story, except to note that he didn't call himself an area boy; he said he was a street child.

'He's on tour in the States soon, isn't he?' Subu asks.

'So I hear.'

'They've been making a lot of noise about him. I don't understand it.'

'He's definitely over-hyped.'

'Have you met him?'

'I'm administrative staff. We don't meet anyone.'

She has not met any of LINK's benefactors and won't have cause to meet their beneficiaries unless a fieldwork review is necessary.

'So people need him to tell them to give money?'

'Apparently.'

'I'm sure there will be an ABC concert.'

'And ABC T-shirts and ABC CDs.'

'Of course the concert will be held in South Africa.'

'Where else?'

'And of course they will invite Mandela.'

Deola laughs. 'If we can get him.'

She would rather not say any more. Most Nigerians she knows abuse celebrities involved in African charities. They accuse them of looking for attention or knighthoods. If they talk about the plight of Africa, they are sanctimonious. If they adopt African children, they are closet child molesters. She has heard all the arguments: charities portray Africans as starving and diseased. Western countries ought to give Africa trade and debt relief, not aid. The drug companies should reduce the cost of their medications. The churches ought to shut the hell up with their message of abstinence and start distributing condoms. Africa T-shirts are just designer wear for the socially conscious.

Africa Beat gets funding from churches and pharmaceutical companies. Their posters of Africa can be simplistic, but so is most advertising, Deola believes. Her experiences may also be negated, but Africa does suffer, unduly, unnecessarily, and if all she has to cope with is the occasional embarrassment about how Africans are portrayed, then she is fortunate.

'What's going on, Shoe Boo?' she asks again.

Subu shrugs. 'We're fine, we're here.'

Today they have little to say to each other. They seem to have exhausted their friendship now that they don't have their simple left-wing–right-wing rows any more. Deola is thankful when Subu leaves. There is a melancholy about Subu and she is aware how contagious it can be.

When she was a student at LSE, she went out every weekend and how ridiculously young she and her friends were, living in their parents' flats, running up their parents' phone bills and driving cars their parents had bought them. They spent their pocket money on memberships at nightclubs like Stringfellows and L'Equipe Anglaise so they could get past bouncers, and threw raucous parties after midnight until their neighbours called the police.

Nigerian boys carried on like little polygamists, juggling their serious girlfriends and chicks on the side. Well-brought-up Nigerian girls were essentially housewives-in-training. They dressed and behaved more mature than they were, cooked for their boyfriends and didn't party much. Useless girls slept around. A guy had to rape a girl before he was considered that useless and even then someone would still go out with him and attribute his reputation to rumour. There were rumours about cocaine habits, beatings and experimental buggery. The guys eventually got married.

None of her boyfriends counted until Tosan, whom she

met during her accountancy training. He graduated as an architect at the beginning of the post-Thatcher redundancies and couldn't find a job. He shared a flat with some friends in Camden and cycled around, even in the winter. Deola was working in the city and studying for her exams. After she bought her flat, Tosan spent weekends with her. He cooked and cleaned up. He had her listening to francophone African music and reading Kundera novels. He owed her money for plays they'd seen, like *Hamlet* with Judi Dench and Daniel Day-Lewis and *Burn This* with Juliet Stevenson and John Malkovich. He smoked marijuana and she didn't. She told him he had to do that at his own place. She also drew the line at going to the pub.

She had never met a Nigerian who enjoyed a rundown, dirty, smelly, mouldy English public house as much as Tosan did. She didn't go to pubs with him because they would end up not speaking. She embarrassed him whenever she checked her wine glasses for lipstick stains. Tosan went to pubs on his own, but he also needed company. He talked a lot, too much. He was always going on about arts and culture and punctuated everything he said with a 'You know wha' I mean?' Sometimes she wanted to say, 'Actually, I don't.' Other times, she just wanted him to be quiet. She barely had time for him while she was studying for her final exams and that was probably when he began to look around.

He got a job in Watford and began to stink of honey. He left traces of it on her couch and in her bed. The smell terrified her. She accidentally traced it to a Boots counter. It was a lotion for dry skin and Tosan never used lotion. That was a joke between them: his legs and arms looked as if he'd been carrying cement. Of course he denied he was sleeping with someone else and she chose to believe him, but they fought. They fought when he arrived late on Saturday nights and when he left early on Sundays, supposedly to play football in Hyde Park: Nigerians versus Iranians. Mostly they fought over the money he still owed her. 'Where is my money for bloody *Burn This?*' she would ask. Or, 'Where is my money for frigging *Hamlet?*' One night he said, 'Stop shouting. You're always shouting. There is no need to shout.' So she punched him. She never believed she had a right to hit a man with impunity and she didn't stop him when he walked out. The next day she donated the Kundera novels he'd lent her to charity and threw out his *soukous*, *kwassa kwassa* (or whatever it was called) cassette tapes.

He was sleeping with someone she knew. Not a close friend but it left her with a misplaced distrust, of which she was not proud, because it wasn't proper to talk about the treachery of women. She ate a lot of jellybeans and played sad Sade songs. She saw Tosan again, at a party, and rather than admit what he'd done, he went on about sexuality, or was it Eros? Yes, it was. Eros was at the root of politics, religion and art, he said.

She has since had other boyfriends. One was so passive she went as far as to shake his shoulders, pretending that she was joking and hoping she might get a reaction out of him. Another reminded her too much of her mother. On the first date, he was going on about looking for a woman who was marriage material. Another was a liar. Not even a serious liar. He lied about acquaintances and name-dropped people he didn't know. It became awkward.

These days, she no longer goes out on dates and she rarely gets an invitation. Her married friends throw parties for their children. The last time she was with a group of them was at a seventh-day ceremony. The couple, both Nigerian dentists, hired a rabbi to carry out their son's circumcision because they couldn't get one done at the hospital where he was born. The wife burst into tears and the husband made some suggestive comment, which Deola ignored for fear of being labelled a home wrecker.

She wishes she had been more adventurous. For her, there will be no chance meetings in bars or sex with strangers. Within the social network to which she belongs, love is so contained, so predictable, and marriage might be as banal and unsatisfying as her career.

During the week, Bandele calls. She hasn't heard from him in months. He either bombards her with phone calls or avoids her phone calls. She fondly refers to him as her grumpy writer friend. She is getting undressed when her phone rings. She stands before the mirror in her bedroom as she speaks to him, stripped down to her underwear, and pulls her stomach in.

'My love,' she says.

'Old Fanny,' he says.

His voice is hopelessly public school. It sounds like one low rumble of thunder after another. She panics as she inspects her back view. Is her arse beginning to sag or is it just the way she is standing? It looks uncertain, like an uncertain arse asking, 'When?' as if it won't be long before she gets the answer everyone dreads, 'Soon.'

She tells him about her new job and he says he is trying to get published.

'You are?'

'It surprised me, too. "Never, again", remember? Now, I'm

back to submitting work. And I've been short-listed for an African writers prize.'

'Hey!'

'No "hey". I don't want to make a fuss or anything. You know, in case it doesn't work out. It's been a bit nerve-wracking. We've had all these readings lined up.'

'You took part?'

'I had no choice. The last one is on Saturday, near Calabash. Remember Calabash?'

'Sure.'

It was a restaurant at the Africa Centre in Covent Garden. She saw him read there when he published his first novel, *Sidestep*. He stuttered a lot, which was unusual for him. Readings made him nervous and back then he didn't want to be associated with African writers.

He says he found out about the competition through an online forum for Nigerian intellectuals, which he ended up leaving because they kept getting into tribal spats. He had not encountered Nigerians like them before: people who were capable of debating about Derrida and Foucault, but unable to contain their primal urges to clan up and wage war.

'They were a vile bunch.'

'Sounds like it. So where is this reading, then?'

'A bookshop.'

'I'll meet you there,' she says.

'Meet me afterwards,' he says. 'These things can be tedious and it will be impossible to talk.'

He gives her the address.

'I'll pick you up,' she says. 'Let's say nine? We can go somewhere. I want to hear what you've been up to. What were you short-listed for anyway?'

'A novel. The first five thousand words. The winner gets ten thousand pounds and a book contract.'

'Wow! What's the title?'

'Foreign Capitals.'

'That's a good one,' she says, though she is not sure.

'Yeah?'

'Yes. I can feel it. You will win.'

'Thanks. I needed to hear that.'

'See you soon.'

She takes a bath before she goes to bed. Her bathwater is lukewarm. She spreads her legs and arches her back. She has missed the weight and warmth of a man. Sometimes, she climaxes in her dreams and she looks at children differently, as if they could be hers. She brushes against her walls for contact.

When she met Bandele, she couldn't have imagined they would be friends. She had a crush on his elder brother, Seyi. Seyi was her brother Lanre's friend. They were dayboys at Saint Gregory's College when she was a boarder at Queen's College. She overheard senior girls talking about them. They were cool Greg's guys, heavy, dishy guys.

The summer after Form Three, Seyi showed up at the house. He was gorgeous in his white uniform, tall, and he didn't have those weak calves that Nigerian boys had. Even her mother was taken. 'Such a lovely boy,' she said, 'the Davis boy.' His nickname was 'Shaft in Africa'. His father was a retired labour minister and his mother had a boutique at Federal Palace Hotel.

That holiday, Seyi drove his mother's old Mini around. He and Lanre would somehow squeeze themselves into it and find their way to Ikoyi Club to play squash and chase chicks. Seyi called Lanre 'Whizzy', after a song by a Greg's band that landed a record deal with EMI. Lanre wasn't allowed to drive and he always refused to give Deola a lift. 'The driver will take you,' he would say. 'Wait for the driver.'

She would have to wait until the driver returned from whatever errand he was on. She would get to the club late in the afternoon and find Seyi and Lanre smoking and drinking beer in the rotunda. Lanre would stub out his cigarette, as if she were likely to tell on him, and Seyi would sit there looking amused and red-eyed.

Seyi played in squash tournaments with middle-aged brigadiers. Sometimes she watched him play pool in the games room. Under-eighteens were not allowed in, but they bribed the waiters and, during the day, anyone else who might report them was at work. Seyi would prowl around pool tables in his worn-out T-shirts and jeans. He drank beer from bottles and bent low to shoot.

He was just a boy and someone ought to have talked to him about drinking. Once he saw her at the newsagent and announced, 'My sweetheart,' and hugged her. He was drunk again and she held him tightly, but that was as far as she went with him. He had a girlfriend called Tina, whose mother was Jamaican. Her hair reached her shoulders, so he and other guys made a fuss about her.

Then one day, Bandele came to the house. 'Is Lanre in?' he asked. No 'please' and he pronounced Lanre's name 'Lanry'. He sounded completely English and all she knew about Nigerians who spoke that way was that they looked down on Nigerians who didn't. 'Lanre is not in,' she said. She was wearing jeans and a long T-shirt. Bandele asked, 'Is Madam in, then?' Deola said, 'You mean my mother?' He looked her up and down. 'I thought you were the housegirl.'

Bandele had the same features as Seyi, but they were not nearly as symmetrical and he was shorter. Lanre later explained that he was Seyi's younger brother who was sent off to an old-fashioned school in England called Harrow. Now he was so lost that even Seyi was ashamed of him. Deola did notice how Bandele hung around the expat crowd at Ikoyi Club. They called him 'Daily Davis'. He called himself 'Daily Davis'. His English accent made him effeminate, as far as she was concerned. He didn't even recognize her after that day – the same way some expats couldn't tell one Nigerian from another.

She turns off the hot water tap as she remembers the night Seyi Davis died. There was a film show at the club that night: James Bond. She was there with her friends. Seyi and Lanre left the rotunda early. It was raining and they had been drinking beer again. They went off to the Floating Bukka on the marina. After the film, the driver came for her. She got home and Lanre had not yet returned, which wasn't a surprise. She ate the pork chops her mother had left in the warmer and went to bed. Her mother stayed up to watch *April Love*. She heard the theme song. It must have been eleven-thirty when the phone rang and her father answered it. It was Seyi's father. He said Seyi and Lanre were in an accident on Kingsway Road, Lanre had lost consciousness and Seyi was lost. That was exactly how her father delivered the news: 'Unfortunately, we have lost Seyi.'

Lost him where? she thought.

The Davises restricted Seyi's funeral to family members. No one else was allowed to attend – not his godparents, not their friends, not even his friends from Saint Greg's. Lanre was bedridden. He had a concussion and black eyes. Her parents went several times to pay their condolences at the Davises' house, but their steward would open their door dressed in a white uniform and say, 'Master and Madam are resting.'

Seyi's funeral caused a scandal in Lagos that summer. After the obituaries and tears, people began to abuse his father in private. They said he was too English. He didn't know how to mourn properly. Her father saw him on the golf course practising his swing. Her mother bumped into Mrs Davis at Moloney Supermarket and was finally able to speak to her.

Deola's mother banned her from the club for the rest of the summer, so she didn't know if Bandele went there or not, but the holiday ended and Bandele must have gone back to Harrow. She still didn't know how to react to Seyi's death, so she wrote a poem dedicated to him and buried it by the pawpaw tree in the backyard.

She didn't see Bandele again until she was in her final year in university. She met him at a black-tie dinner in Pall Mall. A mutual friend had her twenty-first birthday at a gentleman's club there. The gentlemen looked like retired generals and diplomats. She spotted Bandele taking his surroundings a little too seriously and looking rather like a penguin. She asked him, 'Aren't you Bandele Davis?' He said, 'I am, and who might you be?'

He was with a blonde with puffy taffeta sleeves. Deola was with Tosan, who suggested to the blonde that if she really enjoyed lover's rock, she ought to try a fantastic club in Hackney called the All Nations Club. Deola asked Bandele what he was studying. He said he was not in university; he was writing a novel. 'A real one?' she exclaimed, thinking she didn't know one Nigerian student who was writing books or bypassing university. 'The question is, are novels real?' he asked, lifting his hand.

Tosan was so convinced he was gay.

On Saturday evening, she arrives late at the bookshop. She has driven around Covent Garden trying to find a parking spot, and it has turned cold enough to wear a jacket. She rubs her bare arms as she hurries towards the entrance. There are globes and travel maps in the window. Indoors is a café where the reading is advertised on a poster. Were these people at the reading? There is a woman with long frizzy hair, another with a grey ponytail and a navy wrap, and a man with a comb-over. The rest look half Deola's age. They have dreadlocks and braids and are dressed in hip-hop clothes, ethnic prints and black. There is a lot of black (individualists always look as if they are in mourning). She stands out in her tracksuit; so does Bandele in his prim shirt and tie. His haircut belongs on an older face. He has a mischievous expression, but his eyes are subdued. It took him a while to find the right medication for his depression. One dried up his mouth and another bloated him up. They all make him lethargic. Most days he doesn't get up until noon.

'What's this?' he asks, patting his chest. 'You're . . .'

'Don't start,' Deola says.

She is wearing a new padded bra. A woman approaches him with a copy of *Sidestep*. She has a nose ring and her lips are thick with gloss.

'Sorry,' she says, wrinkling her brows.

'My pleasure,' he says.

He autographs his novel on the nearest table, shakes her

hand and returns. Deola predicts he is about to make a rude comment and she is right.

'Let's go,' he mumbles. 'I can't take much more of this.'

A group of people has formed a bottleneck by the door. She enjoys the close contact and mix of scents, but Bandele grips her hand until they are outside, where he breathes out.

'Was it that bad?' she asks.

'You have no idea. I'm sitting there pretending to listen to their inane discussion.'

'About?'

'About being marginalized and pigeonholed. Then some writer, whom I've never heard of before, starts yelling at me during my question-and-answer session.'

'Why?'

'Something about Coetzee's *Disgrace*.'

'What about Coetzee's *Disgrace*?'

'Oh, who cares? Coetzee's a finer writer than that dipstick can ever hope to be. What does he know? He writes the same postcolonial crap the rest of them write, and not very well, I might add.'

Deola laughs. 'Isn't our entire existence as Africans post-colonial?'

'They should give it a rest, the whole lot of them. Africa should be called the Sob Continent the way they carry on. It's all gloom and doom from them, and the women are worse, all that false angst. Honestly, and if I hear another poet in a headwrap bragging about the size of her ample bottom or likening her skin to the colour of a nighttime beverage, I don't know what I will do.'

He is a Coetzee enthusiast. *Sidestep* was about a nineteen-year-old Nigerian who slept around. She found it funny and sweet. He never denied it was autobiographical and the women in the novel were skinny blondes with AA-cup bras. They wore ballet flats and had names like Felicity and Camilla.

'What a waste of time,' he says, as they approach her Peugeot. 'I should never have come. That's why I've never liked going to these black things.'

'Black things?'

'Black events. They always degenerate into pity parties.'

'Where do you want to go now?' she asks, shaking her head.

'Home.'

'Home?'

'If you don't mind. I'm worn out.'

She paid for two hours' parking, but she is used to him changing plans.

They pass a man who is shouting out theatre shows in an Italian accent: 'Lion Keeng!'

The *Lion King* posters have African faces covered in tribal paint. The street is teeming with cars and people. There are cafés and shops on either side.

Bandele lives in a council flat in Pimlico. His estate has a community centre and launderette. He was in Brixton temporarily, but he threw a tantrum and demanded to be moved. He told his social worker he was only familiar with Belgravia and black people scared him, which was true, but his social worker just assumed he was showing signs of paranoia.

'How's the job going?' he asks.

'Not bad,' Deola says, turning into Charing Cross Road.

'So you're doing charity work.'

'No, I work for a charity.'

'In Brent.'

'Wembley, actually.'

He sighs. 'Why Wembley?'

'What's wrong with Wembley?'

'It's zone four!'

'It's an easy commute for me.'

'I'm just saying. With your qualifications, you ought to be working right here in the city for . . . for Rothschild or something.'

'Rothschild is not an accountancy firm.'

'Saatchi and Saatchi, then.'

'Saatchi and Saatchi is not an accountancy firm. And who says they would employ me?'

'Come on. You're selling yourself short. You're always selling yourself short. Stop selling yourself short. Of course they would employ you. Of course they would. With your background?'

'What background?' Deola says, stepping on her accelerator, instead of admitting she is aware of how mediocre her career is. She is heading in the direction of Trafalgar Square.

'Calm down,' he says. 'I'm just saying. You ought to aim higher. You're too self-effacing. You go for a job like that and you'll end up leaving. It's the same way you found yourself working with a bunch of yobs wherever.'

'Holborn. A consultancy firm in Holborn.'

'With NHS clients in Wolverhampton.'

She slaps his hand down. She can't tell him anything.

'Sorry,' he says. 'I didn't mean for it to come out that way.'

'Hm.'

'May I smoke?'

'No.'

'Out of your window, I mean.'

'I said no.'

He rubs his forehead. 'God, you're such an old fanny. So what is it then, you struggle with the world of commerce and industry or the world of commerce and industry struggles with you?' His American accent is dodgy.

'Who are you quoting now?' she asks.

'Baldwin.'

'What did Baldwin have to say about that?'

'He didn't ask you the question.'

He is also a James Baldwin enthusiast, but he considers Baldwin's experiences American, unlike his, which he might describe as aristocratic English because his grandfather was knighted by the Queen. His snobbishness is exasperating. Everyone is a yob to him. He won't accept that racism exists in England. 'It's just an excuse for the West Indian immies not to work,' he once said. 'Class is everything over here.'

'My job is not bad,' she says. 'I get to travel. I've just come back from the States. Before that I was in India.'

'India?'

'Yes, and I'm going home in a week.'

From the little she saw of Delhi, it was cleaner and better organized than Lagos, but there were similarities, like the crowded markets and the occasional spectacle of someone defecating in public.

'Where is home?' Bandele asks.

'Where else?'

He rubs his chin. 'Nigeria is not *my* home.'

'It's home for me.'

'Good luck to you. I haven't been back in so long I'd probably catch dengue fever the moment I set foot in that country.'

'More like malaria.'

'Nigerians, ye savages.'

'Your head is not correct,' she says.

This slips out and for a while her remorse shuts her up. Bandele has been hospitalized for depression once before, but even at his lowest he was never incoherent. He also appeared physically fit, yet his depression was often so crippling he couldn't get out of bed. Now, he says it is manageable. He calls psychiatric patients 'schizoids'. If she protests, he says, 'What?'

His flat is in a state when they get there – not abnormally so. There is dirty laundry in his living room, a clutter of plates in his sink and a saucer with cigarette butts. He works in longhand and writes it up on a computer, but he has never learned to type properly. He has paper all over the floor, sometimes crumpled up in balls. He writes everywhere as if he is addicted, in notebooks he carries, on paper napkins in restaurants and on cinema stubs in the dark. He goes to Pimlico Library to borrow books and to his local Sainsbury's to buy frozen meals. He heats them in his oven because he doesn't have a microwave. His flat smells of lasagna and cigarette fumes.

'Does the writing help?' she asks.

'Help what?' he says, throwing his keys on a chair.

Her hands are in her pockets. 'I mean in expressing yourself.'

'It's not about expressing myself.'

'What is it about, then?'

'I just don't want to feel so worthless any more.'

'You're not worthless, Bandele.'

'I am.'

'Don't say that.'

'But I am.'

'No, you're not. You're working and it's not like having a job you absolutely loathe.'

He searches the floor. 'I absolutely loathe writing.'

'You do?'

'Of course I do and I loathe publishing even more.'

'Still?'

'Mm, I have an intimate knowledge of its ugly side.'

Again, the dodgy American accent. He can't imitate, but he has an astonishing ability to recall quotes. For her, quoting is like picking flowers instead of admiring them.

'Baldwin again?' she asks.

'You've got that right, sister. Have you read any of his books?'

'*Go Tell It on the Mountain*, and the Beale Street one. The one with the pregnant woman.'

'What did you think of them?'

'I liked them.'

He staggers backward. 'Liked?'

'You and Baldwin today.'

He raises his hands. 'I'm having a séance with him.'

'I thought you didn't believe in all that.'

He was an existentialist when last she asked. She cannot tell if he is erratic or just working himself up into a creative mood. She wants to find out if he is under stress from writing again and if he has a new girlfriend. She would like to ask about his medication and his social worker. But more than that she'd rather just excuse herself and leave because she can't cope with what he might tell her.

'It's a mess here, isn't it?' he asks, looking at the floor.

'It's fine,' she says.

'No, really, it's a mess.'

'It's fine.'

'Just say it is and I'll clean up.'

'I'll help.'

As they tidy up, she tells herself not to worry about him. Every Nigerian she knows abroad is to some degree broken.

'I don't write to express myself,' he says, picking up papers. 'If I need to express myself, I'd sooner take a shit on one of these.'

'I only asked,' she says.

Bandele has never held a job. He had one after *Sidestep* was published because he wasn't earning much in royalties, but he fell out with his manager within a week. He said he couldn't possibly take orders from a yob like her, quit, then had trouble drafting his second novel. His agent stopped returning his calls. He went to her office and whatever happened there led to his hospitalization. His parents came from Nigeria to visit him. He called his father a fucking kleptocrat and his mother a mercenary cunt. They flew back to Nigeria as soon as he was discharged from hospital.

That was when Deola returned to work in London. She was on a tourist visa. She was applying for accountancy jobs, the only jobs for which she could apply for a work permit, and she called Bandele at his parents' house in Belgravia. She was catching up with friends and finding out who else was around. He kept her on the phone for hours telling her what happened. 'It was brutal, brutal in there,' he said. 'Dickensian and the nurses looked as if they were men dressed in drag.' He said his father had given him six months to find somewhere else to live. It was easy for her to blame his father. The man was too Nigerian, she decided.

Bandele's father went to Cambridge and Bandele was expected to go there, but instead he wrote the novel. His father never mentioned the novel, as if doing so might prove Bandele right. After Bandele moved to Pimlico, he invited her to the Tate Gallery for exhibitions: David Hockney, Francis Bacon, someone or other. She persuaded him to come to Brixton for a Fela concert at the Academy. Tosan didn't care if he tagged along. He was so sure Bandele was gay. In fact, he thought that was the cause of Bandele's breakdown, while her friends referred to Bandele as 'the *bobo* who went mad because he couldn't accept the fact that he was black'. It got worse if she ever tried to defend him.

Over the years she has discovered that Bandele tells just enough of the truth to get sympathy. His father is known as a thieving politician, for instance, but he is a well-respected one, as they all are. His father may also have disciplined his children with a cane, but no more than the average Nigerian parent did. Sometimes she can't tell Bandele's natural grandiosity from the symptoms of his illness. He has since learned to live with the black people on his council estate, but she no longer blames his family for giving up on him. The cunt business was just the beginning. He called his sisters (who were known for buying the affections of guys who were far better looking than they were) ugly whores. She keeps in touch with him by phone, but she can go for months without seeing him. His ridicule of Nigerians is hard to take, and she once attributed it to the sort of self-loathing that only an English public school can impart on a young, impressionable foreign mind.

Overall, she finds Bandele testy, but his talk about schooling and artistic expression prompts her to call Tessa during the week. Tessa Muir, or Tessa the Thespian, as she used to call her when they were roommates in boarding school. Sometimes it was Tess of the d'Urbervilles. This was during O levels, when Tessa, like Bandele, didn't have the normal preoccupations like choosing what A levels to study or going to university. Tessa later left boarding school for a tutorial college in London so she could audition for acting roles. She didn't actually get any roles, or A levels, but it was fabulous.

The last time Deola saw Tessa on stage, Tessa was playing Lily St Regis in *Annie*. She sang 'Easy Street'. Tessa does voiceover work now. Once in a while Deola recognizes her voice in an advert, when Tessa is not sounding like someone else. It brings her back to when they were fifteen-year-old girls.

School was in Somerset, and their boarding house was in Glastonbury. They had a housemaster with hair full of Brylcreem who peeked through keyholes to check if girls were misbehaving and a housemistress who was too vacuous to understand the implications of this, but she made the best apple crumbles ever. A bus shuttled students to and fro. Deola's classes had ten students at most, compared to the thirty-odd girls she was used to at Queen's College. There were boys in her class and no school uniform, which meant she had to think about what to wear in the mornings: skirt or trousers, cardigan or sweater, penny loafers or boots. She had a Marks & Spencer duffle coat and her mother's old Burberry trench coat, both of which she found frumpy.

She was fresh from a boarding school in Nigeria, where girls stuck their bottoms out and walked around with Clearasil on their faces. Now, she was sharing a house with girls who flipped their hair from side to side and ran around with Nair on their legs. She found them just as funny to observe. Tessa came from a drama school with her own special antics, which quickly earned her a reputation for being a weirdo. The only girl weirder than Tessa was a Californian who wore an ankle bracelet and said, 'Far out, man,' and sniffed her spray deodorant.

First thing in the morning, Deola would be lying in bed, tucked under her duvet, reluctant to brave the cold. She slept near the heater. Outside it was invariably dark. Tessa would get up early to avoid the shower rush. After her shower, Tessa would strut into the dormitory, grab her hairbrush and start singing some annoying chorus from a musical, like 'Um diddle diddle diddle, um diddle ay,' and Deola would shout, 'Will you shush?'

They were both in the drama society and Tessa had major roles in the school productions of *Guys and Dolls* and *The Importance of Being Earnest* that year. At Queen's College, Deola was in the drama society. She once played Hamlet in the 'To be or not to be' scene. In England, she always ended up with female or black roles and usually as an extra. One night in their dormitory, she thought she'd show off her acting skills to Tessa and recited the 'The 'squire has got spunk in him' scene from *She Stoops to Conquer*. Tessa laughed until she drooled. The trembling nasal voice Deola used became a voice of reason of sorts.

They couldn't agree on what music to play. Deola had a stash of cassettes, most of which were badly dubbed from soul LPs and labelled 'Mixed Grill'. Occasionally, Radio One played a song with a dance beat, like 'Funkin' For Jamaica';

otherwise, she had to tune into Radio Luxembourg. Tessa was into bands like Led Zep and Pink Floyd. Deola had never heard of them before and Tessa did not know who Teddy Pendergrass or George Benson were. In the end, they didn't agree to take turns to play their music; they just enjoyed whatever was on and that was how Deola learned that those obscure choruses from her childhood, like 'Goodbye, Ruby Tuesday' and 'Ob-La-Di, Ob-La-Da', were from songs by the Stones and the Beatles. She'd grown up believing they were Nigerian folk songs.

She calls Tessa and they arrange to meet for tea on Sunday in a café off Haymarket. They sit by the window, which is thick enough to reduce the noise of the traffic to a hum. The café is cozy. There are mirrors on the walls and Deola can see her profile as well as the back of her head. The tea is overpriced and the sugar is caramelized, as if to compensate. She eats a cheese danish as Tessa butters a scone and slaps on strawberry jam. Tessa's red hair is pulled back with a black band. She has a slightly crooked nose that makes her look striking. Her dark denim jacket contrasts with her pale freckly skin. She wears a ruby cabochon ring on her middle finger; it is too loose for her ring finger. She has been engaged to Peter for several months now and they are yet to set a wedding date.

'The trouble is,' Tessa says, 'we can't decide where to live. It's either Pete moves here or I move to Australia, right? So Pete doesn't like the climate here and you know I can't stand the heat. But I really don't have to live here to work and Pete can basically live anywhere.'

'So?'

'So it's unsettling. It's such a long way away, Australia. Such a long way from home. He will build me a studio, though, if we move there, so I can work.'

Tessa and Peter live in a mews in Notting Hill Gate. Peter buys houses in London with a business partner, fixes them up and sells them. He left school at seventeen, wanting to be a wildlife photographer, and travelled throughout Asia taking carpentry and building jobs to sustain himself.

'They have that huge theatre, don't they?' Deola asks.

'Which one?'

'The one at Sydney Harbour.'

'Yes, the opera house.'

'Australia,' Deola says. 'My neighbours downstairs are from Australia.'

Tessa puts her teacup down. 'Are they?'

'I think so. Stay here, Tess. What if you get another big role?'

Tessa bites her scone. 'Mm, mm. The . . . roles . . . aren't . . . there any more.'

'You got *Annie*.'

'Yes . . . but that was ages ago.'

'So?'

'So in a couple of years I'll be old enough to play Miss Hannigan.'

'Remember when you were Adelaide?'

'Adelaide,' Tessa says, unenergetically.

She misses being on stage. She has had more luck in festivals than in the West End. She eventually turned to BBC radio and the voiceover work came out of that. A review said her singing voice was 'soulful', and Deola secretly took credit for that. Who exposed her to soul music? Who took her to see the High Priestess, Nina Simone, at Ronnie Scott's?

'You know who I'd really love to play?' Tessa says.

'Who?'

'Piaf. But I'm too tall to play her. She was tiny, Piaf.'

Tessa as Édith Piaf doesn't surprise Deola as much as Tessa as a housewife. Tessa gave Peter an ultimatum before he agreed to get married. He is six years younger than Tessa and his father is not pleased about that. Peter's mother died of melanoma when he was a boy and he and his father are more like brothers. They get drunk together, which Tessa at first thought was sweet. Now she says it's unsavoury.

'What made you change your mind?' Deola asks.

Tessa wipes her fingers on a napkin. 'About?'

'You know.'

'I'm ready,' Tessa says. 'I want the husband, the kids, the whole lot.'

Deola thinks of the clapping and skipping games she learned as a girl and chants like 'When will you marry? This year, next year' and 'First comes love, then comes marriage.'

'I know we've been brainwashed,' Tessa says, reading her skeptical expression. 'It's biological. I don't want to wait until I have fossils for eggs.'

'Please don't mention eggs around here.'

'Why not?'

'There's no hope for mine.'

'Don't be silly, darling.'

'Seriously. There's no one in London.'

'What do you mean? There's someone. There's someone else.'

A group of Japanese tourists are walking past. One stops to take a photograph with his Canon camera.

How to begin? Deola thinks. The closest she got to talking

to Tessa about race was telling Tessa she danced well, considering. Tessa, of course, thought Deola was a fantastic dancer. Deola didn't dance that well, just better than other girls in school, who danced out of rhythm. Tessa got curious about the word '*oyinbo*', having overheard other Nigerians using it and it was awkward for Deola to confess it meant white, Westerner, Westernized, foreign. Tessa blushed. The British won't have any of that, stirring up stuff.

'You must have had an image of what your prince looked like when you were a girl,' Deola says.

'I'm sure I did,' Tessa says.

'Well, mine was no Englishman.'

Tessa laughs. 'What?'

'I want to be with a Nigerian.'

'Oh, don't be daft.'

'It's a preference.'

'Don't be daft, darling. Who ends up with her prince anyway?'

Deola gesticulates. 'It's about . . . having a shared history.'

In her college days, who wanted to be the odd one with the *oyinbo* boyfriend at a party, explaining to him, 'Yes, yes, we like our music this loud. No, no, we don't make conversation, we just dance'?

You were either pathetic or lost if you were with an *oyinbo* boy. She never went out with any in school. She had crushes. There was the golden-haired American tennis player and the Welsh rugby player with bowlegs. Tessa went out with a pimply pseudo-intellectual who walked around with a paisley scarf wrapped around his neck. He seemed harmless enough until he spread a rumour that Tessa stuck her tongue so far down his throat she practically extracted his tonsils.

In a way, Deola was glad she was saved from that nonsense: who fancies whom and who got off with whom. Boys called her 'mate' and slapped her on the back. They might have wanted to hug her, but it was safer if she were one of the lads. Sometimes they introduced her to a Nigerian boy who came to their school for an away game. They would endorse him as 'good fun', mispronounce his name ('Addy Babby Lolly') and no matter how unattractive she found him, they would grin at him, and her, as if expecting them to copulate.

She concentrated on studying for her O levels. At the end of term, while Tessa was busy getting upset over some boy who'd slow-danced with some other girl at the school disco, Deola was looking forward to travelling home. She knew she wasn't going to be overlooked for much longer. On the last day of term, they shared a bottle of scrumpy on Glastonbury Tor.

She was specific when she started dating and she still is. Her men must taste and smell as if they were raised on the same diet and make the same tonal sounds. Similarity on all fronts is essential. She won't even be with a Nigerian like Bandele, who might end up asking her, 'Pardon?'

'What's wrong with a different history?' Tessa asks. 'What's wrong with two histories?'

'Nothing, if they really are shared.'

'Come on. That is so . . . I'm sorry. I'm not precious that way. I'm just not.'

Tessa's father is Scottish. Her mother's family emigrated from Italy. She has an uncle on her father's side whom she calls a disgusting old fart because he complains about his new neighbours who are Pakistani, spies on them from behind his curtains and once called the police to say he suspected them of terrorist activities. Before Peter, she dated a Trinidadian artist who looked Chinese, then a French merchant wanker, as she called him after they broke up. Tessa would not know what it means to be nationalistic about love. She thinks it's racist to talk about race. She is unapologetically prejudiced against actors, though. Her first boyfriend was one. He was in his forties, and married. They met in bedsits for years. She swore she would never get married after she broke up with him.

'What if I said that to you?' she asks, blushing. 'What if I said that about Nigerian men?'

'It's not the same,' Deola says.

'Why not?'

'Because it's not. You don't live in Nigeria, for a start. Imagine if you did.'

'Why?'

'Just imagine you lived there in a community of expats for years. You know how you're not sure about moving to Australia? That is my whole life here.'

'It's not like you haven't had time to adjust! You went to school here!'

'You have no idea what it was like for me in school.'

The man at the next table glances at them. His nose is bulbous and the skin on his neck droops from his chin. Tessa's moment of anger subsides.

'Does being a redhead child actress come close?' she mumbles, as she eats the other half of her scone.

'It's not the same,' Deola says.

Tessa's hair is not the same shade of red as it was. It is darker now, less orange. She is going grey, so she dyes it. As a girl, she was in adverts for lemonade and toothpaste. Her teeth were perfect and her hair was coarse and curly. She envied child actresses like Patsy Kensit who had straight blonde hair. Actually, she hated Patsy Kensit. She wanted to be the girl in *The Great Gatsby* and people kept telling her she would make a wonderful Orphan Annie, whom she also hated. A West Indian woman at an audition suggested she use TCB conditioner to tame her hair and Tessa's mother had to go all the way to Shepherd's Bush to find some.

Tessa has had her hair blow-dried straight for auditions and worn wigs for roles. When they were roommates, Deola was amused that girls wanted cornrows after they watched the film *Ten*. She could either see it as a fashion trend or an insidious undoing. A boy who called her his mate asked if he could rub her Afro for good luck. She has had to get her hair chemically relaxed for interviews. A partner in her accountancy firm commented that her braids were unprofessional. Not once did she think her hair was the issue at hand.

'I mean,' Tessa says, dusting her hands, 'all my life I haven't been right for the roles I've wanted. If it's not my hair, it's my age. If it's not my age, it's my height. It's been like that from the very beginning, rejection after rejection. Never mind what I said in school. I was such a little liar then.'

'Weren't we all?'

'I actually thought you fitted in more than me.'

'Me?'

'You were a right little miss. "Would you please keep the noise down?" "Would you please not leave clothes strewn all over the floor?" I mean, what fifteen-year-old uses the word "strewn"?'

Deola steadies her teacup as she laughs. What she remembers is the careers adviser in their school telling her Africans were not intelligent enough to go to university and the drama teacher asking her to sing 'Bingo bango bongo, we belong back in the jungle' in an end-of-term musical, and trying to convince her that it was a satire.

Tessa did also have a reputation for lying. She said her parents had a mansion in Richmond. The mansion in Richmond turned out to be a semi-detached in Twickenham. She said she had to leave school because she was missing out on roles. Her mother was a music teacher and her father was a cellist. Tessa was on a scholarship. They withdrew her from boarding school because they feared she was losing her self-confidence. She was embarrassed about her upbringing, which she could claim was unusual until she met international students like Deola, who grew up overseas. 'My life is so blah,' she would say to Deola, or 'I'm so pale. I wish I could swap skins with you.'

Deola didn't want to swap skins with Tessa, nor did she believe Tessa would consider it a fair exchange. She thought every boarding school had the same sorry array of international students and had seen them at their loneliest, sobbing over a mean comment someone had made. All of them were levelled by their desire to go home.

'I've known you for so long,' Tessa says. 'You have to be a bridesmaid.'

'Of course.'

'There will be fittings.'

'I will be there for each one.'

'Our colours might clash.'

'That's not fair, Muir.'

'What? You started it. When will you be back from Nigeria?'

'In a week.'

'When would you like to be measured then, the Saturday after?'

'Make it the Saturday after that. I usually need two weeks to recover.'

Tessa makes a fist. 'Do us a favour, if you meet someone over there . . .'

'Um, I think it's a little precarious for one-night stands.'

'"I think it's a little precarious." See what I mean? It won't kill you to have one before you die.'

'Tessa.'

'What will you do otherwise?' Tessa asks. 'You might not get another chance if you're so picky about your options here. What's that look for?'

It is almost parental, the way Deola considers what she can bring up about her experiences as a Nigerian in England. Tessa would probably feel guilty, without realizing that Nigerians are as prejudiced as the English, and more snobbish. Nigerians, given any excuse, are ready to snub. Without provocation and even remorse. They snub one another, snub other Africans, other blacks and other races. Nigerians would snub aliens if they encountered them.

The first time she was ever aware her race mattered, she was in Nigeria. She was in primary school and must have been about eight. She was taking ballet classes at another school for expatriate children. The girls in the class were mostly English, but there were Chinese, Lebanese and Indian girls as well. Deola was one of a few Nigerian girls. The ballet teacher was English. She walked around clapping in time to the music, and ordering, 'Tuck your tails in,' as girls practised *pliés*. She would pass the Nigerian girls and say, 'I know it's hard for some of you.' She would pass the other girls and say, 'Good work!'

The next time, Deola was fourteen and in a summer camp in Switzerland. She shared a room with a blonde girl from Connecticut who was always getting into trouble with counselors and calling her parents in tears. Deola was combing her hair with an Afro pick one night when the girl pointed at her and laughed. This surprised her because during the day the same girl was constantly throwing her arms around a boy who looked like the youngest Jackson 5 brother, until he said she was so fat that if she jumped in the swimming pool, half the water would splash out. He was from Chicago. Deola, too, was infatuated with him. But one afternoon, they were at horseback-riding when he started dancing around her with his knees bent, flapping his arms like chicken wings and chanting, 'Ooga shaka ooga shaka.'

She went to boarding school in England a year later. In English class, she sat next to a boy who was forever cracking jokes. She noticed how her classmates called him 'Jacob', wrinkling their noses, as if his surname were a cough syrup. She knew he was picked on for a reason neither he nor they may have been conscious of. Then one day, they were taking turns reading *Look Back in Anger* out loud, and he asked a question about 'wogs' that she didn't catch. 'Now, now,' their English teacher said, with a smile. 'We don't say "wogs" here. We say "Western Oriental gentlemen".'

None of these experiences are worth mentioning, Deola decides. They are laughable.

'Want another scone?' she asks. 'I think I'll have another danish.'

Tessa's thirteen-year-old niece is a Dára fan. She is a fan of hip-hop in general and she does the hand signals and calls girls she doesn't like 'biatches'.

'She is such a silly sweetheart,' Tessa says. 'You just want to give her a clip around the ear. She says to me, "Can you ask your Nigerian friend to get me Dára's autograph?" So I ask her, "What do you see in him?" And she says, "He's gangsta." My brother and his wife are going spare. I told them not to worry. It's like rock and roll, really, this whole hip-hop thing.'

'Dára is not gangsta,' Deola says. 'He's just a college dropout.'

'How funny. I can see what she sees in him, though.'

'You can?'

'Mm. There's something about him. Something . . . very noble about his looks.'

Deola doesn't know what to say to this. The man at the next table with the bulbous nose looks noble to her, like a Roman emperor.

'How's your dad?' she asks.

Tessa's father is much older than her mother and he has Alzheimer's. He can no longer play the cello.

'Dad's not doing well,' Tessa says. 'That's one reason why I have to make a decision about this wedding soon. Mum's doing her best. It's something to witness, something to aspire to, the love between them. I just hope Pete will be there for me if anything like that happens.'

'He will,' Deola says, sincerely.

One night that week, she catches the end of a television interview with Dára and studies his face. He is not beautiful, but he may have crossover appeal: big eyes, a well-proportioned chin and a nose that doesn't change shape when he speaks. His face is still as a mask. Could that be seen as nobility? He is talking about his debut CD.

'The response,' he says, ''as been amazing.'

His chest is pumped up and the watch on his wrist is as thick as a handcuff. His interviewer, Abi Okome, is also well known. How he resists looking at her breasts is a mystery. They are propped up like bread rolls on a platter.

'In what way?' she asks, smiling.

'What way?' Dára says.

'Yes,' she says. 'Tell us how exactly.'

'Well,' Dára says. 'People recognize you. You can't just walk down the street any more. They call your name. At first, I was not sure 'ow to react, but I mean, I am sort of getting used to it now.'

His accent is a mixture of Cockney and Yoruba. He looks self-assured, but his smile ends and there is a moment when he lets out a giggle, as if he still can't understand what the fuss is about.

'So is England home for you now?' Abi asks. 'Because you're originally from Nigeria and my family is originally from Nigeria.'

Her hair weave barely shifts when she tosses it back. She is an attractive woman and she has that essential smile, that big smile that shows a lot of personality.

'Sure,' Dára says. 'England is 'ome for me now.'

Abi faces the camera. 'And Sir Paul said it wouldn't last! Give it up for hip-hop sensation Dára!'

Deola changes channels as the audience gives it up and woo-woos. England has changed. It's a long way from finding her way to the only record shop in Soho that sold soul imports. It's not just Nigerians; Black culture is everywhere now, but she is not satisfied. She turns off her television, mistaking her boredom and sense of unbelonging for an uncontrollable urge to sleep.

Foreign Capitals

On her overnight flight from Heathrow Airport to Lagos, she sits next to a woman who is reading a Bible. The woman started before the plane took off, mumbling psalms to herself. When the plane is about to land, the woman brings out a white rosary from her handbag and begins to pray out loud. The engine drowns out her voice. Passengers unclasp their seatbelts as the plane taxis. They grab their hand luggage from the overhead compartments. A flight attendant, who has not bothered to dye her hair in a while, ambles down the aisle saying, 'Please remain seated.' No one pays her any attention.

The moving walkway in the airport is stationary. Deola hurries past rows of blue chairs and down the escalator, which is also immobile. She is first in line at Passport Control, which means she has to wait longer for her luggage. Two flights have arrived this morning. Passengers sit on the edge of the carousel, hissing and sighing. Their suitcases emerge between cardboard boxes, which are untidily taped. The air conditioner is not working and the spot where Deola is standing reeks of armpits.

A gap-toothed man walks past her shouting on his mobile phone: 'Our luggages were delayed! I said our luggages were delayed! I can't make it until tomorrow!' He laughs and pats his handkerchief, which is hanging out of his jacket like a limp tongue. 'My prince! My professor! No, it's not New York I went to this time. It was London. For business.'

Deola cherishes her homecomings because of characters like him. She loves her fellow Nigerians, especially this one with his white pointed shoes. His arse is halfway up his back and his jacket almost reaches his knees. His oblivion is a spectacle of beauty. She can't stop looking at him.

She eventually gets her suitcase and wheels it towards Customs. The customs officers are men. One scratches his head and asks, 'Sister, *wetin* you bring come?' He eyes her midriff as his colleague chews on a toothpick.

'Nothing,' she says.

They wave her through. Her mother is in the crowd waiting on the other side of the automatic doors. She hugs her and they rock from side to side. She could easily lift her mother up, yet she is somehow able to lean on her.

'What happened?'

'There was a delay with our luggage.'

'We've been waiting for over an hour now.'

'Sorry.'

'I was beginning to worry. The driver has been circulating outside.'

Her mother, Remi, wears a navy T-shirt, white trousers and wedge-heel espadrilles. Her perfume is musky and she has a braided chignon attached to the back of her hair. A small woman, she parts the crowd while raising her hand in a stately manner and ignores the touts who call out, 'Yes? You need cab?'

Outside, she asks, 'Where is this fellow for heaven's sake?' and signals to the driver, who is standing behind the barricade. He waves to indicate that he will bring the car around.

She turns to Deola. 'So how are you, Miss Adeola?'

'Fine,' Deola says, feeling as if she is back from school with a report card that doesn't quite measure up.

'Is this a new hairstyle?'

Deola smiles. It is a prelude to a disagreement they have had too many times. She has been through experimental phases: twisting, dyeing and perennial braiding with extensions. Her hair once fell out after a relaxer.

The air is humid this morning and she sweats in her shirt and trousers. Her pashmina scarf hangs on her bag and her loafers pinch. The driver manages to park by the barricade. He loads her suitcase in the boot of the Range Rover. She and her mother climb into the backseat.

'Is this new?' she asks, pressing the leather.

'It's your brother's,' her mother says. 'He lends me his driver once in a while.'

'What happened to yours?'

'I sacked him.'

'What if he needs his?'

She is conscious that they are talking about the driver as if he is unable to hear them. She sees his eyes in the rearview mirror. He seems to be concentrating on the traffic ahead.

'You do what you must,' her mother says.

'At night? With armed robbers?'

Her mother shrugs. 'How for do? They attack in broad daylight.'

Deola straps on her seatbelt. 'You still don't use a seatbelt, Mummy?'

She is surprised by the resignation she encounters at

home. Her mother's eyesight is poor, yet she won't wear glasses, except to read. The roads in Lagos are full of potholes. Why would a seatbelt matter? Her mother says she doesn't use them because they wrinkle her clothes. Deola starts to object and her mother raises her hand and says, 'Jo, please.'

The driver slows down over speed bumps and turns up the air conditioner. They pass Church of the Ascension and a sign that says, 'Welcome to Lagos, a place of aquatic splendour.'

The city is shrinking, or perhaps it is just more crowded. It is rainy season, which makes Deola wonder why she ever called this time of year summer. The streets are waterlogged. Some of the sights along the way are new to her, like the organized labour mass-transport vans, but most are familiar. There are yellow taxis and vans, buses with biblical messages like 'El Shaddai' and 'Weep Not Crusaders', lorries dripping with wet sand, unfinished buildings and broken-down cars. People are crossing the central reservation of the highway and rams are feeding in troughs. The stalls in Oshodi Market look like prison cells and the skyline is cluttered with billboards advertising shippers, banks and computer colleges. Smoke rises behind a bush of palm trees. From Third Mainland Bridge she sees a cluster of houses and the University of Lagos. The edge of the lagoon is crowded with canoes and fishing nets.

'Are the street lights working now?' Deola asks her mother.

When she lived in Lagos, Third Mainland Bridge was a deathtrap at night. Drivers used to just slam into stationary vehicles, even with their headlights fully on.

'Nothing works,' her mother says, in a tone that approximates smugness. 'We thank God if we're able to get from A to B.'

'How are the plans for Daddy's memorial going?'

'We're keeping it simple. Otherwise, it's hopeless. In the morning, we go to church. In the afternoon, we have lunch. That's about it.'

'What about Aunty Bisi?'

'Bisi? Bisi is busy with her husband.'

Aunty Bisi is her mother's younger sister, who spent holidays in their house when she was in university. The guestroom was hers. She taught Deola and her siblings songs like 'Ruby Tuesday'. Once in a while she saved them from punishments. Her mother paid for Aunty Bisi's university education and training as a chartered secretary. Aunty Bisi must have felt indebted from then on because she was always around, helping with Christmas parties, weddings and other family functions.

Aunty Bisi is in her fifties now and for years has been involved with one of her clients, who is known as an industrialist and philanthropist. She is not actually married to him. He is a Muslim and has other wives. She has a son by him, and he supports her financially.

'What about Brother Dots?' Deola asks.

'Dotun?' her mother says. 'He's fine. He's flying in on Saturday. Why?'

'Nothing. I just wondered.'

Her father was married before. Brother Dots is her half-brother, who grew up with his mother. He is an engineer and he works for an oil company in Port Harcourt. He was a huge Jimmy Cliff fan in his teens. He had her and Jaiye playing backup singers and choreographed their moves.

As they drive into Ikoyi, Deola notices the oil-stained pavements bordering the road. It is Sunday, so the road is less congested, but there are hawkers and newspaper sellers. There are also beggars, who will become peripheral once she becomes habituated. Signboards are perched on buildings that were once residential: Phenomenon Clothing, FSB International Bank and Sherlaton Restaurant.

'*Na wa*,' Deola says. 'Ikoyi is practically commercial now.'

'You have no idea,' her mother says.

There was a time Deola could walk down the main road here. She ran errands for her mother at Bhojson's Supermarket and got her cholera inoculations from a Lebanese doctor whose practice was across the road. She would stop for a banana nut sundae at the ice cream pavilion in Falomo Shopping Centre further up the road. Sometimes, late in the afternoon, she rode her Chopper bicycle to Victoria Island on the other side of Falomo Bridge. Victoria Island was mostly anonymous streets and unclaimed plots then. Now it is as cramped and commercial as Ikoyi.

They get home and the driver waits as the watchman unlocks the gate. A Pentecostal church has occupied the house next door. Someone has painted 'Jesus is Lord' rather sloppily on the wall. The church is in the middle of a Sunday service. Deola hears a man (or woman) singing off-key into a microphone, 'Oh Lord, my God, how excellent is your name.' There is a chorus of electricity generators, which means there has been a power cut. Her mother has complained about the noise from next door, but she never thought it was this raucous.

'What is this?' she asks.

'The born-again Christians,' her mother says. 'I told them,

"The Bible says love thy neighbour. Is this any way to love thy neighbour?"'

Their original neighbours were an elderly French couple who owned a yellow Citroën with a sunroof. They returned to France and a succession of Nigerian businesses has occupied the house next door. The first was a hair salon and the second a boutique. For a while, the place was vacant, then it was an art gallery, which folded before the church moved in.

The pastor of the church has had the front yard cemented and the back of the building extended. If anyone complains about the increase in traffic caused by his congregation, he shows them his planning permit and invites them to join his church. On Tuesday evenings, he holds a spiritual clinic and on Thursday evenings, a revival hour. The family that lived on the other side of the church couldn't tolerate the caterwauling, as her mother calls it. They moved away. Her mother refuses to. 'I brought my children back from hospital to this house when they were born,' she told the pastor. 'I lost my husband in this house and I will not leave this house for you.' The pastor said, 'Well, madam, this church is God's house.'

Her parents' house was built before Independence and has the colonial features of others in this part of Ikoyi, including a chalet and boys' quarters. There is gravel in the driveway and crimson bougainvillea on the surrounding fence. The front door is glass with a framework of iron bars that are more protective than decorative. Indoors, with the electricity generator and air conditioner on, Deola can still hear the man (or woman) singing, 'Count your blessings' this time. She puts her suitcase under the stairs as her mother calls Lanre and Jaiye. She speaks to them on her mother's mobile phone and walks around glancing at the shelf of leather-bound books, the tapestry in the living room, the piano where her teacher made her play Bach's Minuet in G Minor over and over until she broke down and cried. Outside in the garden, her mother's tiger lilies are doing well; so are her traveller's palms.

Lanre and Jaiye ask routine questions about her flight and she answers 'yes' and 'no', enjoying the proximity of their voices. The Sunday newspapers are on the dining table. The headlines are about trade and politics, not the news she is used to reading overseas about Nigeria, which is about Internet fraud, drug traffickers, Islamic fundamentalism and armed militants in the Niger Delta. Here, the newspapers are specific about which states they are referring to in the Niger Delta: Rivers State, Bayelsa State or Delta State.

Small by small, she reorients herself.

Lanre and Jaiye show up before noon, Jaiye with her children. Deola teases them about raising a second generation of heathens. When they were children, they never wanted to go to church on Sundays. Instead, they looked forward to going to their beach house on Tarkwa Bay, where they would swim, drink fresh coconut milk and eat toasted cheese sandwiches. Lanre maintains his membership with Lagos Motorboat Club.

'What ever happened to the house on Tarkwa?' Deola asks him.

'It's there,' he says.

'Do you go?'

'Tarkwa? Hardly ever.'

'Ilashe Beach is the place to go now,' Jaiye says.

They are at the dining table. Jaiye's children are in the

sitting room. Deola gave them their nicknames, Lulu and Prof, which have stuck. Prof has astigmatism. He has worn glasses since he was a toddler. He sits cross-legged on a chair, sipping apple juice with a pensive expression. Lulu is lying on the sofa with her dress above her waist. She will only wear dresses, but she won't keep them on. Deola's mother pulls fluff from her hair. Lanre's sons are with his wife, Eno, for the day. Eno and her mother run a nursery that supplies flowers for weddings and funerals. Jaiye's husband, Funsho, has travelled to South Africa. Funsho works for a telecommunications company and their headquarters is in Johannesburg.

'He's always there,' Jaiye says. 'He is thinking of buying a house.'

'That would be nice,' Deola says.

Jaiye looks bored. 'There's too much crime.'

Jaiye is fashionable, even at work. She wears high-heeled shoes and jewellery with her doctor's coat. Today, she is in a *boubou* and her face is bare of makeup. She says there is a new community of South Africans in Lagos, and Kwara State has just adopted a group of Zimbabwean farmers who lost their land under Mugabe.

'So long as they don't bring their racial *wahala* here,' Deola says.

'What racial *wahala*?' Jaiye asks.

'It's the Chinese I'm worried about,' Lanre says. 'You know the Chinese. Before you know it, they take over your economy. Very soon they'll be telling America to shut up.'

'We're used to the Chinese,' Deola says.

The spring roll was as Nigerian a snack as puff-puff.

'Hong Kong Chinese,' Lanre says. 'These ones come from the mainland and, by the way, they hate each other.'

He still has a scar across his forehead from the car crash with Seyi and his patch of white hair has broadened. He has her father's tall stature and has over the years developed her mother's composure.

'I hear South Africans don't care much for Nigerians,' Deola says.

'I don't blame them after what Nigerians have done over there,' he says.

Lanre and Jaiye have not spent as much time abroad as Deola has. Jaiye studied medicine at Lagos University Teaching Hospital and Lanre got his degree from the University of Warwick in England. He worked at Trust Bank for a year and went back to England to get his master's degree from the University of Manchester while Deola was in Lagos; then he came home for good after she left. They regard her as a radical for raising issues like this: the négritude sister. Their lack of awareness doesn't surprise her. She was exactly like them when she was at LSE, and was surrounded by other Nigerian students who were the same way. Despite their academic competence, they were so averse to seeing themselves as subjugated or victimized in any way that to say race had any relevance to them was an admission too lowly to contemplate. In fact, if anyone was in the habit of bringing up racial issues, Deola might have accused them of having an inferiority complex. It wasn't until she started earning a living in England that she began to reassess her experiences there. Here, she is virtually colour free and she hopes to remain that way.

Lanre stretches lazily. 'That's one good thing about this place. We don't have any of that racialism rubbish.'

'I see too much of it abroad,' Deola says.

'Ignore it,' Lanre says.

'Come home more often,' Jaiye says.

Neither of them has left home, Deola thinks. Jaiye is thirty-five and Lanre is forty-one. Everyone they work with knows they are Sam Bello's children. They live in houses they inherited from him. Lanre's is on the other side of Ikoyi and Jaiye's is in Ikeja, where Deola's is. Hers is rented out for now.

Jaiye's children migrate to the dining room. Deola enjoys being their fun aunt. She can't tickle Prof under his chin, as she used to, so she wrestles with him. Lulu is too heavy to toss in the air, so she teaches her to say 'Wassup' in a raspy voice.

After a while Prof asks Jaiye, 'May I have more apple juice?'

He pauses as if he has asked an in-depth question. Jaiye goes to the kitchen to get him some as Lulu dances to another hymn blaring from the church.

Higher, higher, higher,
Lifting Jesus higher.
Higher, higher, higher,
Lifting Jesus higher.

As they eat lunch, they talk about the arrangements for the memorial. Her father's burial was overwhelming in comparison, from publishing the obituaries to organizing the wake-keeping and funeral. There were hundreds of guests to feed. Jaiye couldn't stop crying and Lanre, who confused his sadness for a foul temper, threatened to beat up a distant cousin who was bossing everyone around. Aunty Bisi was busy distributing the *aso ebi* and collecting payments. Another aunt accused her of having a profit motive. Someone else complained about the quality of the *aso ebi*. Deola didn't want to wear *aso ebi*, just as she didn't want to dance at her father's funeral reception. His funeral was communal, well beyond their control.

'None of that fuss,' her mother insists. 'We are remembering your father, not trying to bury him again.'

What Deola remembers are road trips to the house in her father's hometown and singing songs like 'Mama Look-a Boo Boo' on the way. The harmattan mists in the mornings and the smell of boiled corn in the afternoons. She also remembers family holidays in their flat in Cádiz, which they have since sold. Lanre was always chatting up local chicks and Jaiye once peed in the swimming pool. Jaiye was a cute girl, but she had a bladder problem, and she was lousy at Marco Polo. Her father was a glamourous man with a cigar in one hand and a crystal decanter of whisky in the other. Her mother wore big round sunglasses and wrapped silk scarves around her head. People in remote villages mistook her for an actress. They came out and stared as she spoke awful Spanish: 'Done-day-ester . . .'

The *Señora*. All she ever wanted was to find the nearest butcher where she could buy an ethnic cut of meat. On one holiday, she went as far as La Línea de la Concepción to buy pigs' feet and tripe.

Today, her *eba* and *efo* stew is delicious. After lunch, Lulu and Prof go upstairs to watch a DVD and she calls the house-girl, Comfort, to get more water.

'Comfort, will you get yourself in here?' she says.

Whenever Comfort falls asleep in the kitchen, her mother calls Comfort lazy. Comfort wakes up at six-thirty in the morning to sweep the floor and she doesn't stop working until nine at night.

Comfort walks in pouting. 'Yes, ma?'

She wears rubber flip-flops and her navy gingham uniform is too tight. She circles the table looking for a space where she can lean over and retrieve the empty bottle. Lanre hands it to her.

'Why are you staying in a hotel?' he asks Deola.

'I'm here on business,' she says.

'So?'

'I have to keep things official. No one at work knows I'm here for a memorial.'

'You can't tell them?'

'I've just started working there. I can't take time off.'

'England is too strict, man.'

'I swear,' Jaiye says.

'Bring a cold bottle this time,' Lanre says to Comfort.

Comfort returns to the kitchen. Deola recalls being that dependent on house help and quarrelling with truant drivers, who were nearly always rude to her. 'I'll tell your daddy,' they would say, snapping their fingers. She would snap her fingers back and say, 'You'd better respect me.'

Now she would be embarrassed to order anyone around, but she won't put up with the everyday inconveniences her family is accustomed to. She discovered the hotel online. It is a boutique hotel on Victoria Island, converted from a house. At night, her mother turns off the electricity generator. The hotel has two generators – or so its website claims. It has 24-hour Internet access and a restaurant, which means she won't have to wait for food to defrost. Her mother freezes everything to prevent rot during power cuts, sugar included. The hotel also has a car-hire service for guests, with drivers. She would find it impossible to get any work done otherwise, and if she stays at home, her mother might see that as an opportunity to nag her about settling down.

'I need to check in and have a good look at the place in daylight,' she says.

'I'll take you there,' Jaiye offers. 'You can see the new car Funsho bought me.'

'Is it nice?'

Jaiye pulls a face. 'Wait and see.'

Her mother calls Comfort to clear the table and goes to the sitting room to stretch her legs. Lanre says he has 'a meeting' to attend and reads his text messages.

'We all know it's your wife checking up on you,' Jaiye says.

'While the cat's away,' he says.

He is less serious than he appears. This is his playboy routine, which he should have outgrown, but he comes back to it whenever he needs to fool himself into thinking that he is still a bachelor.

'See your brother?' Jaiye says. 'This is what he does, then he disappears.'

Deola laughs. In her teens, she would have been the one at loggerheads with Lanre. She was forever confronting someone at the dining table: Lanre, for not helping in the kitchen; her mother, for letting Lanre get away with that; her father for being in favour of the IMF loan or some other government policy. She would call him a capitalist and he would completely ignore her. Her mother would ask why she was getting upset and Lanre, who had a knack for slicing through a person's tender parts, right between the ribs, would answer, 'Because she is a *lepin*,' a loser.

'Worry about your own husband's whereabouts,' he says to Jaiye.

His comebacks are more expedient than malicious. He forgets what he says within minutes.

'Jaiye,' her mother asks. 'Did you submit the memorial to *The Guardian*?'

'Yes.'

'Full page?'

'Half.'

'Why half?'

'Half is big enough,' Jaiye says.

'What did you write?' Deola asks.

'In loving memory and all that,' Jaiye says.

'What?' her mother asks.

'In loving memory and all that,' Jaiye snaps.

Deola shakes her head. She is back home.

'Did she e-mail it to you?' Lanre asks.

'No,' she says.

'Why didn't you e-mail it to her?' Lanre asks.

Jaiye frowns. 'Who has time for e-mail?'

'What do you mean you don't have time for e-mail?' her mother asks.

'Don't worry about it,' Deola says.

'I would have e-mailed it to you,' Lanre says.

'You should have e-mailed it to her,' her mother says.

Jaiye slaps the table. 'Lanre could have e-mailed it to her!'

'You people,' Deola says. 'It doesn't matter.'

The singing stops, which means the church service has ended. Deola goes to the shelf of leather-bound books before she and Jaiye leave. They are English literature classics her father bought in the early seventies. She chooses *Pride and Prejudice* over *Sense and Sensibility*. She was an Austen fan in her teens. She considered herself the sensible sister, but Jaiye was the pragmatic one in the end. Jaiye was able to settle. She, Deola, has been capricious in her relationships as well as her career. The moment she is not happy, she leaves. For her, there are worse situations, but none more preventable than being stuck in a job or marriage.

Lanre does not go to his meeting after all. He follows her and Jaiye to the hotel in his aged Volvo estate. Jaiye's new car is a Mercedes, which Deola suspects is meant to appease Jaiye for another affair. Inside, Jaiye turns the CD player on and begins to nod to 50 Cent's 'P.I.M.P.'.

'You listen to this when the kids are in here?' Deola asks.

'Of course.'

'Why?'

'Why not? They love it.'

'Have you heard of Dára?' Deola asks.

'Who?'

'Dára, the rapper.'

'Oh, him! He was a student at LASU, wasn't he?'

'So I hear. He's on tour in America.'

'Is he?'

'Yes. They're really promoting him over there.'

Jaiye hisses. 'He's not a rapper. He can't rap like the Americans. He can only sing hooks and not even well. He's not the best Afro hip-hop singer around. The *bobo* sounds like an intoxicated mullah.'

She slips on her sunshades and begins to sing, 'I don't know what you heard about me.'

Deola has trouble figuring out what 50 Cent is saying, but she no longer tries to impose her views on Jaiye. And Jaiye can be a tyrant these days, especially when she is at odds with her husband. Still, she doesn't see how Jaiye, who might cradle her children's heads to carry them into her car, can play music like this when they are around.

'I'm a motherfuckin' P-I-M-P,' Jaiye sings.

'When is Funsho coming back?' Deola asks.

'I don't know.'

'Will he make it for the memorial?'

'He says he will.'

'What's he doing in Johannesburg anyway?'

'Ask him.'

Jaiye steers away from potholes on the road. For as long as they have driven on it, the road has not been repaired. It is a measure of the decay and ruin in Ikoyi.

Deola thinks of her generation that was raised here, oil boomers, as she calls them, because they came of age during the oil boom and benefited from it. Does she have any remorse about dancing throughout dictatorships, taking orders like 'shake it but don't break it' and 'throw your hands in the air and wave them like you just don't care'? No, just a longing for the good old days when she had no responsibilities and didn't spare a thought for the future.

At LSE, one lecturer or the other would approach her and say, 'Shame about the coup in Nigeria.' She always got the impression they were snickering behind her back. After all, how had Nigeria governed itself since Independence? Two failed attempts at civilian governments, a four-year civil war and God knows how many military regimes in between. She would say, 'Yes, it is a shame,' wondering what their reaction would be if she revealed that 'Ain't No Stopping Us Now' (the extended version) almost brought their little section of Lagos to a standstill and 'One Nation Under a Groove' ruled for years. Kurtis Blow came along with 'The Breaks' just as the economy took a turn and slide, slide, slippity slide they did into a recession, yet oil boomers continued to rock throughout the eighties, chanting, 'The roof, the roof, the roof is on fire.'

They were the Ikoyi crowd and those who were in school abroad were 'Aways'. There was some resentment and contempt for them, but she never thought they should be held in awe as they sometimes were. She still doesn't because she has seen their ineptitude rather than elitism. They have access to the best Nigeria can offer, the best education and professional training the world over. Yet they can't get the country to function, or even preserve their little havens, like Ikoyi, which keeps on deteriorating.

Of the Ikoyi crowd, she is one of the few living abroad. The rest fly in and out and educate their children overseas. In the summer, they go on family holidays to get away from the rain. Dubai is the latest destination because Nigerians love to shop. They say things are bad in Nigeria, but there is money in the oil industry despite the grand larceny that goes on. There is money in the telecommunications and banking industries. There is money in the churches and non-governmental organizations. There is money for those who own their own professional practices. And for those who do not care to go through the normal apprenticeships or be burdened with public accountability, there are political positions in the Third Republic.

The hotel is a guesthouse. Its sense of intimacy remains intact despite its conversion into separate suites. It has modern stone walls and hardwood floors, a gym, a bar and an outside swimming pool. She can visualize a family living here, walking up and down the stairs and sitting at the dining table to eat. The other guests she sees in the lounge are diverse: there is a couple, Belgian most likely, who have adopted a Nigerian girl. The girl could pass for a boy. She wears denim shorts and her hair is shaved. There is an elderly black American woman who looks like an artist. She is dressed in a tie-dyed *boubou* and her hands are stained with paint. A young Nigerian guy, probably on a business trip, talks on his mobile phone while keeping an eye on his laptop. At the reception, a Hausa man checks out. An *oyinbo* woman with bleached hair accompanies him. She is dressed in a short, tight dress. Jaiye says she is a call girl.

After Deola checks in, Jaiye says she has to go back and pick up her children before returning home. She doesn't want to get caught in the traffic to the mainland. Deola sits with Lanre in the lounge and they get into a childish argument when he comments on his wife's weight.

'Eno's just getting fatter and fatter.'

'What is wrong with you?'

'But she is.'

'Why are you so wicked to the woman?'

'She's not taking care of herself.'

'Isn't she taking care of your children?'

'Wait until you see how fat she is.'

'Look at your stomach!'

'It's the fish and chips she keeps feeding me!'

'Isn't fish and chips what you wanted?'

Lanre denies it, but Deola remembers how he and Seyi went crazy for the girls with foreign blood: half English, half Jamaican, half bloody Cameroonian.

Eno's mother is English. Her father, a pediatrician, died when Eno was young and her mother remained in Nigeria. Eno was raised on fish and chips.

'She can't cook, man,' Lanre says. 'And she never uses enough pepper.'

Deola sighs. 'Let's change the topic. I don't want to hear any more of this.'

These clashes with her brother are inevitable. So also is his way of calling her 'man', as if she is an honorary one and ought to side with him. It is discomforting to be in a hotel with a man. The staff avert their eyes as if she is guilty of impropriety.

Lanre says Trust Bank is planning another share offer and advises Deola to buy more shares. The value keeps rising and the bank declares a dividend every year. She asks about Summit Bank, Nigeria, which has recently collapsed.

'Their directors were using the bank vault as their personal stash of cash,' Lanre says.

'Their auditors must have known.'

'Auditors,' he says dismissively.

He tells her Summit Bank was heavy with unsecured loans and buckling under bad debts as its directors misappropriated funds. Deola's threshold of morality drops. You cannot complain about corruption in Nigeria, she thinks. You dare not. Members of your family are corrupt, some of your best friends are corrupt. The only people who claim they are not corrupt have not had an opportunity to be corrupt, which is why they complain. They feel cheated in the midst of all the corruption around them.

When she worked for Trust Bank, she would get anxious about some of the bank's clients, which included corrupt politicians and dictators. She would ask her father, 'But isn't he . . .?' She is unable to finish her question, '. . . one of the biggest thieves in Nigeria?' And her father would answer, 'This is business. There is no such thing as clean money.'

It is incredible to her that anyone bothers to follow laws in Nigeria. They are optional. Lanre says the Economic and Financial Crimes Commission is cracking down on corruption, but the Summit Bank directors have not been charged and their depositors and investors are still trying to recover their funds. He then drifts into the usual about how difficult life in Nigeria is and soon he, too, says he has to leave.

'Why are you running away?' she asks.

'Armed robbers,' he says.

'Is it that bad?'

'Are you joking? My colleague at work, they woke him and his wife up with machetes. Just last week, they were shooting down the road from me.'

'You'd better go,' she says.

She was partial to Lanre when she was a ten-year-old. His games were a change from 'Red Rover' and 'Not Last Night but the Night Before'. She shared his interest in superhuman heroes who battled evil and saved the world. He was Batman and she was Robin. He always had to be the one who jumped out of hiding places, shouting '*achtung*', but she didn't mind falling down and playing dead for him. He thought she was tough for a girl – until she developed breasts. Then she became Triple Six and Moaner Lisa.

Lanre knew things: why planes flew longer in one direction and how fast piranhas could devour a human body. If he didn't feel like answering her questions, he would curve his arm and say, 'Ask-ology is the science of asking questions.'

The summer after Seyi died in the car crash, Lanre began to surround himself with boys who were notorious for smoking marijuana. He was sixteen. Her parents had no clue. Lanre was smoking at home in his bedroom, out of the window and using towels to block the draft under his door. He was also sleeping and eating more than usual. Her father was at work for most of the day and if ever Lanre got into trouble, he would say, 'Leave the boy alone. He's been through a lot.'

Lanre got suspended before the Christmas holiday, for sneaking out of school with friends, then during the following Easter break one of his friends ran down a motorcyclist. There was a court case, which was covered in the newspapers. Her father found out that the defendant in question was the same boy who kept showing up at their house, as if he had no parents to answer to, secretly bearing videos like *Emmanuelle* and *I Spit on Your Grave* because he couldn't watch them on the Betamax in his house. He could recite every line of Dr Fritz Fassbender's in *What's New Pussycat?* and of Popeye Doyle's in *The French Connection*.

Her father chased Lanre around the sitting room with a cane, warning him with each stroke, 'I, must, not, see, any of those louts in this house again. I have given you a long rope and you will not hang me with it.'

'I'm depressed,' Lanre yelled.

'You are not depressed,' her father said. 'You're stupid and I will kill you before you end up killing yourself or someone else.'

Her mother begged, 'Sam, don't beat my son. Please, don't

beat my son,' which was odd because only a few years ago, all Lanre needed to do was loiter in any part of the house and it was whack, whack, whack from her before she even asked, 'What are you doing here?'

Lanre cried out, 'I'm not a donkey,' gave her father a hind kick in the groin, and claimed it was a muscle spasm.

It wasn't funny then. Deola and Jaiye were in tears upstairs. They didn't speak to her father for days. Once he recovered, her father walloped Lanre for all the times he wanted to and didn't, walloped him in anticipation of more wrongdoings. He walloped Lanre so that he might not end up harming himself by drinking and driving, then he decided to send Lanre to school abroad for his A levels, to stop him from getting out of control.

Her father suggested that Deola go abroad for her O levels so that Lanre wouldn't be alone. Deola didn't mind, but Lanre was at Concord College in Shrewsbury and they hardly saw each other until the holidays, when they flew back to Lagos together on British Airways, usually not on speaking terms. Her father had them in separate schools intentionally, so they would learn to appreciate each other, which they did.

When Lanre turned seventeen, he was allowed to drive, but he was not allowed to go to Ikoyi Club without taking her. Perhaps her parents thought she might keep him in check, but she would sit with him and his new friends in the rotunda as they drank beer and talked about girls: who was fat, who was loose and who got *bensched*. She joined in with them because she despised girls, who were turning against her. One cow who was at Roedean, where Jaiye later went to school, would walk up to her, tap her nose and say, 'Powder.'

It was a confusing time. Eno was a skinny girl in drain-pipe jeans. She was in her final year at Holy Child College in Lagos. Lanre called her 'A Taste of Honey' because she looked like the bassist in the band, but he was two-timing with her classmate, who, according to Jaiye, had such a terrible reputation her name was an adjective and a verb. Jaiye was a junior girl at Holy Child. Lanre would ask her and Deola to lie to Eno whenever Eno called. Deola noticed how her mother took pleasure in announcing, 'Lanre, *one* of your girlfriends is on the phone,' and how his friends made comments like, 'You know, Deola, you'd be all right, if you'd only just learn to shut up.'

They were not interested in her in that way. They called her 'Small Girl' because she was a couple of years younger. She didn't socialize much with boys her age because their mothers would think she was loose. She tried to and one mother said, 'Don't ever call this house again.' Another asked, 'Why don't you wait for him to call you?'

She couldn't come to terms with why these mothers who had once patted her head now considered her a temptress, and she began to size up Lanre's friends who judged girls by their looks. One had a bottom as wide as the wings of a Boeing 747 and the other was as short as Tattoo on *Fantasy Island*. She stopped sitting with them and tried to form friendships with girls who were not vicious, but they were too goody-goody for her. They wouldn't even talk to boys. It was like belonging to the Scripture Union after a while, and she also lost patience with Eno, who stayed with Lanre even though he continued to two-time her – or have shows on the side, as he called it.

With Jaiye it was different. Deola didn't get along with Jaiye from the start. She bullied Jaiye. Her earliest memory of Jaiye was of her holding a stick with a piece of banana ice pop, crying, 'It's not fair, you took the bigger half.' Jaiye was always crying and telling. On Sundays, Deola had to oil Jaiye's hair and she hated doing that. Jaiye would cry, 'It's paining me,' and Deola would push her head. Jaiye would howl even louder, until her mother would come in and threaten to box Deola's ears or to throw her down the stairs.

She fought off other kids who called Jaiye names or tried to beat her up only because she considered that a personal affront. 'You wounded my sister?' she would say smacking her chest. 'I'll kill you!'

Jaiye grew up and began to preen and read magazines like *Vogue* and *Harpers & Queen* and Deola would order, 'Read a book.' She thought Jaiye was in danger of becoming vain. She would call Jaiye 'Popular J', popular jingo, to tease her, and Jaiye would call her 'Over Z', overzealous, to retaliate.

Jaiye started going out with Funsho, and Funsho had several shows on the side. His excuse was that girls were constantly hounding him. Funsho was known as a fine boy at University of Lagos. Two of the hottest Unilag chicks had got into a physical fight over him. Jaiye would walk into parties and stare her rivals down. She married Funsho soon after she graduated from the medical school. Deola could have told her that was a bad idea, but she didn't want to be accused of being overzealous, or worse, jealous. Lanre wouldn't discuss the matter, and her mother immediately began to plan a wedding, though her father didn't approve of Funsho. 'I don't think that boy is capable of kindness,' he once said.

Her father was capable of kindness. He would get her mother wet towels whenever she had headaches. He would shell her mother's pistachios and indulged her long-term infatuation with Harry Belafonte. 'Your boyfriend is on television again,' he would say and her mother would squeal, 'Ooh!'

Jaiye was Daddy's girl. He called her 'Doc'. He was worried that her marriage to Funsho would not last. He gave them the house in Ikeja as a wedding present anyway, but he made sure the house was in Jaiye's name alone.

Funsho, at least in the beginning of his marriage to Jaiye, was capable of going out at night and not coming back until morning. Deola told Jaiye to speak up and Jaiye did, quoting her. 'You see?' Funsho said. 'That is why your sister is not married. Her mouth is too big for her own good.'

This evening, there is a pleasant smell in the foyer of the hotel, like meat pies baking in an oven. Deola takes a bath and changes into sweatpants before coming downstairs for dinner. The tables in the restaurant are laid out with screen-print cloth and several paintings by local artists hang on the walls.

She orders a steak and sees the young businessman at the bar. He is with a woman who has a long hair weave and a bracelet just under her bicep. The woman is in her twenties, a Hollywood celebrity clone – or is it a hip-hop video-girl clone? It is hard to tell any more, but her confidence is admirable. She doesn't seem conscious that her jeans are so low they barely cover her backside.

Deola orders a bottle of Eva water and goes to the lounge to wait for her meal. A Nollywood film is showing on the Africa Magic channel. She watches for a few minutes when a man joins her in the lounge. She hears him laugh, but she doesn't turn around.

By now, she has figured out the plot of the film, which is about to end: prosperous and honourable man duped by his conniving wife and mother-in-law, who practises juju. His mother-in-law's juju backfires on her and she confesses to a priest who is brandishing a Bible. The film ends with a warning: 'Wickedness will not be rewarded. BEWARE!!!' Its credits are preceded by a message: 'To God be the glory.' Only then does Deola turn around and she discovers the man is not one of the guests she has come across.

'They all end the same way,' he says.

His moustache and beard are a dark shade of grey and he wears a white shirt. She pulls her T-shirt down, conscious of her sweatpants.

'What?' she asks.

'Nollywood movies. God takes care of everything.'

He puts his hands behind his head. He is not wearing a ring. She has seen several Nollywood films in England and has yet to decipher how much they approximate reality. The tragedies are comic, the comedies are tragic. The scripts are definitely written by men.

'It would be nice to see one that portrays women differently,' she says.

She couldn't care less. Her shrug gives her away.

'How so?' he asks.

'We're not all into witchcraft.'

He smiles. 'How's your room?'

'My room?'

'You're safe here. No need to worry.'

She returns his smile. 'I don't need your assurance.'

'Sorry,' he says, standing up. 'I didn't mean to be rude. I'm Wale Adeniran. I'm the owner of this place.'

She shakes his hand. She was attracted to him from the moment she saw him, but only when it occurs to her she has not met anyone this attractive in years does her heart begin to act up.

'It's a good thing I didn't badmouth the service,' she says, her voice higher than normal.

'How is your room?'

'Fine, fine.'

'And dinner?'

'I haven't had dinner yet.'

'Are they keeping you waiting?'

'No, no.'

Keep your head straight, she thinks, resisting the temptation to tilt it, as she remembers how easily a man can sense desperation in a woman.

'Let me know if there's anything I can do for you,' he says.

'Sure.'

She forgets to tell him her name and tries to hide her saggy sweatpants as she walks away, suspecting she looks as if she is wearing a baby's nappy. He can easily find out her name if he wants to anyway, and she is curious meanwhile. Why is he staying here?

She goes to the dining room and a waiter soon serves her food. Her steak is tasty and so filling she is sure she will sleep well tonight, but she doesn't. The generator that comes on at night doesn't carry her air conditioner well. After midnight, it begins to rain. She hears the drops on her window and worries about mosquitoes, but none surface. She takes out *Pride and Prejudice* and begins to read under her flickering bedside lamp. The lamp continues to betray her. She curls up wishing she were in her own bed and falls asleep at the purgatory hour, just before dawn, when she is most aware of how alone and vulnerable she is.

The next morning at breakfast, her eyes are swollen and her voice is hoarse. She eats a croissant that is a little too heavy and has two helpings from the fruit bowl, while nodding at the other guests as they appear. The black American woman is again dressed in a *boubou*. The Belgian couple is eating with their daughter, who smacks her lips. The young businessman is on his laptop again.

Deola goes to the front desk to check up on the car she has hired for the day and the receptionist asks, 'How was your night, madam?'

'Restful,' she says, reluctant to complain.

The receptionist has small eyes and full cheeks.

'Mr Adeniran says we should take care of you.'

'Why?'

'It's our policy, madam.'

'Oh, I see. Thanks.'

Her driver arrives. His Peugeot smells of his flowery cologne. It should take him only half an hour to get to the office, but the road is flooded and blocked with rows of cars, which are parked in front of businesses. One reverses on the street and blocks it. Car horns go off and the driver of the offending car pretends he can't hear them. When he's satisfied with the commotion he's caused, he drives off. Deola's driver turns into a road where residential homes are hidden behind rusty gates.

Victoria Island is the banking hub of Lagos. The traffic is so bad that people can't drive out of their homes during rush hour. There are fewer cars on the new road. Cigarette stalls are set up under almond and mango trees. GLO and MTN phone card sellers sit under umbrellas.

The office is in a block of flats with a cemented yard. No signboard, but the security guard confirms that she is in the correct place: Plot 400. He opens the gates and allows her driver to park inside.

'De malaria man?' he asks, when she asks for Dr Sokoya.

'The malaria man,' she confirms.

'First floor,' he says.

She walks up the stairs. The walls are smeared with handprints. Dr Sokoya shares the floor with a travel agency. He has a Ph.D. in public health. His certificate hangs next to a Chinese calendar. He is bald with a taut face and, for someone who is looking for funding, not cordial. He clasps his hands together on his table and watches his knuckles as she introduces herself. The fluorescent lights are harsh on him and a bottle of Eva water sweats on his desk.

'I thought you were expecting me this morning,' she says.

'I was,' he says, his gaze shifting to the whirring air conditioner.

She will give him a chance. She has often discovered that what she mistakes for hostility is simply nerves. Sometimes clients are simply trying to look busy.

'So you're London-based,' he says.

'I am.'

'You're lucky.'

'Am I?'

'Of course. To escape all the hardship.'

She agrees. London is not paradise, but that isn't the point.

'You are Yoruba?'

'My mother is Yoruba.'

'So *gbo* Yoruba?'

'Mo *gbo* Yoruba.'

'I'm surprised.'

She ignores his putdown, but he grows more inquisitive.

'You grew up in Lagos?'

'Yes.'

'Where in Lagos? Don't tell me, Ikoyi?'

'Yes.'

'I can always tell.'

He smiles and so does she. Worse than the smell of privilege is a cheap attempt to mask it.

At Trust Bank, she worked with men like Dr Sokoya. They immediately took a dislike to her. No matter how brilliant they were and no matter how much she admired them, an accusation would always come: 'I'm not from a rich family.' She would get upset. It felt like a judgement. Her father, who did not grow up rich, would warn her, 'It's envy.' Lanre would advise her on tactics similar to those used to tame wild animals: 'You have to know how to approach them. You have to come down to their level of thought and establish who is in control from the beginning. Any sign of weakness and they will pounce on you.'

Lanre was an heir to the throne at Trust Bank, but he did not earn that position. He had to prove he deserved respect from his colleagues, who got where they were by being competitive, not by stepping into Daddy's shoes. Her father's only encouraging words to him throughout his thirties were, 'A fool at forty is a fool forever.'

How annoying she must have been, practically apologizing for being the chairman's daughter. Her father and his peers were responsible for the new banking class that emerged after the banking sector was deregulated. Now that some of her former colleagues have risen in Trust Bank to become senior managers and directors, and now that Lanre has told her how quick they are to become pompous and ostentatious, she realizes that yes, it was envy all along.

Dr Sokoya introduces her to his employees, a skinny graduate and a woman her age who wears a wig. Deola is pleased that he is not particularly well dressed and doesn't have an expensive car parked outside. The security guards know what he does for a living. This points to his legitimacy, though she is certain he set up the NGO to create a job for himself.

He rubs his hands together. 'If all goes well, we are looking to expand next year.'

'Is there any reason why all shouldn't go well?'

For the first time he is animated. He waves his hands.

'Ah, no! I didn't mean it that way!'

She recognizes she is not the vulnerable party, coming from abroad and being in a position to decide whether his application for funding can go forward.

'I'll be in your way for two days,' she says.

'You're not in our way,' he says. 'Everything you need, we will provide.'

The right elements of internal control have been incorporated into their daily processes. They have paper trails, authorizations and separation of duties. Malaria does not get enough funding, Dr Sokoya says, and there are resistant strains because of the fake drugs imported from Asia.

'I hear it's the same with HIV,' she says.

'Yes,' he says. 'But that is mostly because people are

non-compliant. Even if the drugs are not fake, they don't take their medication regularly or they can't afford to continue to take the drugs.'

'Hm.'

'It is bad, but HIV gets more attention.'

'Malaria is also communicable.'

'Not in the same way. It is a parasite, not a virus.'

He is eager to explain what he calls the pathogenesis of the disease. She already knows about the female anopheles mosquito from secondary school biology. As a boarding student, she slept under mosquito nets. She would spray a cloud of repellent inside her net and wait for it to subside before going to sleep. If her net had a hole, she would patch it up. Malaria meant a few days off school. Solid food was out. The nausea was severe and the headaches and chills were worse in the evenings.

'So we're still fighting malaria with nets,' she says.

'It's the cheapest way,' he says. 'And prevention is always better than cure.'

The nets he distributes are pre-treated so there is no immediate need for mosquito repellents. She is sure she will be able to recommend his organization. She does not tell him this, though.

'I'll have to come back tomorrow,' she says.

'We'll be here,' he says, smiling. 'Maybe we can treat you to dinner afterwards, a local delicacy to fire up your London taste buds?'

This throws her every time: after the accusations come the propositions and they are delivered with such aplomb. She wonders why any man would want to date a woman he disapproves of.

'I doubt we'll have enough time,' she says.

'We'll see,' he says, undaunted.

The traffic is worse this afternoon, especially along the route her driver takes. They pass people queuing outside the Embassy of China. Perhaps they have given up on getting British and American visas, she thinks. On another street, also filled with potholes, she notices several car dealerships and it occurs to her that the terrain here actually resists development. It is a passive-aggressive landscape. There are no earthquakes, volcanoes, tornados or hurricanes, but a car dealership opens and the road in front of it splits, as if to say, 'I told you I couldn't handle it.' A mall is built and bundles of sticks and stones line up along the pavement and apologize, 'Oops, excuse me. Oops, don't mind me, I'll be out of your way soon.' A restaurant gets popular and a banana tree at the entrance wets itself and whimpers, 'I can't help it,' as mosquito larvae flourish.

The land is too damn African, stubbornly so. People can continue to develop it if they like, but it will find ways to expose any sign of urbanization as a façade.

She tells the driver to take her to Ikoyi to see her mother. At this end of the bridge, there are caged puppies for sale by a botanical garden. At the other end of the bridge, children beg for money by the police barracks.

She gets to her mother's house and her mother is furious because she has not heard from the caterer.

'That's your sister for you,' she says. 'She has to go and hire a caterer. I told her I didn't want a caterer. "Just go to the market, find me four women and they will do what they need to do." Oh, no, she has to go and get a caterer. "Oh, Mummy, she is a professional. Oh, Mummy, she has an office. She has staff. She has a mobile phone." Now, I can't get the woman to return my calls.'

It is not yet dusk. Her mother has taken her afternoon siesta and she is in the sitting room, dressed in a *boubou*. She is wearing burgundy lipstick. Deola can't recall the exact colour of her mother's lips, but she remembers crystal glasses stained with that shade of lipstick. Her mother is drinking a gin and tonic. At night, she might have wine with her dinner.

Deola calls Jaiye to ask why the caterer hasn't been in touch. This feuding between Jaiye and her mother is unsettling.

'Don't mind Mummy,' Jaiye says. 'She's joking if she thinks I have time to start looking for any women in any market. She wants everything done now, now. She just has to be patient. The caterer will call her.'

'She wants to know when,' Deola says.

'Tell her to cancel the caterer!' her mother says.

'Look,' Jaiye says. 'She'd better not annoy me today. I have told her before that those market women are unhygienic. I have seen people end up dead from typhoid.'

'Come on,' Deola says.

The market women were the only option before caterers came along. Their hygiene standards are not perfect, but their food is tastier.

'She's driving me crazy,' Jaiye says. 'You don't know what I've been going through with her. Listen, I have to go.'

'Wait.'

'I can't. I have a clinic.'

'Okay, okay.'

It is the stress of Lagos, Deola thinks, and the nature of

her family. They are a volatile lot. Didn't she once accuse Jaiye of betraying her as Judas did Christ? Didn't Lanre once swear he would throttle her if she so much as opened her mouth? She called him a drunk because he was breathing beer on her. Yes, and she was always getting into one disagreement or another with her mother, after which they would end up glaring at each other until they looked like gargoyles.

She hangs up and faces her mother. 'She says the women are unhygienic.'

'Don't mind your sister,' her mother says. 'The minute she has tension at home, she takes it out on everyone else. Are you staying for dinner?'

She is suspicious about the casual way her mother throws this in, as if to catch her off guard. This is how her mother works. She used to encourage her mother to work on her father this way: feed him first and then slip in your request.

She turns away from her mother's gaze. 'My driver has to leave at six.'

'It's rice and chicken stew,' her mother says.

'Don't worry, Mummy. I'll eat at the hotel.'

'I'll get Comfort to fry some plantains.'

'Mummy, the man says he has to go.'

'Call your brother, then. Call him and tell him you need his driver.'

'He might need his driver.'

'How do you know?'

'It's a weekday.'

'So? Call him and find out.'

'I don't want to bother him.'

'How do you know you're bothering him if you don't bother him?'

'Mummy,' she says. 'Don't worry. I'll eat at the hotel.'

If she stays for dinner, she can guarantee her mother will start prying again.

'I'll drop you there,' her mother says.

'It's not necessary.'

'I'll drop you . . .'

'But armed robbers . . .'

'What is this "armed robbers, armed robbers" about? They're part of our lives. You don't stop doing what you have to do because of them.'

'Mummy, the traffic is terrible and you can't see at night.'

Coming from abroad, she can never be right about Lagos. Everyone complains, but the moment she says things are bad, someone will say things are not so bad.

'If only I didn't have to sack my driver,' her mother says, giving up. 'The fellow had body odour, such awful body odour. I gave him antiseptic soap to wash, but he never made use of it.'

His name was Monday. Her mother also made him disinfect the steering wheel before she drove her car because he didn't always wash his hands after using the toilet. Monday didn't seem to mind. If her mother forgot, he reminded her, 'Mummy, don't forget the Dettol.'

Deola regrets leaving her mother drinking alone, but her mother has always done that, even when her father was alive. After her siesta, she would head straight for the cabinet, and pour herself 'a little something'. By nighttime, when her father arrived and they drank wine with their dinner, her mother would be toasting in foreign languages, saying, '*Salud*', '*Santé*', '*Salute*', even when dinner was stewed goat's intestines.

This evening, she sees Wale again, but not in the lounge. She is there for a while, watching *Idols West Africa*, but she can't be fooled into laughing at the contestants. They are over the top. One of them sings 'I bereave I can fry', and rather than suffer the procession of hopefuls, she goes to the bar and orders a bottle of Eva water.

Wale shows up at the reception. He is dressed in an *ankara* tunic and trousers. He talks to the receptionist, then heads for the lounge.

Should she or should she not? Deola thinks.

'Mr Adeniran,' she calls out.

'Yes, sir,' he says.

She laughs. 'I was just saying good evening.'

'Good evening.'

'How come you're a guest in your own hotel?'

'I stay here whenever I am in Lagos.'

'You don't live in Lagos?'

'I live in Abuja.'

'Don't tell me you're a politician.'

'Why?'

'I'd rather sit with an arms dealer.'

He sits on the barstool next to hers. She tells him she will be in Abuja on Thursday. His company is based in Abuja. He supplies computer hardware and he comes to Lagos to see clients. She guesses his clients are either foreign multinationals or the government.

'Sometimes I surprise them here,' he says, leaning forward. 'I make a reservation and they don't know it's me until I show up.'

She does not normally go for men with moustaches or beards, but they frame his mouth beautifully. His lips are darker than his skin. She likes his eyes most. They are sincere and his lashes are unusually straight. He could pass for a Hausa man.

'That's very sneaky of you.'

'You know how it is. You have to stay on top of things, otherwise.'

'Why didn't you just rent it out?'

'I thought about that, but there are businesses all over the island and not many reasonably priced places to stay. This way, the house works for me and I have somewhere to rest my head.'

'How long have you been in Abuja?'

'Six years. Six years now, but I have been going there for about sixteen. The first time I went there, all we had were the politicians and their entourage. Kingmakers, government contractors and prostitutes.'

'Commercial sex workers.'

'What?'

She smiles. 'Commercial sex workers. That's the correct terminology.'

'Is it?'

'Yes. And now?'

'Now?'

'Now, in Abuja, I mean,' she says.

'Now, we have traffic, armed robbers, the whole lot.'

Her father bought land in Abuja in the late seventies. It was the new federal capital then, but the government ministries had not yet relocated from Lagos.

'I've never been to Abuja.'

'No character whatsoever.'

'Seriously?'

'None at all.'

'Is corruption really as bad as people say it is over there?'

'You know how bad people say it is? Multiply that by a hundred. What are you going there for, business or pleasure?'

She tells him about her job at LINK, wondering if he thinks she belongs to an industry that thrives on an Africa that panders to the West. But computers don't necessarily make for progress. Not in basic humane ways. Not in ways that matter. All they have done in Lagos is create work for Yahoo Yahoos.

'I have to make sure our money will be in safe hands.'

'It's necessary,' he says. 'I get around and I'm telling you, the nongovernmental sector is becoming a racket. Here, take my card. You should give me a call when you get in. I'm leaving tomorrow morning.'

She doesn't read his card and she still hasn't told him her name, but she is sure he knows who she is.

'Do you prefer Abuja to Lagos?' she asks.

'My work is there and my daughter is in school there.'

'I see.'

She has misread their conversation. He is married with children.

'Do you have anyone there?' he asks. 'Friends? Family?'

Her tone is less casual as she tells him her family is in Lagos. As if to remind herself, she adds that her father's memorial is on Sunday.

'I'm lucky to be able to come home,' she says. 'Imagine trying to explain to an English boss the significance of a five-year memorial.'

'I know,' he says. 'My old man died in '86 and I was in the States.'

'Which state?'

'New York.'

'That must have been nice.'

'It was, but I was almost at the end of my course when my father died. I had job interviews lined up and everyone was telling me to come home. So, I came home. I've been hustling ever since. Nothing I learned abroad has been of any use to me. I have friends who still live there. Their parents die and they fly in for a couple of days. I think the English are more sympathetic than the Americans are about these things.'

'Was your father ill or . . .?'

'He had cancer.'

She drinks her Eva water. Their parents were taken down by cancer, heart attacks and strokes. Respectable diseases. She assumes Wale inherited the house. With the reconstruction work, it must be worth about a million pounds.

'So many fathers are dead,' she says.

'Mothers, too.'

'All I ever see are widows. Where are the widowers?'

He pats his chest and she covers her mouth.

'It's all right,' he says. 'It's been a while now and my daughter and I are doing well.'

'What is her name?'

'Moyo. Or you mean my wife? Her name is . . . was Ronke. I'm never sure if it is "is" or "was".'

His voice trails off and she can't think of something suitable to say.

'I should go.'

'Make sure you call when you get to Abuja.'

'I will,' she says.

—

On Wednesday evening, she meets her cousin, Ivie, at a hair salon on Victoria Island. The salon, converted from a shipping container, is on a rented plot. Indoors, the air conditioner is on. The white walls are chipped and the ceiling is peeling. Samba music is playing. A hairstylist sings along as another, a man, heats up curling tongs. The supervisor is behind a desk, collating receipts.

Two stylists are braiding Ivie's hair with extensions. Ivie is remarkably pretty and slim. She incurred wary looks from other patrons when she walked in, followed by a general slighting. Deola wondered if Ivie was aware. She has observed how Nigerian women use their fluency in silence to isolate women who, by their mere appearance, suggest they are not willing to obey the order, no matter how trivial, idiotic or catastrophically destructive the order is. Ivie looks like a woman who would have no qualms about breaking up a marriage.

'I've never heard of him,' Ivie says. 'Wale Adeniran?'

'Yes.'

'And his wife died?'

'Yes.'

'And he hasn't yet remarried?'

'Not to my knowledge.'

His marital status may not be a consideration for Ivie, who has been living with a married man, Omorege, for years. She was with him before he got married. Omorege is a senator and is separated from his wife, Patricia.

'He sounds suspicious to me,' Ivie says.

'Why?'

'There are no men like that in Lagos.'

'What do you mean?'

'He is single, owns a hotel and no one has snapped him

up yet? Do you know how many single women there are in this place? This is not a matter of scarcity. Men like that don't exist. Or is he . . .'

Deola winces. 'Gay?'

'He might be, especially if he lives in Abuja. What? That is their home base. Everyone knows they go there to look for government contracts.'

The stylists laugh as Deola shakes her head. She will never understand Nigerian attitudes towards gays: even the most decadent and perverted Nigerians vilify them, while those who are more open-minded worry about their proliferation as if they were an infestation of mosquitoes.

'Nigerians,' she says. 'Why are we like this?'

Ivie glances at the male hairstylist and whispers, 'Me, I have no problem with them. It's when they marry that I have a problem. I don't like confusion. It's bad enough man to woman. You have to declare your stance, that's all I'm saying.'

'He's not gay.'

'How would you know?'

'I can tell.'

'How?'

'I just can.'

'Okay, how are you so sure his wife died, then?'

'Why would anyone lie about that?'

'He might have killed her. Seriously, there have been cases like that. They give their wives rat poison. Look, one man I know did it and he got hold of his wife's inheritance. Why are you laughing? You have to be careful these days. You meet a single man in Lagos and it's best you check with Interpol. The worst part is that they are not like our fathers. At least our fathers tried to take care of their families. These ones don't care. As for women, they've gone nuclear. If you can't provide, they will find someone on the side who can. It's true! Alternative energy sources!'

Deola laughs. 'Please, don't kill me.'

Ivie's Omorege was a victim of that. He met his wife, Patricia, when they were both students in university. They came from the same town in Bendel State. Patricia won a Miss Nigeria pageant. Her guardian was a family friend she called 'Uncle'. Uncle was a retired brigadier. He became a governor after a military coup. He was ousted in a subsequent coup, but he made money while he was in office. He helped Patricia financially and bought her a car. He said he was taking an interest in her studies. He turned out to be her sugar daddy.

Omorege found out after he got engaged to Patricia. He broke off their engagement, and at first Patricia said he must have known all along; then she got down on her knees and begged. Omorege refused to take her back. He met Ivie and started going out with her. Patricia tried to kill herself by swallowing aspirins. Omorege visited Patricia while she was hospitalized and she seduced him during her convalescence: she bought fertility drugs on the black market and pierced a hole in his condom. All this became public knowledge after she delivered triplets. Omorege married her because they were Catholic, but they have separate homes and he continues to live with Ivie, who has not been able to have children.

Marriages in government circles are like Nollywood scripts to Deola. Lagos is still captivated by the news of a minister who has been in every administration, military and civilian, since the Second Republic, doing nothing useful and getting richer. The newspaper reports accuse him of sleeping with his daughter-in-law. Deola doesn't doubt he is capable of having an affair with his daughter-in-law, but she can't believe the manner in which the reports relay the details, showing the same photograph of the woman in question, with a hair weave and deep cleavage, and referring to her as 'the delectable thirty-four-year-old'.

The supervisor changes the music to what initially sounds like another samba number, but turns out to be a catchy gospel song. A customer, who is eating a takeaway meal that resembles chicken piri piri, begins to sing along to the chorus, 'The best, is yet, to come! The best, the best is yet to come!'

Ivie reaches for her bottle of Coca-Cola and mumbles, 'They've started.'

Ivie attends a Pentecostal church, but she dislikes pious displays. She was previously with another church, 'Church of Curses', as she now calls it. She might have joined because of her infertility problems, but the pastor told her someone had put a demonic lock on her womb, so she left.

The woman continues to sing, 'Today is the first day of the best days of your life! Today is the first day of the best days of your life!'

Nigerians are usually tone-deaf, but her voice is beautiful.

She gets higher and higher, 'You ain't, seen nothing! You ain't seen nothing yet! You ain't, seen nothing! You ain't seen nothing yet!'

Deola browses through a magazine, *Metropolis*, crammed with photographs of camera-ready people. 'Celebrities on the Red Carpet', the heading reads. They are TV personalities, Nollywood actors, musicians and singers, carrying on as if Lagos is Los Angeles.

'So there are no normal couples here,' she says.

The Coca-Cola deepens Ivie's voice. 'My dear, everyone is sleeping around.'

Ivie also mixes with the financial circle in Lagos that is concentric with the government circle in Abuja. She says single women party in Nigeria. They may pray to get married and to have children, but they don't sit around waiting for God to deliver them. They share men. They don't deceive themselves as married women do. Are they better off? thinks Deola, as Ivie then demoralizes her with halfhearted gossip about couples who are either separated or divorced, husbands who beat their wives and wives who are having affairs. Some woman has just poured boiling water on her husband and no one knows why. The number of stories about widows who were said to be visiting their boyfriends when their husbands died is disturbing.

'So someone can't die without his wife being maligned,' she says.

'What scares me the most,' Ivie says, 'is that you don't even know what people die of these days.'

'*Na wa* for Naija marriages,' Deola says.

Ivie is her paternal cousin. Ivie's mother is her favourite aunt who ended up with a man from Benin City who beat her. He beat her so hard she would run into the street to escape him. She relocated to Port Harcourt, where she married an elderly polygamist.

When they were younger, Deola saw Ivie as her out-of-town cousin who was funny but forward. Ivie would order Deola around and Deola, herself a little bully, would tell Ivie, 'You're not my leader.' They became close when Ivie got a job at Trust Bank during her national service year. They stayed in the chalet and went to work together. They also went to parties together.

Ivie looked like a model. Miniskirts and leggings were in, and invariably, guys would approach Deola and ask, 'Who is that?'

But Ivie had no time for Ikoyi guys, especially the Aways. She thought they were immature and trying to impress her, 'disturbing her with their nonsense', as she would say. She had so much parochial pride. Omorege came along and he was a little older. He was a managing director of a finance house, which went bankrupt. The rumour was that he cleaned out his clients, though he denied this. Ivie fell in love with him and no one in the Bello family could believe it. Barely a few months in Lagos, and she was carrying on with a married man, who then disappeared to London for about a year, abandoning his wife and triplets to avoid facing charges under a failed bank decree. For a while Ivie was the bad girl of the family, but now everyone seems to have forgiven her.

It takes two hours to braid her hair and she drives Deola home afterward. Deola wants Ivie around so she can avoid having the marriage talk with her mother.

Is it her imagination, or has she been hopping from one luxury car to another here in deprived Africa? Ivie's is also fairly new, a BMW, which Ivie says is nothing compared to the cars some of her colleagues have.

'It's all show in this place,' she says. 'We're all caught up.'

'Naijas in England are like that,' Deola says. 'They're even worse in America.'

'Don't trust what you see,' Ivie says. 'A Nigerian may not have a kobo to his name and you will never know.'

It is not whether people here can afford luxury cars; it is the state of the roads. Ivie has to drive on the sidewalk at one point. Only an army tank could survive the potholes along the way.

'But aren't people doing well in business?' Deola asks. 'All I hear is that people are doing well in business.'

'Don't let anyone fool you,' Ivie says. 'There is no real business here. All we have is oil money circulating in our economy. The whole banking sector is running on laundered money. The whole of Nigeria is.'

Ivie is the corporate relations director of her bank. Deola has heard that Victoria Island is sinking. She has had nightmares of hurricanes submerging the island, neighbouring Lekki Peninsula and Ikoyi, along with their overvalued properties and inhabitants.

Tonight they get home and Deola's mother is fussing about the canopies she has rented. She is sure it is going to rain on Sunday. Deola is never indulgent whenever her mother is like this, working everyone up about problems that may not occur. Her mother's ability to get attention in any given room and have everyone consoling her is astonishing.

'The canopies are going up on Saturday,' her mother says. 'I should have rented a hall instead and had it indoors, given my guests lunch and be finished with it. I don't know why I didn't think of that before. They will tear up my grass. The rain falls for one second in this place and your heels just sink in.'

'Don't worry, Aunty,' Ivie says. 'It won't rain, by God's grace.'

'I hope not,' her mother says to Ivie. 'I have my gardener coming in tomorrow. But surely, one shouldn't pray for no rain.'

'It didn't rain on the day of Uncle's funeral,' Ivie says.

'Oh, it did,' her mother says. 'That morning and that night, remember? We were spared in the afternoon. This time of the year is no good for any type of outdoor function. Remember Jaiye got married this time of the year and it rained so heavily?'

'It didn't rain that much,' Deola says.

'I remember,' Ivie says.

'You remember? We couldn't get out of church that morning, and the ushers with the umbrellas. We were all wet. We had the reception at that restaurant on the lagoon.'

Deola's mother is intentionally ignoring Deola and as for Ivie, this is typical of her. She grovels to her elders. Deola remains silent as her mother goes on about the likelihood of rain, but she snaps when the subject turns to her trip to Abuja the next morning.

'It's in and out with this one,' her mother says.

'I have work to do,' Deola says.

'She comes in on Sunday,' her mother says. 'Now, she's off to Abuja.'

Ivie laughs. 'Aunty, Aunty!'

'In and out. That's your cousin. She comes home and moves straight into a hotel.'

'You don't have a driver,' Deola says.

'You could have borrowed your brother's driver,' her mother says.

'He needs his driver and I had to e-mail my boss. You don't have e-mail.'

'She will be back on Friday,' her mother says to Ivie. 'On Sunday, after the memorial, she takes off again.'

Deola shrugs. Her mother stayed home and raised children. Now, she controls shares. She dresses up for meetings at Trust Bank, walks into the boardroom and everyone stands up and calls her 'Madam'.

'If you're going to Abuja,' her mother says, 'you might want to check up on your father's land to see what has become of it. The government has given us a certain amount of time to fence it; otherwise they will seize it.'

'I won't have time,' Deola says.

'You might want to make time,' her mother says. 'The land is worth a considerable amount, as you well know.'

They eat shrimp curry and coconut rice for dinner. Ivie drives Deola back to the hotel. There Deola e-mails Kate to say she has reviewed Dr Sokoya's NGO and will be in Abuja tomorrow. She has two scam messages in her inbox, which she is sure came from an Internet café somewhere in Lagos.

In the foyer, she passes the receptionist, who asks, 'Is everything okay, madam?'

'Yes,' she says.

'You're still checking out tomorrow?'

'I am. Thank you for taking care of me.'

'You're welcome. I was worried that something was wrong.'

Deola thought she had a smile on her face. The receptionist was probably worried that she was annoyed about the bartender, who was on the computer, surfing the Internet before she got online. She was busy thinking of her conversation with Ivie on the way here. Ivie asked her to be more understanding, as her mother was upset at having lost the love of her life. Deola thought that was typical of Ivie, to completely romanticize a tense family situation, then she conceded for a moment. Then she went back to seeing her mother as a manipulator, taking any opportunity to interfere in her life.

She can't bear her mother's disappointment. Her mother's enduring disappointment. She wants to distance herself from it. She doesn't even want to rebel against it because it might end up defining her, if it hasn't already.

The young businessman is in the lounge, speaking French on his mobile phone.

'*Oui, oui*,' he says. '*D'accord*.'

She can't understand what he says after that, but she enjoys listening to him. He is probably in marketing or some other trendy job.

She is suspicious of the term 'brain drain', which she first heard at LSE. For her, it was a polite alternative for people who might want to say 'Go back to Africa'. She has always thought there are enough brains in Africa, at least in Lagos. People who may not do much for the common good, but they achieve so much for themselves. She runs into old friends, most of whom are married with children, and marvels at their accomplishments – lawyers who are jewellery designers on the side, doctors who just happen to be manufacturing beauty creams, accountants who produce Nollywood films. They make the opportunities overseas look like a joke.

In her room, she recalls her father's reaction when she resigned from Trust Bank after Ivie did. 'You as well?' her father asked, as if Ivie's behaviour and hers were on par. Then he concluded, 'You children are too flighty.'

Her mother called her friends and told them Deola was going back to England. She gave every relative that came to the house a full report. Aunty Bisi stepped in to mediate telling her, 'Stay, stay,' until Deola finally said, 'Oh, come on, you people. I'm going to join an accountancy firm, not a pop group.'

They treated her as if she were still in boarding school and at home on vacation. But she was twenty-two and still living at home. Even if her parents approved of her moving out and renting a flat, she couldn't afford to rent in any decent part of Lagos. On her salary, her options were to find a sugar daddy or hustle for a government contract, which would probably not be awarded without a sexual favour. That was not the Nigeria her parents returned to, a Nigeria where they were feted just because they were graduates and offered jobs with housing and car allowances. She had all that at Trust Bank, but she couldn't sustain herself with an out of control inflation rate to contend with, so what was the point of staying? What sort of privilege was it to live off her parents?

Some of her colleagues found her decision to leave Trust Bank predictable. It confirmed what they thought of her: pampered and sheltered. What was all this talk about independence? Why couldn't she just ask her father to pay for an MBA? Then, after she left, circumstances changed for a minority of them. Their salaries became higher than hers in England, despite an exchange rate that was unfavourable to them. They climbed out of the recession and up the corporate ladder and the longer she stayed in England, the more difficult it was to return and compete with them. She held on to her independence there, even as her independence began to look more like loneliness.

Her father wanted her to work for Trust Bank after she qualified as an accountant, but she was reluctant to: her colleagues would never give her credit as the chairman's daughter. 'I don't know why you care,' her father said. 'There isn't a single one of them who wouldn't want to be in your position.'

His family were farm folk. He grew up with a hoe in his hand. He bragged about how he would walk miles to get to school, wearing hand-me-down plimsolls and carrying books on his head. He had two khaki uniforms to his name. When he washed one, he wore the other. His parents couldn't read or write but they managed to send him to Durham University. He left for England on a cargo ship. He was not interested in starting a practice when he returned to Nigeria as a qualified accountant. He worked for United Africa Company and acquired shares in foreign companies during the indigenization era in the seventies. He went into banking when that sector was privatized in the eighties. He told her he was a millionaire when the value of the naira to the pound was one to one. He was badly hit by the devaluation of the naira, but he recovered by capitalizing on foreign exchange deals. He might have sensed what she didn't know at the time, that she was unwittingly in competition with him. She wanted more than he could offer.

'You can never rise to the top as an African overseas unless you do exactly as you're told,' he used to say.

'I will, Daddy,' she would say. 'You'll see.'

She packs *Pride and Prejudice* in her suitcase. When she first read it, the Bennets were fascinating to her. Now, they could well be a Nigerian family. She pulls out Wale's card from the pouch where she keeps her underwear. His full name is Adewale and his middle initial is also 'A'. She wonders what the 'A' stands for as she transfers his card to her wallet. Her mother would like him. A good man from a good family.

The next morning, she takes the first flight to Abuja. The air is drier there but with the hills, palm trees, cornfields and red soil she could be anywhere outside Lagos. On the way from the airport, she passes bundles of sticks, laundry laid out to dry, bungalows with corrugated-iron roofs and dwarf goats. A group of girls carry pots on their heads and a lone elderly man sits under an umbrella to protect himself from the sun. This is Islamic territory. In the villages, men wear skullcaps and women are wrapped up.

She thinks of her old friend Fatima, who lives further north in Kaduna. Fatima was known as a cool Hausa chick, a forward-thinking Muslim because she drank beer and smoked cigarettes in private. They were classmates at Queen's College. They met up during national service and have since been out of touch. Deola was surprised to hear that Fatima agreed to an arranged marriage after national service. Her wedding was a seven-day affair attended by sultans and emirs. Her bridesmaids got their hands and feet dyed with henna. The president made an appearance at the wedding prayers. The marriage didn't last. There was some talk that Fatima's husband discovered she wasn't *virgo intacta*, but people said he wouldn't know the difference because he drank too much – so much that he would wet himself in bed. Fatima had a daughter by him and moved out. She started a law practice in Kaduna and became an advocate for underage Northern girls who were forced into arranged marriages. The girls she represented were in their early teens. Her NGO was Daughters of Islam, Women for Islam or some pro-feminist, pro-Islam name that didn't quite add up. She started covering her hair, which may have been a ruse to continue her subversive activities, but people laughed at her and called her a born-again Muslim.

As the city approaches, there are more motorcycles, vans and lorries. In the distance is a cluster of houses with blue roofs. The taxi driver points out Millennium Park and Aso Rock, where the president lives. There are rumours that the president, a former military head of state, is seeking an extra term in office. Lanre claims he is sweetening the Senate and House of Reps and money has been moving around mysteriously in banks. She understands what Wale means about Abuja lacking in character. Close up, the buildings are new and incongruous. Some look as though they belong somewhere in Florida.

At the Hilton, she checks in and takes another taxi to the office of Widows In Need. She is early for her meeting with the CEO, Mrs Nwachukwu, and her vice president, Elizabeth Okeke.

Elizabeth seems friendly. She wears a shin-length flowery dress and is possibly in her thirties. Mrs Nwachukwu is definitely in her fifties, portly, and her glasses are perched on the tip of her nose. She is dressed in an elaborate up-and-down.

'From where are you?' she asks.

Deola's first instinct is to say 'Nigeria', as she does in London. Then she remembers that here, she is from whatever state her father is from. She has never lived in Kwara State, so she says, 'Lagos.'

'Are you Yoruba or Hausa?' Mrs Nwachukwu asks.

Deola smiles. 'Does it matter?'

'Just out of curiosity. "Deola" is Yoruba, but "Bello" could be Hausa.'

'It's not Hausa.'

Mrs Nwachukwu shrugs. 'As I said, it's just out of curiosity. If you hear my surname, you will be right in eh, assuming I am Igbo, but Elizabeth here is not. She is from Plateau State.

Okeke is her marital name. You see? So I thought, "Okay, Bello must be her husband's name, then."'

'I'm not married,' Deola says, keeping her smile intact. 'I consider myself Nigerian and I hope we can be united in the face of this epidemic that threatens us.'

She is always thrown by ethnic distrust, though she has read enough newspaper editorials about the next elections to understand how much ethnicity still matters politically. Pressure groups are vying for equal representation in the government. She suspects she sounds just as bombastic as the editorials. What did any of that mean? *I consider myself Nigerian. United in the face of this epidemic.*

Predictably, Mrs Nwachukwu is noticeably offended, taking in Deola's pearl earrings, black linen dress and pumps as if the overall understated effect is a plot to undermine her flamboyant, traditional look.

'Kate Meade is your director, eh?' she says, stroking her gold pendant. 'Yes. I've been communicating with Kate Meade.'

Mrs Nwachukwu's mobile phone rings a cheerful calypso tune. She indicates she needs privacy and Elizabeth ushers Deola out of her office as Deola scolds herself. She and Mrs Nwachukwu have one Nigerian trait in common, the tendency to jeopardize an opportunity out of sheer arrogance and still expect a suitable outcome.

The friction works in her favour. Outside in the corridor, Elizabeth whispers, 'Don't mind her. She is a difficult woman. You know she was a midwife?'

The corridor is empty but for the two of them. Deola steps away from the door and keeps her voice low.

'I know.'

'I'm her in-law. She is well known within the family for being troublesome.'

'I'm just here for a review.'

'That's what I'm trying to tell you. She collected money for HIV education to start WIN.'

'So . . .'

Elizabeth pats her chest. 'So I'm saying the women are from my town. I was the one who told her about their predicament. Their husbands drove lorries. They travelled up and down the country. They followed prostitutes. Everyone knew why they died. No one needed any education.'

'Education can't do any harm.'

'I know that, but they are not prostitutes. That is what I'm saying. She collected money to educate prostitutes. The foundation came from the US to inspect. She said the women should pretend they are prostitutes. I said, "How can they pretend they are prostitutes?" The very people who caused the problem in the first place.'

'No one caused the problem.'

Elizabeth turns away. 'Unless you don't want to say the truth. You should know that wives are not in the same category as prostitutes.'

'So what is it you are saying?'

'I'm saying let her educate prostitutes if she wants to. That is her own business, but she shouldn't put the women of WIN in the same category. They need medicine. They haven't seen any medicine yet. Some are sick. They don't know what to do. They can't afford to go to hospital. But most of them are well and they don't want education.'

'How can LINK help?' Deola asks.

Elizabeth shakes her head. 'I can't tell you.'

'That's what I'm here for.'

'Microfinance. Have you heard of it?'

'Yes.'

Elizabeth glances at the door. 'She says she is not interested. Me, I don't know. I'm not the one collecting money all over the place for all sorts of purposes. I'm not the one with a big, big house. See this place? It belongs to her brother. So who is collecting the rent? Who benefits from WIN? Ask yourself these questions. Me, I'm not an enemy of progress. I'm just telling you what I know.'

The office block is four stories of whitewashed concrete and reflecting windows, but the rent may be less than what WIN might pay in Lagos. Elizabeth puts her finger to her lips when she hears Mrs Nwachukwu calling her name.

Deola is not surprised that there has been misrepresentation of purpose and misdirection of funds in the past. A review of their fieldwork by the US foundation would have uncovered that. For now, she is concerned that WIN is renting an office from Mrs Nwachukwu's brother, so she focuses on their administrative costs, which are disproportionately high. She suspects that Mrs Nwachukwu's salary is understated, but what bothers her most is that every purchase order, every receipt and cheque has been signed by Mrs Nwachukwu alone.

'What is Elizabeth Okeke's job description?' she asks later.

'Elizabeth?' Mrs Nwachukwu says. 'Elizabeth is, well, eh, officially, Elizabeth is my VP, but in actual fact, she is a jack of all trades in this office. Yes. As a matter of fact, she is invaluable to us. We would not be able to function without her.'

'She says you have not been able to get any medication.'

'She did?'

'I asked her.'

Mrs Nwachukwu frowns. 'Well, she knows we are following up on that. The problem is fake drugs. We don't want to end up with fake drugs.'

'What happens to those who are sick meanwhile?'

'They go to the churches or they go to the herbalists.'

'And their children?'

'Children? Let us not even begin to talk about them.'

Deola can't imagine an entire town devastated by AIDS. Clusters, as they are called. In Lagos, there are too many people. Depopulation might go unnoticed. She has heard Nigerians say that the rates of infection are higher wherever Westerners flock to in Africa: the port cities and the countries with cooler climates. Nigerians were furious with the press reports that said the virus originated in Africa, livid when the reports said the virus was traced to monkeys. Who did they think Africans were? Dirty perverts? Didn't they know that to piss off an African, all a person needed to do was mention any species of ape or make any kind of simian reference? Now that the virus is here to stay, no one seems to care where it came from. She has seen numerous posters declaring that AIDS kills and signs advertising bogus cures, so perhaps education about treatment is another area where funds can be directed.

She is almost certain she will not recommend WIN after her review. Why come all the way from England, only to return with a report like that? she thinks. What a waste of money and a letdown for the women.

She calls Wale when she gets back to the Hilton. He doesn't answer his phone and she doesn't leave a message after his recorded greeting, which ends with him saying, '*Shalom*'. She is walking into the bathroom when her mobile phone rings and she runs out. She sees Wale's number and takes a breath before she answers.

'Hello?'

He sounds angry. 'Did you just call my number?'

'It's Adeola Bello.'

'Hey! You're in town?'

'Yes.'

'I thought someone was flashing me again.'

'Flashing?'

'You've haven't heard of flashing? When you call, hang up and wait for a call back?'

She smiles. 'Not used that way.'

'So how are you, Adeola Bello?'

'Very well. I was hoping we could meet for a drink.'

'When?'

She wrinkles her nose. Why is her heart beating faster?

'Tonight?'

He laughs. 'Where?'

'I'm at the Hilton. What's so funny?'

'I didn't expect to hear from you.'

'Why not?'

'I didn't ask for your number. It might have seemed . . .'

'It didn't seem anything.'

'Good. I didn't want my staff to think I was, you know.'

'You were fine. You weren't flirting.'

'Who says?'

'So, I'll see you later?'

'What time?'

'Eight?'

'Eight, then.'

She struts around her room, then she pats her cheek. She mustn't look desperate.

She has dinner at the hotel restaurant and returns to her room to take a bath and change. She sprays perfume on her wrist, smacks her lipstick in place. Her earring needs securing. She smoothes her eyebrows.

The front desk calls to say he has arrived and she goes downstairs again, this time pretending to take an interest in the décor in the lobby, which is reminiscent of a dictator's palace, with its crystal chandeliers, faux Louis Quatorze chairs and white marble floors. The light reflecting on the marble blinds her and she worries about slipping. There are a few expatriates and many Nigerians walking around in that lethargic manner that is typical of loiterers in hotels.

Wale is by the front desk. He has made an effort, his shirt and trousers are pressed. He looks naturally trim. He stands with his back to the lift, which might be deliberate, and she is tempted to pinch his bottom and throw him off balance, but she taps his shoulder instead.

'Have you grown?' he asks, looking her up and down.

'My heels,' she says.

He smiles as if she is a statue he can't quite take seriously.

'*Shalom*?' she says.

'*Pele*, then,' he says. '*Pele*, if you prefer.'

'Not really.'

Pele doubles up as an apology. *Pele* might also mean he feels sorry for her.

In the lounge she orders a Cointreau. She has never had Cointreau before. It is strong and tastes of oranges. He has a neat brandy. She doesn't just like his eyes; she likes his way of looking at her as if she is a solo act. She is also aware of the stares she gets from the security guards who size her up as she tells him about her day at WIN.

'What pains me is that I now have to go back and admit to these people that Nigerians are fraudulent.'

'She's just hustling like everyone else. She and the other woman, who might be trying to sabotage her.'

'You think?'

'Of course. Even microfinance is a hustle now. The people who are meant to get it don't. It's all about competition here.'

'They won't see it that way. All they know is Nigeria, corruption, 4-1-9, Internet crime. It's embarrassing.'

'It is.'

'And Elizabeth made more sense. Of course the women would want to do business. Of course they would. Business is what we do in Nigeria.'

'We do.'

Is she talking too much? She can't get away from the idea that she has failed the women, but not enough to disregard the irregularities she noted at WIN. She takes another sip and winces. The Cointreau is too concentrated for her.

'Your father's five-year memorial is on Sunday, isn't it?' he asks.

'Yes.'

'How are the preparations going?'

'Fine. Everything is fine.'

'It's good that we do that, remember those who have died.'

She finds the idea of a five-year memorial artificial. She remembers her father when she smells a combination of whisky, cigars, aftershave and perfume: the 'grown-up party' smell. Or when she hears the music he listened to:

his Ray Charles, Dave Brubeck and Dvořák. In her teens, they argued over music. 'Who is this Teddy Pendergrass?' he would ask. 'Have you heard Otis Redding?' 'Who is this George Benson? Have you heard John Coltrane?' He pitied her because she didn't appreciate juju music. 'Children of nowadays,' he used to say. 'You have no roots. You go any way the wind blows.'

She would love to find his Bally slippers again, knowing that all he had to do was think where he last left them before asking her to look for them. And to watch Wimbledon on television with him. Every summer he was in London in time for Wimbledon, knocking things over while cheering and getting names wrong ('Matilda Navratilova').

'How old is your daughter?' she asks.

'Fourteen.'

'Is it just you and her?'

'Her and me, that's it.'

'Fourteen. People say thirteen is the tricky age, that you're still adjusting to the whole teen thing at thirteen.'

'Which is why I have no intention of complicating her life further by making her a half-sister or stepchild.'

He seems to be addressing someone else and this agitates her. They are talking too much about family.

He puts his glass down. 'I have just put you off, haven't I?'

'No, no.'

'See me. I have white hairs all over my head. No more raps.'

'Some of us are not interested in being stepmothers, wicked or otherwise.'

He smiles. 'I didn't mean you.'

'Please,' she says. 'I meet someone I like. Why would marriage be a consideration?'

His expression reminds her of the boys she chatted up as a teenager. They knew bad girls didn't talk as much.

'What?' she asks. 'You're underestimating me? I've had many men. I'm a very passionate lover.'

He laughs loud and claps, causing people to turn around.

She retaliates. 'Isn't it dangerous for you to leave a teenager at home on her own this late with armed robbers prowling?'

'She's with her cousins.'

'You might want to pick her up soon,' she says, reaching for her glass.

'Her cousins are in Lagos.'

'So there is no reason to run home tonight.'

'No.'

She crosses her legs. It is not as if she has misinterpreted him or vice versa. She imagines his skin against hers, his hands, his tongue and hard-on. Her desire is insistent, almost jeering. Why the small talk? Why not now? She gave up her virginity when she had no more use for it. Losing her virginity was like discovering her hair was not her crowning glory.

She is heady from the Cointreau, but more so from the thought of having a safe indiscretion. A security guard in the lobby gives her the same meddlesome look she encountered when she sat down. That can happen in a Lagos hotel, but here there's also Sharia law, which can make men act in overzealous ways.

'What if security stops us?' she asks.

'Who, these ones?'

'It's me they are watching, not you. Weren't there riots here when the Miss World contest was supposed to be staged? The fatwa on the journalist and all that?'

'*Haba*, things are not that bad.'

'Who says?' she asks. 'Don't they sentence women to death for fornication in these parts?'

'No one would dare sentence a woman like you.'

'That's good. I don't want to be disgraced meanwhile.'

'My house is not too far.'

'I can't go to your house.'

'Why not?'

'I said I can't go to your house.'

'I asked why not?'

'How do I know you're not a killer?'

'Can't I kill you here?'

She laughs and slaps her thigh.

'I will speak to the front desk,' he says.

He finishes his brandy. She abandons her Cointreau and goes ahead of him, so as to be sure she won't be stopped.

In her room, she takes off her sandals and rubs her feet. They are smooth enough. Her clothes are padlocked in her suitcase and her makeup is in a bag. She hides her vitamin C-and-ginseng night cream.

He knocks on her door moments later and she lets him in. He says the service in the Hilton is better than he expected. She admits she has never had Cointreau before.

'Neither have I,' he says.

'I didn't like it much.'

'Why drink it, then? Let's see. Let's see here.'

He kisses her, tasting warm and of brandy. He smells of an unimaginative sandalwood deodorant.

'I like your hair,' he says.

'Why?'

'It's all yours. Those fake hair extension things, you get in there and it's like shrubbery underneath.'

'What kind of women do you meet in that brothel of yours in Lagos?'

'What?'

'My bra is padded. That I fake.'

He runs his hands over her to check, searches under her top and unfastens her bra. She slides her hand down to his zipper.

'Stranger,' he murmurs, when she finds him.

They undress by the bed. Bra off, she wriggles out of her panties to distract him from her back view. He is not flawless, but his stomach is tight and his arms are toned. He could be a cyclist. She has always been attracted to athletic-looking men.

He turns away to roll his condom on.

'Why do you have to do that?'

'I don't want to shock you.'

'I've seen bigger.'

'Are you nervous?'

'Me? Why?'

'You can't stop talking.'

He pulls her towards him and kisses her breasts until she aches.

'What next?' he asks, against her lips.

'Straight sex,' she says.

He obliges. Her toes curl and she could shout from relief. Sex feels, tastes and smells better with a stranger. They lie on their backs exhausted.

'You taste good,' she says.

'You too.'

'I should have had your drink.'

'I should have had Lucozade.'

'This one,' she says, guiding him to her other breast.

'Sweet woman.'

'Sweet man.'

She shifts until she is on top of him. He shakes his head.

'No?' she asks.

'You'll have to be more passionate than that. I can't feel you with this thing on.'

He reaches for her shoulders to turn her around. She is not comfortable in this position, but she moves with him until he withdraws unexpectedly.

'What?' she asks. 'You still can't feel anything?'

'Wait.'

'What?'

'I think . . . I think we've had an accident.'

She pushes him away, jumps out of bed and runs into the bathroom. Now that she is there, she doesn't know what to do with herself. Wash? Pee? Puke? She leans over the sink as he walks in, not caring that she is naked under the bathroom lights.

'Are you okay?' he asks.

'No! Are you sure?'

'Yes. It must have been . . .'

It must have been the position they were in. His face appears lopsided in the mirror. Both their faces appear lopsided. She steadies her breathing as she remembers him joking about being a killer.

'Have you been tested?' she asks.

'Yes.'

'When?'

'Three months ago.'

'Why?'

'I'm on my own. I have a child to raise.'

'Why should I believe you?' she asks.

'I don't lie.'

'Everyone lies about . . .'

Everyone lies about sex. He lowers the toilet seat after he flushes the condom down, then he sits. She can't imagine how he can make a sensible decision. His palms are pressed together. She wants to pray, but she is certain God has no hand in this. She wants to cry, but crying might mean she has reason to.

'Has this ever happened to you before?' she asks.

'No.'

'Why me?'

'Have you been tested?'

'I'd like to be sure of your situation first.'

'I'm okay. Are you? You should get tested. Do that, please, and let me know.'

She raises her hand. 'I beg you. Let me think. Let me think straight.'

She is angry with herself, not with him. She can smell sandalwood on her skin and she is still wet. She crosses her arms when she remembers she is ovulating.

'Shit. I have to take the morning-after pill. Where will I find the morning-after pill in this place? Where will I find a frigging pill in this country that is not fake?'

'I know a good pharmacy. I will take you there, don't worry.'

'Are they open now?'

'Not until tomorrow.'

'Is there anything else we can take?'

'I don't think so.'

She thinks of the antiretroviral drug for rape victims. Isn't she more at risk as a woman? In the bathtub, she fidgets with the tap, talking to herself, 'Shouldn't have done this. Acting so stupid . . .'

'Come on,' he says. 'We're not children.'

She stamps her foot in the water. 'I know! That's why we should have waited!'

'See,' he says, standing up. 'I liked you immediately. I did. I could tell that some of the way you acted, you were putting it on, and yes, it was just a . . . but I saw you and I thought . . .'

She pulls the curtain, shutting him out. He is already speaking as if it is over. How dare *he* speak as if it is over?

'You'll be okay,' he says.

'What if I'm not?'

Her face itches. There is too much steam behind the curtain. The water covers her feet. This could have happened even if she waited, even if they were in love, even if they were married.

'Where is the pharmacy?'

'Not far from here.'

'Can you help me with this shower?'

He draws the curtain back. 'Sure.'

'Turn the hot water down, please.'

He takes a shower after she does. When he comes out, she is dressed in her pyjama top and lying on the bedsheets. Yes, he has been truthful; otherwise he would be gone by now. Finish. End of story. But he has to make sure she is not getting pregnant by him or worse. She eyes him as he dresses. He straightens his shoulders and buttons his shirt. Yesterday, she would have wanted any reason to know him for more than one night.

'Are you staying here till morning?' she asks.

'If you'd like me to.'

'Do you mind if I leave the light on?'

'No.'

'What is the A in your name for?'

'Akinyemi.'

'Which university did you go to in New York?'

'Columbia.'

'Where were you born?'

'Ibadan.'

'What year?'

''62.'

'When last were you with someone?'

'A few weeks ago. Why?'

'I want to know. Are you still with her?'

'No.'

'Why not?'

'She didn't think I cared enough.'

'Did you?'

'Not enough for her.'

'What happened to your wife?'

She doesn't expect an answer. He sits in the chair.

'She died. When my daughter was born.'

'Labour complications?'

'Yes.'

'It messed you up, didn't it?'

She wants to say she is still miserable about her father, but is that comparable?

He pats the arm of the chair, so she makes a show of smoothing his head indentation out of the pillow, telling herself she will take the pill tomorrow, she will get tested when she returns to London and she will be all right.

'Will you be able to sleep over there?' she asks, getting into bed.

'I doubt it,' he says.

But he does. In the purgatory hour while she is still awake. She has given up on praying and is willing the sun to rise. There isn't a sound outside. She hears him breathing and looks over to the chair. He is lying back and shielding his eyes.

The progestin pills are supposed to make her feel nauseous, but what initially sickens her is her interaction with Wale the next morning.

She gets up at dawn, drags the curtains apart and unzips her suitcase. He watches as she grabs her clothes. He stands up and goes to the bathroom. She hears the toilet flush. He comes out, pats his pocket and says, 'I'll see you downstairs, then.'

She says, 'Okay,' without looking.

She finds him in the restaurant drinking coffee. She orders tea.

'You look tired,' he says.

'I am,' she says.

From then on, they don't speak, and breakfast is silent but for the clinking of their cups against their saucers.

He drives her to the pharmacy in some sort of jeep – silvery. At junctions, they look in separate directions like a couple that has been together for too long. They get to the pharmacy and he offers to go in with her. She says she prefers to go in alone. She badgers the pharmacist, who assures her he doesn't sell fake drugs.

After she buys the pill, Wale drives her back to the hotel

without saying a word. He drives too fast, which makes her get out of his jeep quickly.

'Don't forget,' he says.

'I won't,' she says and shuts the door.

Her flight arrives in Lagos late in the afternoon. Lanre's driver picks her up and takes her home. Her nausea doesn't begin until the evening. She has pressure behind her eyes, her throat tightens and her stomach turns. This is why she stopped taking contraceptive pills, and the effects of the progestin pills are more severe. She takes her second dose and her lips begin to tingle and the back of her tongue tastes bitter. She gets dizzy and tells her mother she will skip dinner tonight. She has to go to bed early because she is not feeling well.

'I hope you haven't caught something,' her mother says.

'I doubt it,' she says.

She vomits that night, within the safe period of taking the pill, but she still worries about getting pregnant. She develops a headache, takes a couple of Panadols and wills her father to make his presence felt, but he doesn't, as if he has decided she needs her privacy. Then she has that moment – meaningless, she has always thought – when people stand in front of their bathroom mirrors, look at their reflections and think they ought to change, but they just go back to doing whatever they were doing beforehand. Hers happens after she has washed her face, brushed her teeth and noticed the white tiles on the wall have been changed to a sky blue. Stupid girl, she tells herself, then she smoothes on her night cream with vitamin C and ginseng.

In the morning, she is lying in bed when she hears the workers who are putting up the canopies in the garden. They hammer and shout, '*Oya, oya, oya!* Keep it s'raight! Keep it s'raight!'

Her mother's voice is strident: 'Be careful with my plants!'

'E *ma* worry, ma.'

'E *pele*, Mummy.'

'*Oya, oya, oya!* Hol' it! Hol' it!'

She takes a bath, changes and comes downstairs with *Pride and Prejudice* and returns it to the bookshelf, the story now irrelevant to her. Austen women did not have one-night stands. Austen women did not take the morning-after pill. Austen women took to their beds when they were heartbroken or down with colds.

Jaiye is in the back garden watching the workers. There are four of them, their faces and arms darkened from sun exposure. They have finished with one canopy and are raising another. Both canopies are orange and white with their company name and telephone number printed in black.

'You're awake?' Jaiye says.

'Yes,' Deola says.

Jaiye is dressed in jeans and high-heeled sandals. She has a ponytail attached to her hair. She is naturally shapely, but she is determined to be thin. She goes to the gym three times a week and is on the South Beach Diet, which perhaps is why she is so irritable, apart from the running around she has been doing for the memorial.

'Mummy said you were sick last night,' she says.

'I was a bit. I'm better now. Where is she?'

'My driver took her to the nail salon.'

'Did the gardener show up?' Deola asks.

'Yes,' Jaiye says.

'What about the caterer?'

'I've sorted that out. She is coming here first thing tomorrow.'

'You've tried.'

'Have I?'

'Yes,' Deola says. 'I've done nothing.'

She has to pull herself together. Her nausea has subsided a little, but her breasts ache. She can't dwell on that or on her one-night fall, as she now regards her night with Wale.

'Is Funsho back from Johannesburg?' she asks.

Jaiye hisses. 'Forget that one.'

'Why?'

'Just forget him.'

Jaiye is part of an Ikeja clique of married women. The popular girls of their day, they terrify Deola with their resourcefulness. Their clothes are always well pressed. They can run in six-inch heels, spot a fake designer bag at a distance, disarm an enemy with a 'God bless', cordon off their hearts from straying husbands if necessary, and they keep marching on: *faith, family, friendship, fashion; faith, family, friendship, fashion.*

Deola stays with Jaiye to monitor the workers. Her mother comes back from the salon about an hour later with maroon nails. Lanre shows up in time for lunch with a bootload of South African wine, then he takes off afterward without saying where he is going. Jaiye and her mother grumble about his wife, Eno, who has been scarce.

'I'm not asking anyone to slave for me,' her mother says. 'I don't expect her to come here every day, but she can at least show her face.'

'Leave her alone,' Deola says, instinctively.

'What?' Jaiye says. 'She knows you're here. Why can't she bring the boys over?'

Deola shrugs. 'Lanre could have brought them over.'

'She won't let him,' Jaiye says. 'They're always at her mother's house and he loves it that way, so he can go on his little excursions.'

'Lulu and Prof are always here,' Deola says.

'Don't interfere,' her mother says. 'We know what we're talking about.'

They will all wear white lace *iro* and *buba* for the memorial tomorrow with navy head ties to show solidarity, but Jaiye and her mother are united against Eno.

When Eno stayed at home after Banwo and Timi were born, they criticized her: 'Why can't she just get a job? She is such a lazy girl, that girl.' Deola's mother would complain that Eno was making Lanre work too hard. Deola would argue that not all women wanted careers, without pointing out that her mother didn't have one. Jaiye would say Eno's lack of ambition was abnormal for a Nigerian woman and had to come from her *oyinbo* side.

Women, Deola thinks.

Eno studied fine art at Ahmadu Bello University. She painted children's portraits before she worked for her mother's nursery, but she treated her work as a hobby. For years she would wake up, ask her nannies to get the boys ready, then the driver would take them to school. From then on until they returned, she would waft around the house with a serene air, lifting her chin as if to say, 'I married well.'

For Eno and Lanre's wedding, Eno's mother organized a church ceremony for about a hundred and fifty guests, including a couple of relatives who flew in from England. For Jaiye and Funsho's wedding, a thousand guests were invited to the same church, half of whom were relatives and most of whom couldn't get in the church. They sat on benches outside and listened to the service on a loudspeaker.

The Bello family was furious about Eno and Lanre's wedding. 'What is this?' they said. 'No letter-writing, no engagement ceremony, no night party?' Deola's mother, who spent her entire life playing the African European, who, when she met Eno's relatives from Putney, spoke her crispest phonetics ever ('Lovely to meet you,' 'Yes, it is rather humid, isn't it?'), who didn't even get along with the Bellos (she called them hinterland people), turned around and said, 'Well, this is what happens when you go and marry someone from somewhere.'

Deola's father got along fine with Eno, even when Eno was just one of Lanre's girlfriends. He called her by her full name, Eno Obong. He would ask after her parents and talk about when he visited Calabar, where Eno's father was from. Lanre's other girlfriends didn't get more than a 'How are you?' from him. After Eno and Lanre got married, he would tease Eno, 'When are you going to make *edikang ikong* for me?' Eno would answer, 'I don't make *edikang ikong*, Dad.' She called him Dad. 'Why not?' he would ask. 'Isn't that your specialty in Calabar?' 'My specialty is fish and chips,' she would say. 'Feesh and cheeps?' he would ask, frowning.

Eno humoured him. On his birthday, her driver delivered a pot of *edikang ikong*, which her cook had probably made. He danced around the dining table singing, 'Calabar woman, *na* so so powder, better go follow them, for God's power.' Deola's mother tried only a teaspoon of the stew and asked, 'Don't they eat dogs in Calabar?'

Suddenly, she was suspicious of unidentifiable meats.

She, who wouldn't hesitate to cook an endangered species of animal.

Deola finds her mother and sister's hypocrisy amusing. Jaiye won't go to her mother-in-law's house unless the woman says she is dying. The woman is dying every year, especially around Christmas, when she expects Jaiye to come to her house and help if she is having a family function. Every Christmas, Jaiye pretends to be down with malaria.

Funsho's mother is a proper traditional woman who believes Yoruba culture is superior to all others. Her husband was a chief and she was his senior wife. At home, her sons address her as '*Mama mi*', none of that 'Mummy' nonsense or standing to greet her. They must stoop, avert their eyes, and she doesn't care to speak English in her house.

When Jaiye met her, Jaiye knelt to greet her, but she made the mistake of saying 'Good afternoon' in English and Funsho's mother asked in Yoruba, 'Who is this? What is she saying?' as if she couldn't understand a word. Jaiye refused to kneel after that. 'I don't kneel to greet my own mother,' she said.

The other wives in Funsho's family kneel and they consider Jaiye rude because she refuses to. They shun her in that well-brought-up-Yoruba-woman way. Jaiye says they are backward women who can't face up to their husbands. Funsho's mother, meanwhile, is not impressed that Jaiye is a doctor if Jaiye won't cook for family functions, and she considers Funsho's infidelity a petty matter that Jaiye ought to be mature enough to ignore.

But Deola's mother can't see beyond the roles Eno is meant to perform either. Deola once asked her mother how Eno's art was coming along and her mother said, 'I suppose she's still drawing.' Deola later spoke to Eno and found out she had an exhibition in Lagos, but no one bought her work, so she lost confidence and gave up.

She and Eno have talked about what it was like to grow up with an English mother in Nigeria. 'You're in a different tribe here,' Eno said, plainly. 'It doesn't matter where your mother or father is from, so long as one of them is *oyinbo*.'

Eno's father's family seemed to accept her mother until her father died. Then his relatives came to their house and grabbed whatever they could, including his suits, while her mother was sedated. One of her uncles announced that if her mother thought the house would automatically pass to her, she was joking. He would drive her back to England before that ever happened. Eno's mother stayed in the house regardless. She'd lived there for fifteen years. Her nursery was there. She'd planted some of the trees in the garden, and she gave up her British passport because Nigeria prohibited dual citizenship when she applied for a Nigerian passport.

She got herself a Doberman. Dog eaters or not, her husband's family stayed away from then on. Her nursery business expanded when English roses became all the rage for society weddings in Lagos. She would give her clients the impression her roses came from London, but she flew them in from a botanical garden in Plateau State.

On Sunday, Eno is at church and so are the boys. They have grown: Banwo almost reaches Deola's shoulders and Timi is fast catching up. Now, they have a mixture of their parents' eyes. How does that happen? thinks Deola. They resist her hugs, but they are polite enough to smile and say, 'Hello Aunty.'

'Look at you,' she says, 'you little heartbreakers in the making.'

Banwo laughs nervously and Timi mouths, 'What?'

Lanre describes Timi as his 'Attention Deficit Disorder son'. They both keep close to him, wearing matching light blue *agbada*, and swagger as he does. Eno still has a serene air. She wears her white *iro* and *buba*, without a head tie. She has gained weight, but she is still a pretty woman. Her mother is in an *adire* dress and flat sandals and smiles at everyone, whether or not they acknowledge her.

The service is a regular one and the hymns are a mixture of American and the Church of England. 'Great Is Thy Faithfulness' almost brings Deola to tears. She stops singing and listens as the congregation stretches and vibrates each line as they did with 'Abide with Me' at her father's funeral.

She never saw her father's body. Her family was with him at Lagoon Hospital on the day he died. 'You should have seen Daddy,' Jaiye said later. 'He looked so peaceful, like a boy.' Deola prefers to remember him as he was alive, as he appears in the obituary section of *The Guardian* today, wearing an *agbada* and cap.

After the service, there is a gathering of women in the frontcourt of the church, by a frangipani tree. Most of them are her mother's friends and they look as bright as petals. Deola walks through them and they leave traces of their powder, lipstick and perfume on her. She stops now and then to answer questions: 'Is this you?' 'When did you arrive?' 'How are you, my dear?' 'How is work in England?' There are the reviews to agree with: 'It was a good service.' 'Beautiful.' 'Lovely, just lovely.'

She backs into Brother Dotun, who flew in from Port

Harcourt with Ivie's mother. In his *agbada* and cap, he looks more like his mother, who is absent.

'Brother Dots.'

'Adeola-sco.'

They shake hands. 'What's going on?'

'Work is stressing me out.'

'Are you serious?'

'Work is stressing me out. Can't you see?'

Deola jokes that he has a potbelly, which shows his wife is taking care of him, then she sings, 'Many rivers to cross, but I can't seem to find my way over.' He laughs exactly like her father, his laugh getting higher and higher, as if he is cranking himself up.

She often wonders if Brother Dotun resents her father. Brother Dotun was not left out of her father's will, but he was terribly deprived of paternal attention. His mother did not want to live in England while her father was training as an accountant, so she came back to Nigeria with Brother Dotun and started a bakery business. In those days, people travelled to and fro by ship, from Liverpool Docks to Lagos Marina. Her father didn't see Brother Dotun for years, and when her own mother came into the picture, he divorced Brother Dotun's mother.

Her mother was the one who enjoyed her father's success. Her mother studied nursing in England and was working at St Thomas' Hospital in London when she met her father. She gave up nursing when they returned to Nigeria, while Brother Dotun's mother carried on with her bakery business, struggling each time a military regime banned imported flour.

Deola was vaguely aware that his mother and hers were

politely alienated from each other, as she was of the fact that her mother was an obstacle to any sibling bond she could have with him. Brother Dotun once tried to give Lanre brotherly advice and made the mistake of calling Lanre spoiled rotten. Lanre told her mother and her mother went straight to her father. Brother Dotun was careful about what he said from then on.

'How's your family?' Deola asks.

Brother Dotun's wife, Efua, is from Ghana. She is there with their children for the summer holiday.

'I miss them,' he says.

'You carry them on your head.'

'They're all I've got.'

'What's happening in Ghana?'

'Ghana?' he says. 'It's not perfect. We all have our problems, but I tell you what, Accra is clean, clean and organized, not like this Lagos.'

'What are we going to do about this place, Brother Dots?'

He points at the church. 'It's only God that can save us. Actually, I take that back because things could be a lot worse. God has already saved Nigeria.'

Deola can't confirm that what she observes in Nigeria is the result of answered or unanswered prayers.

Ivie and Omorege walk past. Ivie looks like a first lady in her lace up-and-down and gold choker. Deola exchanges a wave with her. Omorege wears an *agbada* and cap. His cap is tilted as is his grin. He shakes hands as if he is on a campaign trail.

'Deola, *na* you be dis?' he asks playfully, and moves on to the next person without waiting for an answer.

'Isn't that the senator?' Brother Dotun asks.

'Yes,' Deola says.

'I hear he's calling himself Omorege these days. I knew him as George.'

'George?'

'Yes. George. His finance house went bankrupt, didn't it?'

'Yes.'

'He's the one. We started calling him Georgie Porgie when he ran away to London. He's a case, that man. I'm sure he hasn't done a thing for his state.'

Aunty Bisi taps his shoulder. 'Dots, Dots, *kini nkan?*'

'Bis, Bis,' he says, slapping hands with her, '*ba wo ni?*'

Aunty Bisi's lace is sheer and her black bra is showing. Aunty Bisi will not be seen in a short skirt or tight trousers, but she walks around practically naked. She only wears lace *iro* and *buba*. Her lace is either sheer or full of holes. Her head tie adds another foot to her height. Her son Hakeem is with her.

'Hakeem the Dream,' Deola says. 'How are you?'

'Not bad,' he says.

Hakeem's voice is so deep it scares Deola. She carried him when he was a baby and rocked him to sleep. He works for his father's stockbroking firm. His father ought to be here, as an in-law, but the man is too old to get up this early for anyone.

'Jaiye is looking for you,' Aunty Bisi says to her.

'Why?'

'She wants to get back to the caterer.'

'I'd better go and find her,' Deola says.

Colourful hats, head ties and caps block her vision. Some women are bareheaded, and a few are wearing trousers. Trousers in church would have been unthinkable when she lived in Lagos, and for once Deola welcomes the American influence. For too long, Nigerians have held on to social rules that the English have long abandoned.

She sees someone she grew up with, who is in an *ankara* up-and-down. She can't remember her name. Is it Alero? Yes, it is Alero. She was at International School Ibadan, then she went to Cheltenham Ladies' in England. Didn't she end up in a university outside England? Edinburgh or something? Once in a while, she showed up at LSE Afro-Carib events with a head full of braids, which she tucked behind her ears. To say hello, she had to make sure you were 'PLU', people like us.

Alero was the only girl in Lagos to have a coming out party – coming out to which society, no one knew, but they were there, toasting her and saying, 'Hear, hear.' She had a boyfriend who qualified as PLU, presumably because his mother was Norwegian. But he drank a lot and the more he drank, the more boorish he became. Whenever Alero asked him to keep his voice down, he would look at her affectionately and say, 'Oh, shut up with your horse teeth.'

Alero's family was the sort that gave Ikoyi a bad name. They were *oyinbo* to the core. Ikoyi people were not that *oyinbo*. It was too much work. They did not believe *oyinbos* were worth emulating anyway; they only put on *oyinbo* airs to make other Nigerians feel inferior, shifting loyalties to cultures as easily as they changed clothes, unlike Alero's family, who took things too seriously. Even her father did, which was unusual because no matter how *oyinbo* an Ikoyi family was, their father would let them down by saying, 'feesh and cheeps', whipping out a cane to beat someone, or doing something else that would shatter the illusion and remind them where they were coming from.

'Hiya,' Alero says.

'How now?' Deola says.

'It's been so long.'

'Yes, long time no see.'

'So nice to see you again.'

'You too.'

Alero speaks phonetics, almost as if she is encouraging Deola, who cannot be bothered.

'Are you still in England?' she asks.

'Eh.'

'I couldn't live in England,' she says.

'Eh?'

'No, I couldn't live there any more.'

'*Na wa*.'

Deola is sure Alero is still single. Unfortunately, there were not enough of her PLU men to go around. They married women who were younger, prettier and not necessarily PLU. Alero's father wasn't different from others either. In public, he was a salad eater; in private, he had a woman on the side who cooked his cocoyams.

They say goodbye. At the church gates Deola catches sight of Funsho. He is in a black suit and his sunshades are so dark she can't see his eyes. Why is he crouching? she wonders. But he is not crouching. He just has a crouching manner about him.

'Ah, ah?' he says. 'When did you get in?'

'Last Sunday.'

'Ah, ah? When are you leaving?'

'Today.'

'Ah, ah? Why so soon?'

He already knows. His heavy brows jump. Deola struggles over what to say to him and is about to ask where Jaiye is when Jaiye approaches with Lulu and Prof.

'Can you take the kids to my mother's house?' Jaiye asks him.

Lulu and Prof look traumatized by the church service. Lulu is tearful and Prof's glasses are askew. Jaiye brought them to the church. Funsho arrived separately in his car.

He feigns a stutter. 'W-why?'

'Just take them, please,' Jaiye says.

'W-what is your car for?'

Jaiye wags her finger. 'Stop going on about that car, my friend. It's not the only car I've had and I don't need you to buy me one.'

'W-what is your problem?'

'You'll soon know, when I kick you out. Maybe you can take the car with you, so you can have somewhere to sleep.'

'W-what is your point?'

Deola resists looking heavenward. Could Jaiye be more clear?

'Oh, don't be so thick,' Jaiye says.

Funsho turns to Deola. 'You see? This is exactly what your sister does. Then when I say I'm moving out, she'll be begging me to stay and I've told her before, "One thing about me, I give people three chances only."'

How can that be a thing about anyone? thinks Deola. Why three chances anyway? Why not two or five? Funsho does have a tendency to sound thick. 'Life,' he once said. 'You can't live with it, you can't live without it.'

Funsho often brags about money and possessions, his and other people's. For as long as Deola has known him, he has gone on about the property that is due to him. His family is in the business of manufacturing plastic cups and bowls, but there is an injunction on his father's estate following much fighting – not between his mother and the other wives, but between his elder brothers. One allegedly paid an area boy a few thousand naira to 'obliterate', as Funsho put it, the other.

Deola was raised to believe that it was wrong to talk about money. She thought that was a foreign affectation until her father explained it was necessary in Nigeria. 'If you open your mouth in the wrong place, someone might juju you,' he warned.

Deola bends and says to Lulu, 'Wassup.'

Lulu shakes her head. She doesn't want to say 'Wassup'. Deola smoothes Lulu's fingers, thinking how easy it would be to break them. The thought repels her.

'Please,' Jaiye says to Funsho, 'just take them to my mother's house when you finish here. *Oya*, you two, follow your father. I have things to do.'

Deola leaves with Jaiye. The sun is out this afternoon and there are a few clouds, but she has seen rain pour down from a Lagos sky this blue and clear. A group of beggars are gathered outside the church gates. One sits on the ground with his atrophied legs crossed. Another holds up a fingerless hand. She puts money into their aluminum bowls and they pray that Allah will bless her.

Jaiye's car is parked by a street gutter and sandwiched between two cars. Their drivers sit on a bench, fanning their faces with pieces of cardboard. They stand up to direct Jaiye. When she is safely on the street, she slips on her sunshades and turns on her CD player. Deola recognizes the beat, which seems to rearrange her heart rhythm. It's Dr Dre's *The Chronic*. Is this appropriate coming from church, coming from her father's memorial?

Deola fears Jaiye will never outgrow hip-hop. She imagines Jaiye as a ninety-year-old granny dancing to hip-hop. Jaiye was barely in her teens when hip-hop arrived in Nigeria. Hip-hop was milder then, with raps like 'Don't stop a-rocking to the bang bang boogie.' The angriest it got was 'Don't push me 'cause I'm close to the edge.'

Jaiye raps, 'Don't even respect your ass, that's why it's time for the doctor to check your ass . . .'

'You shouldn't *yab* Funsho like that in front of your kids,' Deola says.

Jaiye hisses. 'He's a fool. He'd better not piss me off today.'

'What did he do?'

'He has a girlfriend in South Africa.'

Deola has a surge of outrage as she did when other children bullied Jaiye, but she remembers Jaiye can take care of herself. Her threat to throw Funsho out would have perforated his heart.

Jaiye drives past Tinubu Square. Street hawkers are carrying dishcloths and cutlery sets. A boy of primary-school age holds up *The Complete Works of William Shakespeare.* He scowls when Jaiye shoos him away.

'You still shouldn't *yab* him in front of your kids,' Deola insists.

'Everyone fights in front of their kids,' Jaiye says.

Her parents didn't. The most her mother would say was, 'As you wish.' And her father might come up with, 'Let me relax.'

'It's not Funsho I'm concerned about,' Deola says.

'My children will get over it,' Jaiye says. 'They will just have to. I'm sick and tired of keeping quiet while their father continues to put my life in danger. I've told him, "Chase whomever you want to, swing from chandeliers if you want. Just don't give me any diseases."'

Deola's heart rate increases as she recalls her night with Wale. Jaiye is less restrained than she is about medical matters. Jaiye talks openly about her breast cysts and the consistency of her stool whenever she gets constipated on her South Beach Diet.

'You're all right, *sha*?' she asks.

'I'm all right,' Jaiye says.

As she has in the past, Deola plays a gambling game. She tells herself she will be all right if the car ahead takes the next right turn, which it does. Goosebumps rise on her arms and the sun warms her face. As usual, the air conditioner is too cold for her.

'I'm sorry,' she says. 'Your husband is so . . .'

Jaiye taps her cheek. 'I can't even let him kiss here. I don't know where that dirty mouth of his has been. He disgusts me. Nigerian men disgust me.'

Now she might cry because of the bitterness in Jaiye's voice.

'Nigerian women are not exactly . . .' blameless, she is about to say.

'They disgust me too,' Jaiye says. 'Especially the foolish ones like my mother-in-law, who can't raise a normal human being. His whole family disgusts me. They are typical Yoruba. It's all hierarchy, hierarchy with them. Look, their whole lives revolve around that woman and Funsho can't open his mouth when she's around. Can you believe he thinks our family is *oyinbo*?'

'Us? Why?'

'Because we don't crawl on our hands and knees to greet Mummy.'

Deola has images of herself, Lanre and Jaiye as children yelling, 'My bottom is scratching me!' How could anyone think her family is *oyinbo*? She is never sure what takes precedence in the way Nigerians constantly rank each other according to wealth, education and Westernization, with ambiguous results: this one is bush, that one is *oyinbo*. This one is local, that one is colonized.

'Is this how you will both be in that house?' she asks.

'Yes, until I kick him out. The house is in my name. At least Daddy made sure of that.'

They get home and the Sunday service in the church next door is over. As they supervise the catering staff and rearrange the seating plans, the guests begin to arrive, led by her mother. Soon there is barely any space on the road for cars to get past. Horns go off. People step out of their cars, shake out their trouser legs and dust their clothes down self-importantly. There are about a hundred of them, family and friends.

They ignore the seating plans. Her mother's close friends are the most difficult to manage. They want to sit together and ask that two tables be moved to form one, which becomes the longest table under the canopies.

'Where is the wine?' Aunty Fadeke asks. 'Bring the wine. Make sure the table is steady first. We don't want the wine to topple over.'

Deola has always liked her because she looks as if she is smiling even when she is not. She squeezes into her chair while the others laugh at her.

'Fadeke, girl!'

'What?' she says. 'Remi? Where is Remi? Deola, where is your mother?'

'She is in the kitchen,' Deola says.

'Get her over here. Tell her we have reserved the head of the table for her. She sits at the head today.'

'Yes, Aunty.'

None of them is a blood relation. They ask for more crabs and shrimp, and more wine. She can't pass their table without someone calling out, 'Psst, darling. More wine. Yes, more wine. Preferably red.'

Her mother sits at the head of the table, having taken off her head tie and replaced her shoes with slippers. They congratulate her on the catering.

'Rem, Rem, wonderful job.'

'It took a lot of planning,' her mother says. 'And I didn't have a driver at my disposal.'

'The crab is tasty. Very tasty.'

'And the shrimp.'

'Fluffy rice.'

'Hm.'

Their empty crab and shrimp shells pile up on their plates. Their napkins are stained with lipstick and stew.

'Remi,' Aunty Fadeke says. 'You are disappointing me. How can you forget your namesake on a day like this?'

'What namesake?' Deola's mother asks.

'Rémy Martin, of course! Who else?'

'It's true,' Deola's mother says. 'Where is the brandy? There ought to be brandy floating around somewhere.'

She is deliberately hoarding her spirits. She knows her friends drink like military men.

Deola strays to the next table. Aunty Bisi is taking care of the real relatives and the in-laws like Eno's mother, who are seated there. As usual, Eno's mother is overlooked. Aunty

Bisi gave her special treatment by fixing her a tidier plate and saying a token, 'Hope it's not too peppery for you.'

People on the table don't speak to Eno's mother unless she speaks to them. Her presence may well hinder their conversation because they are not speaking to one another either. She sits there and finishes her food nonetheless. Normally, she would be on the expatriate table with family friends who have now left Nigeria and returned to London, Milan and Hong Kong to spend their retirement years. No more of their mince pies, panettone and steamed dumplings for Christmas. Their wives were honorary aunts: Aunty Jean, Aunty Sophia, Aunty Mrs Wong (Deola didn't know her name). Their husbands were either with multinational companies or working independently as entrepreneurs.

The catering staff is coping well with the guests' demands, but Aunty Bisi insists on waiting tables.

'You have to chaperone your mother's table,' she says to Deola. 'You have to chaperone them. You're not chaperoning them enough. Where is Jaiye?'

Jaiye is in the house with her children. Prof spilled apple juice on Lulu's dress and Lulu threw a fit. Deola heads back to her mother's table to find out what else they need. They seem happy enough, which may be due to the wine they have consumed.

Aunty Simi, who wears Chanel sunshades that cover half her face, asks, 'So, Deola, my dear, any plans to come home?'

'No plans yet, Aunty,' Deola says, skirting the table.

'Why not?' Aunty Yinka asks. 'You're not getting any younger. You have to start thinking about it soon.'

Aunty Yinka wears an emerald-and-diamond ring as big as her knuckle. Her friends call her 'Mappin and Webb'.

'Why should she come home?' Aunty Fadeke asks, knowing Deola is partial to her. 'She is getting along fine where she is. Why should she suffer like the rest of us? Do you have a job waiting for her here?'

Aunty Fadeke studied nursing with Deola's mother and she worked until she retired. Her pension barely covers her phone bills. She lost her youngest daughter a few years ago to breast cancer and her friends raised money for her plane tickets to London while her daughter was receiving treatment there.

'She has Trust Bank,' Aunty Simi says.

Aunty Simi's daughter has always worked for her husband, who owns one of the top law practices in Lagos. He recently received the key to the city of London, opening many more important doors.

Deola's mother is preoccupied with her crab leg. Deola knows she is behind this inquiry. They are the women her mother kept up to date when she left Trust Bank, her mother's childhood friends. They are not always united. Sometimes they get competitive, especially over their looks. Her mother often boasts about not having wrinkles, Aunty Yinka's face is pulled back as tight as a drum and Aunty Simi looks like a walking lesson for abecedarians in her designer accessories with LV, interlinked C's and inverted F's.

Aunty Theresa, who has been rather quiet because every time she speaks, the rest talk over her, says, 'It's your heritage, my dear. Your heritage. You don't turn your back on your heritage.'

She is the only one at the table wearing a dress. She married an Englishman, whose family didn't accept her, despite the fact that she'd attended Oxford University, so she got a divorce and returned to Nigeria in the sixties. A sherry – rather than champagne – socialist in those days, her enunciation is still so impressive that no one understands a word she is saying, which is why they talk over her.

'My father,' she says, and Deola makes out the words 'fought for our independence', 'us pioneer professionals' and 'our children to come back home and follow in our footsteps', as the others drown her out with their chatter.

Aunty Theresa's father, Francisco Blanco, was a renowned nationalist. He was a lawyer-turned-politician like Bandele's grandfather, Sir Cecil Adeyemi Davis, who opposed the movement on the grounds that Nigeria was not mature enough for self-governance, thereby earning himself a knighthood. Francisco Blanco, meantime, was branded a communist by the colonials during the Cold War. Not one of his fellow Nigerians defended him for fear they might be hunted down and blacklisted in the spirit of McCarthyism.

Why anyone would want to follow in the footsteps of a man whose life demonstrated how Nigeria turns its back on its people to kiss the arses of foreign powers is beyond Deola. She is waiting to see what the future holds for Nigerians, now that the government seems to be puckering up behind the Chinese.

'How is your prime minister these days?' Aunty Theresa asks. 'Still standing shoulder to shoulder with the Americans?'

Aunty Fadeke hisses. 'Shoulder to shoulder.'

'Foolish man,' Aunty Simi says.

'God will deal with that Bush fellow,' Aunty Yinka says.

'Well, well,' Aunty Fadeke says.

Deola walks away bemused. First, that her mother's friends are this fired up about the war in Iraq and second, that they are still trying to persuade her to come home. But this is their way. Nigeria is where they are called 'Madam' and treated with respect. They pass on their sense of entitlement to their children through estates. They are Nigerian Tories. Aunty Simi and her husband have houses all over Ikoyi. Aunty Yinka has a block of flats on Victoria Island in addition to her house on Lekki Peninsula. Aunty Theresa, who ought to know better, lives in Yaba on a street named after her grandfather, Senhor Blanco. He was one of the finest masons in Lagos and built houses with stables and orchards. But these days, slums border Blanco Street. After Oxford, Aunty Theresa joined the Colonial Service, then the Ministry of Education, and would have been the permanent secretary had she not fallen out with the British, whom she called 'Cockneys in feathered helmets', and with the First Republic, whom she called 'an old baba's club'. She was retired by the next military regime, reinstated by the one after and finally resigned when she had to work with a Hausa education minister who said the South had too many schools for its own good. She called him 'uncouth and myopic' and his response was that her resignation was timely, and hopefully, she would now go and sit down quietly and collect her pension, instead of speaking big English all over the place.

Perhaps this is the trouble, Deola thinks. Their contemporaries are dying; their society has been replaced by one they could call vulgar. Their network of contacts has been demolished. Semi-illiterates are running the country, which they see slipping out of their grip and they are hanging on to whatever they can – their children mostly. Now they have to deal with people whose nappies they changed, CEOs, pastors, managing directors, attorneys general, senators and governors, whom they refer to as boys and girls. Even if they are wealthy, Nigeria does not belong to them any more.

Deola ends up near the chalet, which is actually a one-bedroom bungalow with a kitchenette and bathroom. Lanre is smoking on the veranda and still checking text messages. She sits next to him.

'You'd better not be messing around,' she says.

He slips his phone back into his pocket. 'It's my colleague, man. She is stressed.'

'For what reason?'

'She's having marital problems.'

'Can't she consult a priest?'

Lanre does not smoke in front of his sons. The smell makes Deola nauseous. From her new position, she has a view of both canopies.

'I hate women,' she says. 'What is she texting you for? I hate that. And I've just been accosted by that group over there.'

'What did they do?'

'"When are you coming home?" "Shouldn't you be thinking of settling down?"'

'They're miserable. Don't listen to them.'

'I mean, who wants anyone to come home when the rest of the country is praying for a way out? And imagine talking to me as if I'm still in school. And Mummy just sat there pretending she didn't know what was going on. It was like the Coalition of the Willing.'

He slaps the cement surface as he laughs. 'Don't kill me.'

'No, cigarettes will do that.'

She has nagged Lanre about smoking and drinking since her father's death. He pulls his cigarette out of his mouth.

'Every bad habit I have, I picked up in this house.'

'I swear. The whole country is full of boozers. Just look at them. Who would even have been standing there, if Aunty Bisi didn't ask me to "chaperone" them?'

'Pity her. She has to sleep with an eighty-year-old man who takes Viagra.'

'He does?'

'Of course.'

Lanre drops his cigarette butt on the ground and crushes it with his shoe. He was always more astute. Perhaps Aunty Bisi's husband does need enhancement. He is in his eighties, and Aunty Bisi was the one who gave Jaiye this advice before her wedding: 'A woman should be a whore in her bedroom and a whore in her kitchen.'

In her heyday Aunty Bisi was at every *owambe* party in Lagos, gyrating in front of Sunny Adé until she abandoned Sunny for Shina Peters. That was how she met her husband. She was dancing to Shina's band at his son's fortieth birthday bash. He walked up to her and sprayed her with dollar notes. Despite his two wives, who were less gregarious, he was demanding of Aunty Bisi's attention, insisting that she cook for him and travel overseas with him until Aunty Bisi, who at first was flattered and enjoyed hobnobbing with him, began to seem more like a hospice caretaker than a paramour.

Lanre assesses her mother's friends dispassionately: Aunty Theresa has probably been celibate since her divorce. He can't imagine any Nigerian man putting up with her phonetics. Aunty Simi has a middle-aged son who can't get up in the morning without sniffing cocaine. He was caught pilfering from his father, whose law practice he was meant to take over. His father disowned him. Aunty Simi pays his rent and provides him with spending money, so he won't go around begging. Aunty Yinka left her husband because he lacked ambition. She had an affair with a government minister in the First Republic and with a state governor in the Second Republic, both of whom were married men. She was finally made an ambassador during the last military regime. Now she is retired.

All those years, Deola overheard her mother talking on the phone about the men Aunty Yinka was 'involved with' and hailing her 'five times a girl' and 'a self-made woman'. She never bothered to question that. She was however able to figure out, while eavesdropping on her parents' conversation, that Aunty Fadeke's ex-husband threw Aunty Fadeke out and moved in her younger sister, whom he was molesting. What her mother said was, 'Folabi was tampering with that girl, and Fadeke knew. She can't pretend she didn't know.'

Deola wished she'd had the courage to confront her mother's friends about their insistence on marriage and coming home. She is still fuming when Lanre receives another text message. He takes his phone out of his pocket.

'She's texting you again?'

He reads the message. 'It's Mama Eno.'

Eno is no longer 'A Taste of Honey' to him.

'Your wife is texting you and she's here?'

'She wants to know where I am.'

'Doesn't she know?'

He keys in a message and sends it. 'Nope.'

'Did you tell her?' Deola asks.

'She's on her way.'

Deola sees Eno walking toward the chalet. Her brother is like a criminal on the run.

'Is it worth the *wahala*?' she asks.

'What *wahala*?'

'Your wife is always keeping tabs on you.'

'Is that my fault?'

'You're texting some other woman.'

'She sent me a text. What am I supposed to do?'

'Ignore it!'

They begin to quarrel. Lanre raises his voice, having lost his composure.

'Why do you and Jaiye keep harassing me?'

'Who is harassing you?'

'I support you!'

'When? When?'

'Didn't I just? Didn't I just?'

'Okay, okay, what would you say if someone treats your sister badly? What will you say when Funsho treats Jaiye badly?'

'I've never cheated on my wife!'

'You did! Before you got married!'

He laughs involuntarily. 'All of you are crazy. How old was I when I met her? Boys play around. That's what they do. Eno stayed. She decided to. Now she keeps going back to what I did over five hundred years ago.'

Eno is closer, so Deola lowers her voice and so does he.

'You had shows until you married her. Yes, you did. Yes, you did.'

'So she shouldn't trust me again for life?'

'Why should she trust you when you're texting another woman?'

'What is wrong with that?'

'Nothing, unless you're betraying her.'

'Who's betraying anyone here?'

Deola wriggles her fingers. 'You and your little disappearing acts.'

'I'm working! What are you talking about?'

'Please,' she says.

Lanre used to tell her that men couldn't help but have shows and the sooner she accepted the fact, the less complicated her life would be.

'I'm a busy man, you know,' he says, lifting a brow to remind her that he has another side to him, a mature, controlled side, where he makes important decisions and is respected by his subordinates.

'How come you have time to text that woman, then?' Deola asks.

'Would my wife trust me if I don't?'

'So why do it?'

He hisses. 'All of you are crazy, I swear, and you contradict yourselves. You support Jaiye and she treats her husband like shit.'

'Funsho treats Jaiye badly.'

'Jaiye is a brat.'

'My sister is not a brat.'

'You don't say a word about Ivie and she's sugary.'

'My cousin is not sugary.'

'She and that shady senator she is with.'

'She's been with him for years! She loves him!'

'Would she love him if he were poor?'

'Why should she love a poor man?'

'What is it? What more do you want? I go to work and come back home.'

'You should. Your father did.'

'Oh, so he never had another family before ours?'

'That has nothing to do with this.'

'How do you know he was faithful anyway?'

'That has nothing to do with what we are talking about here.'

'Every bad habit I have, I picked up in this house.'

'Don't give me that. Not today. Not today.'

'Why not? You see? As usual, you started what you couldn't finish.'

She is tearful. Perhaps her father wasn't always working late, but her father would not lower himself to sneak around as Lanre does.

'Set an example for your sons,' she says. 'It's a different world they have come into.'

Lanre's voice is loud enough for Eno to hear. 'Is your life perfect?'

Eno approaches them laughing. 'Why are you two always fighting?'

No one fights in her family. They are huggers and kissers. Her brother cried at her wedding.

'Don't mind this one,' Lanre says. 'She has nothing better to do.'

He takes out another cigarette and lights up as Deola mopes.

'What happened?' Eno asks.

Deola mumbles, 'I was just getting on his case for not talking sense into Funsho's head.'

'He can't,' Eno says with a smile. 'That would be like the pot calling the kettle black.'

'Hey,' Lanre says. 'Don't start.'

Eno pushes his shoulder. She often comes up with twee English expressions she picked up from her mother like, 'I'll have your guts for garters' or 'Bob's your uncle', and Lanre might say to her, 'You're not having any guts for any garters' or 'Bob is not my uncle'.

Deola leaves them at the chalet when she can no longer stand Lanre's cigarette fumes. She does sympathize with him. She would find it impossible to stay married to someone who doesn't trust her, and Lanre had a difficult time in his teens. He didn't just get his knees dashed; Seyi's death was a plummet. His experimentation with drugs would have followed regardless. So many boys at Ikoyi Club were doing that. They were drinking too much as well and learning they could get away with mistreating girls. They had highly esteemed fathers of dubious morality and were expected to follow in their fathers' footsteps. How many of them discovered they had half-siblings they were not aware of? How many saw their mothers get beaten up? Didn't someone once run into his father and a slutty newsreader in the games room? Wasn't someone else's father, a high court judge, sacked for taking bribes?

She walks over to Ivie's table, her heels sinking into the grass. Ivie is on her own drinking beer and watching other guests. Ivie enjoys a beer, but she won't drink in the presence of her elders. She won't walk around on the grass in her shoes either. They might get ruined.

'How now?' Ivie says, without smiling.

Ivie is withdrawn at family functions, almost as if they take her back to when she was regarded as the bad girl of the family. Her poise ages her.

It is cool under the canopy. Someone has knocked a wine glass over and left a purple stain on the white tablecloth. Deola scratches it. She is worried about Lanre. She is worried about Jaiye, Ivie and everyone. If the statistics on HIV in Africa are applicable here, Ikoyi ought to be a cluster. Everyone in the garden ought to be dead.

'Where's Omorege?' she asks.

Ivie nods in his direction. Omorege is at the relatives' table with his brother Henry. Henry, too, is separated from his wife. He publishes a newspaper that defends the incumbent party, the People's Democratic Party, against its numerous critics. He is unobtrusive and quite the opposite of Omorege. Omorege has the connections and Henry gives him the publicity he needs. They live in Ikoyi with a sense of accomplishment, rather than trepidation, and revel in their children's ignorance of adversity.

'Did you call Wale?' Ivie asks.

'I did,' Deola says.

'What happened?'

'We met.'

'So?'

'He's not for me.'

'Why not?'

'He's not interested in anything serious.'

Ivie rolls her eyes. 'Trap the man. He doesn't know what he is talking about.'

Deola laughs. She would rather be alone for the rest of her life than resort to trapping any man into marriage. She resists checking her phone to see if Wale has called. She could easily fall in love with him under different circumstances and only if he would love her back. It is a choice to love a man, she thinks. Only after the choice has been made does love become hard to control.

'When are you leaving?' Ivie asks.

'At four-thirty.'

'Who is taking you?'

'Lanre's driver.'

'I envy you.'

'Why?'

'Over there, you can manage on your salary. You get your pay cheque and take care of your bills and live comfortably. Over here, it's one thing after another.'

'But you get together here. We hardly get together over there. I can go for days without seeing anyone in London.'

'That's exactly what I want, peace and quiet. There are days I don't want to see anyone in Lagos.'

Ivie's corporate relations work often lands her in the newspapers, whenever she is launching a new foundation or a charity project. Omorege's political career puts her right in the tabloids, with women who are identified by the men they sleep with. They are too old to be called sugar babies, but they once were. Now they seem to have an insight into what prolongs relationships: sex and money. The rest, to them, is histrionic.

'It's true,' Deola says.

In London, she doesn't have peace, but she does have quiet.

She sits with Ivie for a while, and later Ivie's mother waylays her. Ivie's mother has lived in Port Harcourt for so long her pidgin English is perfect and she is not capable of subtlety.

'You,' she says. 'You never born *pikin?*'

Deola laughs. She loves her aunt, but she can't take her seriously.

'Aunty, Aunty,' she says.

'No "Aunty, Aunty" me nothing,' Ivie's mother says. 'Make you just hurry up and born *pikin*. All this book *wey* you *dey* learn for London.'

'I'm working,' Deola says, hugging her. 'Not schooling.'

Ivie's mother makes no distinction between schooling and working, and anywhere overseas is London to her.

'Working, schooling,' she says, 'at least born *pikin* if you no want marry. *Wetin?* Your junior sister, Jaiye, has born *pikin*. Your cousin, Ndidi, has born *pikin*. It's you and Ivie we're waiting for now. Let us see our successors before we die. I've told Ivie, "All this career, career will get you nowhere as a woman."'

Ivie's mother is a retired seamstress. She didn't progress beyond secondary school. Deola has often wondered what would have become of her had she gone to university, as her father and Ndidi's mother had. Ivie's mother was the eldest in the family. Their father did not believe in higher education for girls when she was ready for it. Ndidi's mother was the youngest daughter. She graduated from the University of Ibadan, worked for the Nigerian Broadcasting Corporation and wrote children's books for a while. She has retired from UNESCO, but she still lives in Paris with her second husband, a Cameroonian professor. She hasn't visited Nigeria in years. Ivie's mother calls her '*Français*' and regards her with the sympathy she reserves for intellectuals.

She advises Deola to forget about her career and focus on having a child.

'You hear?' she says, tugging her ear.

'I hear, Aunty,' Deola says.

Her mother's family is more educated than her father's. Her mother's father was a headmaster, so everyone in their family had to go beyond secondary school. Besides her mother and Aunty Bisi, there was Uncle Akin, an economist who was killed in a car crash a year after Deola was born, and Uncle

Bolaji, a historian, who thrilled Deola with stories about Echo and Narcissus, Prometheus and Pandora's box. He drank a lot and died of cirrhosis of the liver. As usual, the men went further than the women, who ended up surviving them, so perhaps the advice Ivie's mother gave her is practical for continuity, if nothing else.

She is packed and ready to leave when the rain begins to fall. Most of the guests have gone home or to other functions. She says goodbye to Aunty Bisi and Brother Dotun. Ivie and Omorege have to make an appearance at a wedding reception. Ivie's mother is staying in the chalet and she retires there. Her mother's entourage moves to the sitting room, except Aunty Simi, who has a night party to attend. Aunty Yinka sprawls out on the sofa.

'I want my cup,' she says. 'Get me my cup.'

She sounds like a toddler. Comfort is handing out commemorative blue plastic cups as keepsakes. Ella Fitzgerald and Louis Armstrong are singing 'Pennies from Heaven'. The air conditioner is on. Deola is aware of the grown-up party smell as she hugs and kisses her aunts. 'Safe journey, my dear,' they say. 'God bless you, darling.' Perhaps they are not remiss. Perhaps they know that this is all people can depend on, coming together to break bread. Aunty Fadeke stands up and secures her *iro*.

'Okay, everybody, I have a speech to make.'

The others make attempts to be quiet, but they fidget. Aunty Fadeke continues, still looking as if she is smiling.

'I have known this family, the Bello family, for . . . for many, many years now. Yes, and I am proud to say that I was there in . . . in . . .'

'Get on with it,' Aunty Theresa says.

'I was there in England when Remi met Sam. Yes, and to us, he was fondly known as Sammy Boy. That was what we called him, but he was born Idris. His family was a prominent agrarian family in Kwara State.'

'Fadeke,' Deola's mother says. 'Keep it short.'

'She's not even coherent,' Aunty Theresa says. 'She keeps hopping from one decade to another.'

'They married on that blessed day in . . . in . . .'

Aunty Theresa raises her eyes. 'Santa Maria.'

She is Catholic and finds this type of Protestant talk undignified.

Aunty Fadeke rounds on her. 'Patience is a virtue. We're not all as we used to be.' She faces her audience of three again. 'Now, sadly, Sam was called to the Land of Canaan.'

'Fadeke,' Deola's mother says, raising her hand. 'Deola has a flight to catch here. Save your speech for later.'

'What?'

'Save your speech for later. Deola has a plane to catch. *Oya*, Miss Adeola, say your goodbyes before it gets too dark outside. There are armed robbers around.'

Deola hugs Aunty Fadeke and her mother. They both smell of wine. She goes to the dining room. Lanre, Eno and Jaiye are there. The children are upstairs. There is more laughter from the sitting room.

'What is going on over there?' Jaiye asks.

Deola shakes her head. 'God knows.'

'Old hags,' Jaiye says.

Even Lanre is stunned by Jaiye's insolence. He seems to have forgiven Deola, though, and he asks, 'Do you want me to come to the airport?'

'Don't worry,' she says. 'It's too dangerous.'

'You're going back to work on Monday?'

'Yes.'

'England is too strict, man. What happened with your NGOs?'

'One of them was questionable. Do you know much about microfinance?'

'Enough.'

'Is Trust Bank involved in any of that?'

'We don't advance money without collateral.'

'But you sponsor community projects. Why not a microfinance scheme?'

'What for?'

'Consider it charity money.'

He nods and she can tell he is approaching her idea from a business angle.

'It can't do our image any harm,' he says.

There are more commemorative cups and food wrapped in foil paper on the dining table, but the faces, smells and sounds are Deola's keepsakes. She sits and absorbs them in her final moments, knowing that the comfort she has here will not last much longer.

She leaves her mother with a full house and Aunty Fadeke sings 'All Will Be Well' in Yoruba, an octave too low. She is glad to be leaving Lagos. Lanre's driver takes her to the airport via Third Mainland Bridge. She is not to tip him too much. That might spoil him. The sky turns orange on the way. She feels queasy with each jolt and pepper burns the back of her tongue.

'Is it bad with the armed robbers?' she asks the driver.

'Very,' he answers.

His name is Mr Mashood. He has a quiet pride, unlike Comfort, who sulks whenever she is called and has to be corrected several times. Comfort parades her discontent, which doesn't earn her much sympathy. Mr Mashood is always courteous, as if he has decided that antagonizing his employer is not worth his while.

During lunch, Deola saw him in the garage, eating his share of the caterer's food with a spoon and clicking it against his top teeth. He bowed slightly to greet her. She might not have noticed him had she not lived overseas and had the experience of being ignored at work.

Now she considers his safety from armed robbers as she sees his eyes in the rearview mirror. Whenever she is on her way out of Lagos, she gets the impression she is emerging from a thick fog she hasn't been aware of. After they have crossed Third Mainland Bridge, she checks her phone for incoming calls and messages and she has none. She returns her phone and remembers Wale's recorded greeting that ends with a '*Shalom*'.

The Business of Humanitarianism

London is unusually hot for this time of the year. Autumn should be sneaking in at the beginning of August, but there isn't even a suggestion of wind outside and the air conditioner inside Kate's office blows out nothing but dust.

'It's global warming,' Graham says to Deola.

This is his explanation for any variation in the weather, even when the temperature drops. There have been longer summers in the past. He stands up and smacks his thigh. Their meeting is over and he is leaving the office for the day as he is flying to Kenya tonight.

'Be prepared for more heat,' Deola says.

'It's winter there,' he says.

'All over?' she asks, wondering if Kenyans call this time of the year winter. 'Where are you going, Nairobi?'

'Mombasa,' he says, widening his eyes.

He takes great pleasure in saying this. His reports on his international travels are a change from embellishing his morning commutes from Kingsbury. He slouches as he leaves the room.

'So,' Kate says, 'we're okay with Dr Sokoya, then?'

Kate has recently had a haircut, which makes her look younger. She also has colour in her cheeks now.

'Yes,' Deola says.

'But not with Rita Wachuku.'

Kate will attempt to pronounce 'Nwachukwu'; Graham won't, despite his familiarity with world cultures. He will struggle over a Russian name, though, and might even bite off his tongue to get a French name right.

Deola didn't bring up Elizabeth Okeke's allegations when he was around and she doesn't intend to. Only with other Nigerians will she admit there is rampant corruption in Nigeria.

'They're not organized at WIN,' she says. 'Rita wants something and Elizabeth wants something else. Elizabeth was talking to me about a microfinance scheme. She didn't want to involve Rita, but I promised her I would follow up with you.'

Kate sighs. 'I got a phone call from Rita while you were there. She said she would like to meet me when she comes here. She's quite keen. She seems really nice.'

'She is.'

Deola won't admit that Nigerians sometimes trust foreigners more than they trust each other, but did Kate not hear her suggestion about the microfinance scheme?

Kate claps. 'Ooh, and I heard from Anne last week. She says Dára made a huge blunder in an interview over there. He said he's for polygamy, or he doesn't think polygamy is wrong, or he would practise polygamy. Something like that.'

'He did?'

'Yes, and they're up in arms about that in the Atlanta office.'

'Don't they have polygamists in America?'

'I'm not sure. I think the polygamists are in states like Utah. I should ask Anne about that. She was pretty upset about the whole business. She doesn't think Dára ought to be our spokesperson any more.'

'Because of that?'

'Yes, that's what I thought, but she's a bit earnest, Anne. Americans can be earnest, and puritanical. I think he's a little green, that's all. He'll get better at interviews.'

'He seemed okay when I saw him on telly the other night.'

Kate wrinkles her nose. 'He's green. You'll know what I mean when you meet him.'

'I'm meeting him?'

'Definitely, at the launch. Do people talk about him in Nigeria?'

Deola nods. Nigerians admire success overseas, even when they don't understand how the success came about or think it is justified.

'Anne's flying in next week,' Kate says.

'So she said.'

'She'll probably tell you more about what happened. Elucidate. You know she and her partner are trying to have a baby?'

'Yes, we talked about that.'

'Oh, you know she's . . .?'

'I know.'

Deola hopes her expression is impartial. She would do the same for Kate, who now pretends she wasn't soliciting gossip.

She points. 'Ooh, and Pam's coming in with her baby today.'

Pam doesn't come in until after lunchtime. She has a shy smile and a rusty voice. Her dreadlocks are tied back with a wrap. She wears silver bangles, which she jingles at her son. He is in a light blue bodysuit and nautical bib. He has so much hair and his eyes are focused. He sucks on a dummy as Kate carries him in the corridor. She coos and rocks him and is about to hand him over to Deola when she changes her mind and hands him back to Pam.

'I forgot,' she says. 'Keep away from Pam. She'll get you pregnant.'

'How would I do that?' Pam asks, laughing.

Kate opens her office door. 'Don't act as if you don't know, Pamela Collins, you fertility goddess you.'

She is barely in her office when Pam rolls her eyes. Do *oyinbo* women do this? Deola wonders. Signal to one another surreptitiously, 'Here we go again'? Pam has only two children. How is she a fertility anything?

'Is he sleeping through the night?' Deola asks.

'Yes,' Pam says. 'He's a good baby. He doesn't give me any trouble.'

On her way home in the tube this evening, Deola thinks of Pam's baby, whose name is Mathew. She would never give her child an English or biblical name. Her family would be mortified. She pictures Mathew's bodysuit. Why light blue? Why not pink? How did that colour code arise? How did it become almost universal and what is the purpose of having separate names for girls and boys?

These thoughts preoccupy her until she walks out of her stop at Willesden Green, behind a couple of elderly Indian women who are wearing jackets over their saris. They remind her of her trip to Delhi.

She tells herself she has to have an HIV test. She will have to if she is to become a mother some day, especially if she has to resort to artificial insemination. She really ought to find out her status beforehand. The side effects of the progestin pills are minimal now, and she expects her period to be earlier or later than normal this month.

At home, she checks her e-mail. On the morning she arrived, she called her mother and sent e-mails to Lanre and Jaiye. Lanre replied with a short 'How are you? Hope you are fine.' He and Eno were off to Portugal with the boys. Jaiye still hasn't replied, which doesn't surprise her. Jaiye is lazy about answering e-mails.

Afterward, she searches the Internet for information about HIV tests. She does not want to go through her GP. She would not want to use a private doctor either. They would keep records. What are the implications? Would her records remain confidential? A clinic would be safer. She could give herself any identity and remain anonymous. She looks for the nearest clinic and finds one in Brent and another in Southwark. She chooses the latter.

As she takes down details, her hand trembles. She would like to pray, but it makes no sense to pray for what might already have happened, or to pray for what countless people have prayed for without getting their desired result. If she is HIV positive, she might never pray again.

She says a quick prayer anyway, in case Wale lied to her, whimpering to herself, 'Help me, Lord,' but this does not calm her down. What if he infected her? What if she infected him? What would happen to his daughter? The ramifications are extensive and possible, so possible that she shakes her head until she doesn't contemplate them any more.

She calls the clinic on her mobile phone. Same-day HIV

tests are by appointment only. She says hers is due to an emergency and she sounds convincing enough because she is genuinely tearful. Going to a clinic has to be right down there with going to a triple-X flick on her own. The receptionist says, 'We have a late cancellation, but please let us know as soon as possible if you're not able to make it.'

'I will,' she says.

She takes a bath and goes to bed, telling herself she can change her mind anytime. She doesn't have to show up. It helps her to fall asleep and she has a dream she can't recall, but she wakes up at the purgatory hour and lies there as blue merges with orange in the sky.

Her appointment is at five o'clock on Wednesday afternoon. She arrives at the clinic early, hoping she will not see anyone. The temperature has dropped considerably this evening and she squints from the wind in her face. Her heart rate increases at the sight of the red-brick building. She walks up the wheelchair access ramp. She played the gambling game on her way here and the traffic lights were in her favour.

There are two men in the waiting room, possibly in their late twenties or early thirties. One has rockabilly sideburns and the other wears cuffed black jeans. The receptionist stands behind the shelf and hands over a registration sheet and a pamphlet.

'Fill this out,' she says, smiling. 'Make sure we have a means of contacting you.'

Deola sits by the water fountain, opposite the men. For her name, she writes 'Angela Davis' and she fakes a date of birth that would make her a mere twenty-seven years old. She gives her mobile phone number. No, she does not want them to contact her GP. Afterward, she skims through the pamphlet, which asks, 'What is HIV?' 'Have you been at risk for infection?' 'Should you have the test?' The pamphlet assures her, 'You cannot catch HIV from hugging, kissing, sharing a cup or toilet seat,' then raises her fears with, 'Test negative or positive?' She stops reading after the list of disadvantages of being tested, the first of which is prejudice and discrimination.

She is reassured when she meets Dr Srinivasan. It is hard to tell her age, but she is certainly not fresh out of medical school. She has shoulder-length hair and shadows around her eyes. Her accent is from East London.

'How can I help you?'

'I would like to get an HIV test. I may have been exposed recently.'

'Recently?'

'Less than a week ago.'

'How were you exposed?'

'Through sex.'

'Anal, oral or vaginal?'

'Vaginal.'

'Were you with a casual or regular partner?'

'Casual.'

Dr Srinivasan's expression is solemn. 'I'll have to ask you a few questions about your previous sexual partners as well.'

Deola lies. She says she had sex six weeks beforehand and has had up to fifty partners. What difference will it make? She has not had any sexually transmitted illnesses. Dr Srinivasan asks if she would like to test for chlamydia and gonorrhea and she answers, 'For everything.'

'For the HIV test,' Dr Srinivasan explains, 'I'll take a blood sample and you'll have to wait outside for the result.'

Deola's heart knocks against her ribs until the sound blocks her ears. She can't hear a word Dr Srinivasan says after this. What about her cough that didn't go away? Her constant fatigue? How will she walk out and drive home if her test result is positive? How will she tell her mother? Who will tell her mother? How will her family cope with the news?

'Are you all right?' Dr Srinivasan asks.

'Yes,' she says, but she wants to cry.

She takes shallow breaths as she changes into an examination gown and shuts her eyes when Dr Srinivasan takes swabs and draws blood from the vein. She is eleven years old again with sore breasts, thinking she has cancer. She is telling her doctor she has a pain in her 'chest' because she can't say the word 'breast'. He is putting a stethoscope to her chest and listening to her lungs and he is saying, 'You're perfectly fine.'

Dr Srinivasan pats her arm and says, 'You can get dressed now.'

When she returns to the waiting room, the men are still there, but there are more people, most of whom are black, except a woman with bleached dreadlocks and a balding man in a brown polyester suit. Her legs tremble as if she has been running in a marathon. She couldn't stop them if she weighed them down with bricks. She could get up and walk down the street, but if she leaves, she might never return. She can't move anyway, not voluntarily. Again, she wills her father to make his presence felt, but he doesn't, so she believes this is a sign. He knows she is HIV positive. Her head aches and her mouth dries up. She stumbles into a psalm:

Please, don't let me be HIV positive. I will be a different person if I leave this place with a negative result. I will, I will, I will. I will change. I will be good to my family and friends. I will counsel them. I will counsel everyone I can. Use me as a conduit. Use me, use me, use me. I will obey Your will. I will be respectful to my mother. Do You want to kill the poor woman? Is that what You want? Well, You will. You will, then You will be sorry. All right, I bow down to You as Your humble servant, then! I said I submit myself to You! What more do You want? Why won't You believe me? How do you expect me to trust You, if You won't trust me? Yes, yes, I have let You down, but that is because Your commandments are too strict. Yes, they are. Yes, they are. Yes, I'm arrogant to say that. Yes, I'm selfish. Yes, I'm a bitch. Sorry I used that word, but You know what I mean. Forgive me for my indifference to my fellow man. Forgive me for my lack of compassion. Aren't You supposed to be all-knowing? Aren't You supposed to be omniscient and omnipotent? So help me! Help me to grow! I'm only human, a mere mortal, a wretch. Yes, I accept that now. I'm a wretch and You created me that way. Yes, You did, in Your image. I didn't mean it that way. All right, I did, and I'm sorry, but I wouldn't be in this position if You were more accessible. You've never been. Okay, that was rude. Okay, okay, I hear what You're trying to tell me, but don't teach me any lesson this way. Take my job, take my pride, take anything you want to, but please, please get me out of this place negative. That's all I ask and I won't ask anything else of You forever and ever . . .

The receptionist calls her. 'Angela Davis?'

She gets up, knees rocking and cold from her head down. The first step she takes calms her. She walks through the door and Dr Srinivasan has the same expression.

'Your test result says you're HIV negative.'

Deola pats her chest as she sits down.

'But you'll have to come back in six months for a repeat test.'

Her physical symptoms have disappeared and her religious doubts are already raising their hands. She was expecting congratulations and would be furious with Dr Srinivasan if she were not this grateful.

'All your test results today are fine,' Dr Srinivasan says. 'I'll go over them with you, but you'll have to make another appointment or contact us in a week to find out about the rest.'

Deola nods. 'Thank you. Thank you so much.'

She is the same way with the receptionist later, almost curtseying when she says she will call in a week. Only when she walks out into the car park, oblivious to the wind, does she spare another thought for the people in the waiting room. What were they there for? What were their results?

As she reverses out of the car park, she sees her reflection in the rearview mirror and stops to rub her dried tears. She is negative. She thought she would toot her horn and flash her headlights, but to rejoice now would be disrespectful to those who are not. She drives, conscious of a world where people are negative or positive. She can't tell them apart on Peckham High Street as they walk in and out of the Internet cafés, kebab houses, MoneyGram shops, black salons and barbershops. There are so many Nigerians here, more than there are in Willesden Green. It is almost like being back in Lagos. She passes Obalende Suya, a food spot she has heard about, and a row of yellow-brick, semi-detached houses with 'For Sale' signs. She imagines the houses were built after World War II, when families slept in the underground and lost their fathers, husbands and sons. Did they accept death with dignity in those days? Or was it that death was more exalted, unlike nowadays, when death is put on display so often that people can see there is no dignity in it. She recalls the news footage of the attack on Baghdad; African and Eastern European countries in the middle of civil wars; villages ravaged by outbreaks of cholera and smallpox; land destroyed by earthquakes and tornados.

In Lagos, people are afraid of death by armed robberies, car crashes and sickness. They are terrified of bankruptcy – financial and the other kind that leads to a permanent loss of hope. They call on God so much because they don't trust that the next day will be delivered free of charge, so they want immediate remuneration, connections and companionship.

These days, Londoners are afraid of terrorism. They are predicting a retaliation, their own 9/11, but London is often a terrorist target. She was in the middle of her accountancy training when the IRA was planting bombs. She was living in her parents' flat when that one went off in Victoria Station. Her family called from Lagos and she told them not to worry. The prospect of being blown up was remote, something to do with governments and their policies. This is different, from a virus she can't see, one that takes over cells and mutates, one that she can carry, transmit and pass on to a child without realizing. For her, this is the greatest terror of all.

Tonight, her neighbours have a party that goes on past midnight and she can't sleep from their laughter and music. The next morning she wakes up exhausted. She does not want to go to work, but she gets ready anyway.

In her kitchen, she calls Wale as she butters toast. If his recorded greeting comes on, she will not leave a message. She doesn't want to hear that word '*Shalom*' ever again, especially from him. He answers after a couple of beeps.

'Hello?'

'Hello, Wale?'

'Yes?'

'This is Adeola Bello.'

He pauses. 'Hello.'

'I just want to tell you I got tested and I'm fine. I found out yesterday.'

'That is good news,' he says, in a subdued voice. 'Thanks for letting me know.'

She returns her butter dish to the fridge, presses the phone to her ear and it gives her a semblance of intimacy.

'Can you hear me?'

'Yes, I can.'

'Clearly?'

'Yes.'

'Where are you?'

'In my office. Don't worry, we are safe.'

She shuts the fridge door. Are they? He has not seen her test result and she has not seen his.

'I also want to ask you a question. Don't take it the wrong way, but it bothered me. I want to know how you could fall asleep that night. I'm not a parent, but if I were, I would not sleep.'

Again a pause. 'I must have been tired.'

Her tap is dribbling. She tightens it until her palm smarts.

'Is that why you were quiet?' he asks.

'That's why,' she says.

'I thought you wanted to be on your own. I was tired that night. That's why I slept.'

She stamps her shoe on the linoleum. He doesn't care. Not enough.

'I'd better go.'

'No. We can talk.'

'I have to get to work. I'll be late if I stay on much longer.'

'Okay, then.'

'I wish you the best.'

'You too.'

He should have kept her on the phone, she thinks, on her way down the stairs. He could have, if he really wanted to. This is the last time she will call him. The banister is shaky and the staircase creaks. Her skirt is short enough to allow her to run down. She stops to button up her jacket and cringes at the dirt embedded in the carpet in the hallway.

Outside, she hurries along with other commuters. Her brisk walk causes her to regurgitate orange juice, only a little, but it burns her. Choosing to love a man may not be conscious after all. It is like breathing. She may choose to hold her breath, but her will will prevail.

Throughout the day, she thinks of Wale. She doesn't need much of a prompt: a tone of voice, a colleague's fresh white shirt or an accidental touch. Even a business card reminds her of his and this thoroughly annoys her. She mistakes her preoccupation with him for desperation. What else can it be? She had just one night with him, if she can call it that. Shouldn't she be more liberated than this?

After work, she has an idea to call Subu and Bandele and tell them to get tested. This she can do for a start, acting as a conduit.

She calls Bandele first when she gets home, but he wants to talk about his writing instead.

'Hey, remember that writer I told you about? The one who was going on about Coetzee the other night?'

'What about him?'

She is lying on her couch in her sweatpants with her knees apart, listening to Rufus and Chaka Khan's *Stompin' at the Savoy*.

'The shithead won the prize.'

'What!'

'Yes, he got the book deal. Can you believe it?'

'Damn. Damn. How did that happen?'

'I don't know, but his novel is about some Nigerian writer who gets murdered in exile.'

'In exile where?'

'Germany or somewhere, by neo-Nazis or something. But guess what his title is?'

'I can't.'

'Just guess.'

'Um, something with "rock" or "river"?'

'The Death of the African Writer.'

'Ugh!'

African novels are too exotic for her. Reading them, she often feels they are meant for Western readers, who are more likely to be impressed.

'Original, ay? I wonder whose bright idea that was. I still can't get over it, but I suppose this is what they want. I suppose this is what they're looking for these days, from those of us of a certain persuasion. The more death, the better. It is like literary genocide. Kill off all your African characters and you're home and dry. They certainly don't want to hear from the likes of me, writing about trivialities like love.'

She shakes her head. Genocide indeed. Over the years, Bandele has whined about unfairly awarded book prizes. She suspects he is jealous as he tells her about the award night.

'I'm sitting there eating chicken and potatoes in what looks like baby's diarrhoea. I have a journalist on one side of me and he was all right, quite interesting to talk to. We had a good chat. I have an agent on my other side and I was trying to talk to her. You know, to get her to sign me on, but the rep from the Nigeria High Commission kept interrupting. On the other side of the table is this literary event organizer, who has a vacant stare throughout, as if she has no idea how she got there, surrounded by all these Africans. You should see the look of relief on her face when she meets the Afrikaner writer. Every once in a while a chap gets up and reads excerpts and there is nothing worse, nothing worse I tell you, than an excerpt from your novel being read out when your bowels are churning. Then this woman, who wears a kaftan and what looks like a plant growing on her head, gives a speech, and I can't even understand a bloody word she is saying, her accent is so thick. She announces the winner and of course it wasn't me. Coetzee Critic shuffles up to the podium in his garb, you know, looking like a real native, as naïve as you please. He gives his thank-you speech: "I yam vary grateful, I yam vary humbled." I could puke at this point. Then the patron of the prize takes a photograph with him. He is smiling away, all teeth. The rep from the Nigeria High Commission abandons me to congratulate him. Prize patron shoos rep away. Prize administrator comes up to me and whispers in my ear, "There was a sense that he needed it more." I'm thinking, What are you running here? A literary contest or a charity drive? And this judge, whom I have no respect for whatsoever – I couldn't get past the first page of her novel – walks up to me and says, "Keep writing." Like that, and I'm thinking, Piss off, you untalented tart! It was torture, pure torture, so patronizing. What's more, the poor bugger who won didn't seem to realize.'

He is jealous. This is first time he has ever acknowledged that race matters. But doesn't he realize Africans know when they are being patronized? Doesn't he know the more naïve they pretend to be, the more they can capitalize on patronage? The poor bugger outplayed Bandele.

She has never worked in the publishing industry, but she imagines the people he encounters there. People who would never tolerate a supercilious upstart African like him. An African who doesn't even have the common decency to entertain them with stories about how awful his country is. Love indeed. She comforts him anyway.

'Love is not trivial,' she says.

'I know that.'

'Love is epic.'

'I know, I know.'

'So what's your novel about exactly?'

'Two people. Just two people who are unsuitable for each other.'

'Are they Nigerian?'

'Is that relevant?'

She struggles to sit up. He is always so defensive about his writings, protecting them as if they were his balls.

'They must come from somewhere in the world. Okay, where is the story set?'

'London . . . and Paris.'

'Paris! I'd love to go to Paris!'

'Why?'

'Why what?'

'Why Paris? Tourists walking around on eggshells, as if it's their fault the French are rude. Piss all over the streets. You hop into a taxi and you're at the mercy of some North African with a chip on his shoulder. Style is all that matters over there. You can get away with just about anything in Paris, so long as you have style. Paris is a cliché.'

Wasn't that a clichéd description of Paris?

'Why set a novel there, then?'

'Because Paris turns out to be more disastrous than their relationship. Only people in books and films want to go to Paris. The only reason I want to go there is to get my scenes right and finally send off this bloody manuscript, if anyone will care to read it. It's not that I'm moaning or anything. It's not that I even care. It's just that I can't get anyone to take a look at what I've done so far. Just take a look at it. And I've been working hard, harder than I have ever worked before. You understand?'

'I understand.'

'So suddenly I am an "African" writer. Suddenly it's the only way I can get ahead in this business, and I can just sense there is going to be an interest in African literature because of this prize. I can just feel it, but it won't be real, if you know what I mean. It will all be about trying to fit into the African literature scene and you either exploit what is going on or you don't. That's all I'm saying. See?'

'I see.'

She thinks of Dára, who crossed over by pretending to be a street child.

'Love is not trivial,' she says. 'Love can be dangerous. Love can be deadly in this day and age, and there are casualties, so write your story. There is no need to fear.'

'You're good to me,' he says.

She finds African literature preoccupied with politics in a way she never was. The fact was she accepted the civil war was the only reasonable option for Nigeria, and from then on witnessed a parade of military and civilian rulers: cowards, reformers, sexual deviants and murderous juju disciples. They were like the stars at night to her. She couldn't deny their significance, but she was hardly dazzled by them. There were times she thought she ought to take more interest in what they were doing, but the death toll from the civil war and years of political unrest combined could not add up to the number of casualties from AIDS, so perhaps her concerns over what was happening between chicks and guys were not so misplaced after all.

'You know I had an HIV test yesterday?'

'Excuse me?' he says.

'I'm fine. But I promised myself I would tell you to get tested.'

'Why?'

'I just thought I should.'

'Why me, I mean?'

'Why not you?'

'Because *you're* all right?'

She did not mean to be smug.

'I'm telling you as a friend.'

He laughs. 'I'm not sleeping with you!'

'It's not by force, Bandele.'

'I should hope it's not "by force".'

'Don't do it, if you don't like.'

'I don't like. So how was Nigeria for you?'

She rolls her eyes. 'Fine.'

'Must have been.'

He is smiling and so is she.

'*Agbaya*,' she says.

'Pardon?'

'You heard me, so you can pardon, pardon all you like. Grow up.'

'Who is he, then? Why do I think he is a doctor, or a lawyer, or an accountant, with a name that begins with "Ade" or "Olu" or "Ola"?'

'Get off my line.'

She disconnects him. He and his Camillas and Felicitys. He will not stop her from being a conduit.

He almost puts her off calling Subu, whom she was saving for later because she expects Subu to be more difficult to persuade. Subu is still at work when she calls.

'Shoe Boo,' she says.

'*Na wa*,' Subu says. 'So you can't call somebody when you get into town?'

'My sister, I've been through a turbulent, torturous, tumultuous period of trial and tribulation.'

'What happened?'

'I had an HIV test yesterday.'

'Why?'

'Don't worry, I'm fine.'

'Thank God. What did you do that for?'

'I had to know.'

'Know what?'

'Forty is fast approaching and I may have to be artificially inseminated someday.'

Subu laughs. 'You're not serious.'

'It's true. We have to start thinking about these things. You should do it, too.'

'Do what?'

'Get tested.'

'Why?'

'To know your status.'

Subu hisses. 'You're not serious.'

'What? Everyone should know.'

'What if I'm positive?'

Deola snaps her fingers. 'I reject that in the name of Jesus!'

'Silly girl,' Subu says. 'Where do you even go to get tested?'

'To a doctor, or a clinic.'

'Me, go to a clinic?'

'I went to one.'

Subu laughs. 'You're a bad girl!'

She tells Subu what happened at the clinic. 'I couldn't even walk straight. I almost collapsed. I thought, what will I do? How will I tell my mother?'

Subu sighs. 'As for me, my mother would be the first person I would tell. I would tell her to get herself here as fast as possible, with her holy water, novenas, candles, all of it. She can come and pray for me.'

Subu's mother is a veteran at prayer, and she loves rituals. She doesn't care what Christian denomination they are from.

She was in London when Deola and Subu got their exam results. They went to Leicester Square that night to buy *The Times*, where the PE II results were published. Newspaper vendors started selling copies around midnight. Before they left, Subu's mother made them kneel down in Subu's flat and she prayed while touching their heads.

'Merciful Father,' she began. 'King of Kings, Lord of Lords, the God of all possibilities, let your children rejoice in the land of the living, in Jesus' name.'

Her prayer was eloquent, but it made no sense chronologically. Their papers had already been marked.

'I actually prayed to be used as a conduit,' Deola says, scratching her thigh.

'Really?' Subu says. 'Maybe you will soon start coming to fellowship with me?'

'That I can't promise. But come . . .'

'What?'

'Doesn't it make more sense to pray before the fact rather than after?'

'Before and after.'

'You are covered on both ends, then,' Deola says. 'Nobody can pray like your mother.'

She calls herself a skeptic, yet she has never taken the time to read a holy book. She tried to read the Bible, but she couldn't get past the 'begats'.

Subu is travelling to Shanghai again this month. She is still considering buying a flat there and will make up her mind on her trip. Deola feels honoured. Subu doesn't normally reveal her plans in case someone gets jealous and jinxes her. She may believe in Jesus Christ, but she also believes in the evil eye.

'I don't have any plan to be artificially inseminated,' Subu says. 'But with all these long-term investments I'm getting into, maybe I should get tested.'

'Promise?'

'Only if you promise to come to fellowship with me.'

'That can't happen.'

'You know there is no hope for you?'

'I know.'

Normally, Deola would ask, 'How would you know?' and that would be the beginning of a religious war between them.

Tonight she lies on the couch listening to the CD until the final song, 'Don't Go to Strangers'. She thinks of Wale again. His composure hides his sense of humour. He might come across as dull. She indulges herself this way, examining him from different angles, and plays the song over and over, telling herself this is due to her loneliness in London. She hopes that by morning, he will be as stale to her as the song will inevitably sound.

She goes to bed early and not until the purgatory hour does she begin to worry, when she wakes up after dreaming that everyone at her father's memorial is lying dead in the garden. Her fridge is humming and a car roars past on the high street. Her bedroom is not entirely dark: the gaps in her curtains allow some moonlight in. She senses a sympathetic presence, which may or may not be her father's. She is virtually asleep again when she imagines the consequences of one of her friends getting a positive result. Her duvet gets hot, her stomach pulsates and her skin moistens. She says a prayer, raps her knuckles on her headboard and buries her face in her pillow.

—

This week she has dinner with Anne Hirsch at a pizzeria. The pizzeria, on Baker Street, has spaghetti Western posters and blown-up black-and-white photographs of Hollywood stars like Frank Sinatra, Dean Martin, Gina Lollobrigida and Sophia Loren. Dean Martin is singing '*Volare*'. On the table is a candle inserted into a wine bottle covered with an avalanche of melted wax. The atmosphere is camp.

'I can't get away from American pop culture,' Anne says. 'I turn on the television in my hotel, and it's all garbage.'

'American culture is everywhere,' Deola says. 'It's your biggest export, come to think of it.'

'No,' Anne says. 'That would be war and violence.'

Anne flew in on Monday. She is returning to Atlanta in the morning. A waiter comes to their table to ask what they would like to drink.

'Wine for you?' Deola asks Anne.

'Water will be fine.'

'I'll have water, too, thanks,' Deola says to the waiter.

The waiters here pretend to be harried to create an Italian ambience. This one keeps twitching. He has blond highlights in his hair.

Afterward, Anne explains, 'I'm a teetotaler for now. You know Ali and I are trying for a baby.'

'Yes,' Deola says.

She would classify this as personal information, but Deola has known colleagues to confide in her at office functions, only to walk past her in the office the next day.

'We've decided that I'm carrying,' Anne says. 'My insurance coverage is better. In the States, we don't have a national health service as you have over here. I think I mentioned that Ali is a florist, didn't I?'

'You did.'

Deola also remembers that Anne will take any opportunity to apologize for America. She seems to admire the English, though. Another waiter returns with their drinks and takes their orders. Anne nods as if she is in the presence of a lecturer as he goes through the menu mispronouncing dishes like *prosciutto funghi e panna* and *pomodorini rucola e prosciutto*. She playfully changes her 'tomay-to' to 'tomah-to' and finally orders a pizza Margherita, so Deola orders a pizza Napoletana.

'Markeriter,' the waiter says, scribbling. 'Naplitaner.'

Other customers in the pizzeria are seated around circular tables similar to theirs. They are well dressed. They would have been called yuppies back in the eighties and are reappearing in London under a European guise.

Anne is eager to tell Deola about Dára's botched interview. She stares through her contact lenses as she justifies why she thinks he ought to be dropped as a spokesperson.

'He was specifically asked about AIDS in Africa and he said, and I quote, "Polygamy helps. When men have several wives, they don't sleep around."'

Deola laughs. 'I don't know about that.'

'I thought, how sexist.'

'He must have been drunk or high.'

'I can't even begin to get my head around it. It makes me very nervous about what he might come up with next.'

Deola tries to understand Dára's reasoning. He probably came up with any answer he could think of. In Nigeria, no one would have paid him any mind, as a college dropout. Overseas, people are asking for his opinions on Africa.

'Don't you have polygamists in the Bible Belt?' she asks.

Anne nods. 'They practise it as part of their religion, but in the States, a man cannot legally be married to more than one woman at a time.'

'Not even Muslims?'

'I'm sure they have ways of getting around the law and you can't stop people from cohabiting.'

Deola pushes the ice in her glass into the water. 'In Nigeria, Muslims are free to practise polygamy. It is legal under customary law.'

Anne shrugs. 'Religion and culture, they're one and the same. How was your trip there anyway? Kate says you were concerned about one of the NGOs you reviewed.'

Kate Meade had to go home after work. Her daughter had a stomach ache. Whenever her daughter falls sick, so does her husband. Deola is beginning to think he is a saboteur not an inventor.

'I was concerned,' she says. 'The CEO wants to raise money for a community. Her VP, who is from the community, is interested in microfinance. I thought that was a good idea.'

'Yes, but that's a shift from what we do. Personally, I think microcredit is a wonderful idea and it's catching on, but within Africa we focus on charity.'

Of course, Deola thinks. LINK is not in the business of making their beneficiaries look self-sufficient. They must evoke sympathy to raise money. This is how charity works. No one gives money to people they are on a par with, so someone has to be diminished in the process.

'It would be nice, though,' she says, 'to show communities like that in a more encouraging light.'

'The reality is,' Anne says, rearranging her fork and knife, 'these communities are at risk and someone has to respond to their immediate needs.'

'But the aim is to enable self-sufficiency in the long run, isn't it?'

Deola asks only because she expects an accusation like, 'It is all right for you to say that.'

'I guess,' Anne says, 'but you would have to be involved in fieldwork to fully understand how bad things are. Women and children are especially vulnerable in Africa. Mothers become sex workers and they pass the virus to their babies. Babies die before they reach their second birthdays. Grandmothers are raising orphans. It is awful what is going on. It makes you so angry.'

Deola interprets this as, 'Shouldn't it make you angry?' It makes her sad. It also makes her scared, too scared to dwell on how much Africa suffers, and it has the same paralyzing effect on her as selfishness would. She does not represent Africa and Anne does not represent the West, but Anne swings easily from guilt to having a monopoly on compassion.

And always over a fairly decent meal, Deola thinks. The manner in which Anne relays these facts is unsettling. Back home, people are more dispassionate when they talk about other people's suffering, which may be more honest. They drop their voices and avert their eyes. They speak with humility, not compassion, and Nigerians are not naturally humble, but they do understand that someone else's suffering could so easily become theirs.

'When are you travelling to Rio?' Deola asks, desperate to change the topic.

'At the end of the month,' Anne says.

'Have you succumbed to a Starbucks latte yet?'

Anne smiles. 'Not yet.'

Deola pretends to be interested as Anne rehashes her fears of corporate invasions. She is suspicious of package positions and Anne seems to have one. She can predict, for instance, that Anne is vehemently opposed to zoos.

Their waiter returns with their pizzas. 'Markeriter?' he asks, and Anne raises her hand. 'Naplitaner,' he says, and Deola raises hers.

The next day, she calls the clinic to find out the results of her remaining tests and she is given the all-clear. She does not see her period, though, which normally begins on the twenty-eighth or twenty-ninth day, but the progestin pills might be responsible for the delay.

At work, Kate Meade calls in sick. Her husband and daughter have a stomach virus and she is feeling under the weather. So is Deola throughout the day, and this evening at home, she is more tired than she usually is midweek. She grills lamb chops with rosemary for dinner and eats them with salad sprinkled with balsamic vinegar and olive oil. She considers having water with her meal and opts for wine, telling herself she has been around too many women who are preoccupied with motherhood. Yes, this is the problem. She is only a day late.

As she eats on her couch, she listens to a Maze and Frankie Beverly CD, *Live in New Orleans*. She holds the lamb chops with her fingers and sucks on the bones. She would not give up moments like this. It was just a matter of time before she got used to being on her own again. She thinks of Wale as she burps with her mouth open and picks her front teeth with her fingernails, imagining his reaction if he could see her. She sings along to 'Before I Let Go'.

After dinner, she calls Subu, who has the latest multi-band mobile phone with this and that feature. Shanghai is hours ahead, but Subu wakes up early to get her prayers in before anyone else, which makes Deola wonder if Australian Christians benefit from waking up before Chinese Christians.

'Shoe Boo,' she says.

'How now?' Subu asks. 'Where are you?'

'At home, but see me, see trouble yesterday.'

She tells Subu about her dinner with Anne Hirsch, struggling to keep her voice low. Her block is quiet and her neighbours might overhear her.

'The woman didn't want to hear anything about self-sufficiency. Anything at all. You think I'm being paranoid here?'

'I don't think she wanted to hear your opinions.'

'I mean, she said Dára's comment was sexist. How can that be sexist? He's just daft.'

'Don't mind these *oyinbo* women. They come with their feminism. When push comes to shove, they turn to their men. Don't trust them.'

'Actually, she's gay.'

'*To*.'

To. End of matter. Nothing left to be said. Deola regrets bringing this up. She should have known how Subu would react.

'I mean, she went on and on trying to take me on her guilt trip, women and children, this and that. "You'd have to be involved in fieldwork to fully understand how bad things are."'

'*Oyinbos*. That's their stock-in-trade. They can't get enough of our suffering. We exist so they can feel good about themselves.'

'It's not that I'm against charity.'

'I am.'

'Since when?'

'Since since. Where has charity ever got us?'

'No, no, Subu. We need charity. We need charity in Africa. Don't tell me this. Aren't you a Christian? Don't you give tithes?'

'Okay, please tell me,' Subu says, 'did you see any beggars when last you were at home?'

'Of course! Plenty, plenty! In fact there were more of them. You know how you normally see beggars on the streets or outside church? This time, I saw them everywhere.'

'Thank you,' Subu says. 'So all these years people back home have been giving beggars money, how come we have more of them, not less?'

'That is a different issue.'

'How?'

'It's a different issue, Subu. That is because our economy is getting worse.'

'Exactly. So why don't we solve our economy problems instead of begging for funds all over the place? Why should Africa always be seen as a charity case? Can't people invest in Africa instead?'

'Invest? Are you investing in Africa?'

'The Chinese are.'

'For what purpose?'

'I don't know, but make no mistake, these charities are dangerous for us.'

'Subu.'

'They are!'

'Subu, why?'

'It's true! I blame them for the lack of progress in Africa. They make us dependent on the money they keep handing us. They do, and their ultimate aim is to hold us back.'

Deola shakes her head. She never expected to get into another left-wing–right-wing argument with Subu. She forgot Subu is as financially conservative as she is Christianly. Her friends are stubborn. They are as stubborn as she is. The fact that they sometimes vehemently contradict themselves proves this. For her, all it takes is for someone to make an assertion and she is ready to object. Perhaps this is partly due to her boredom in London.

'Hear me out,' she says. 'The only Africans I hear complaining about foreign aid are Africans who don't need aid. I don't see Africans who receive aid complaining. I don't see Africans helping each other that much either. How many of us are well off? How many percentage-wise? They expose us, that's all. That is why charities annoy us so much.'

'Expose us how?'

'To the world, for who we are and what we can live with. We don't care about each other.'

'Who said?'

'We don't. If we did, we would be in a better situation than we're in. In fact, all I see around me is contempt. The contempt we have for one and another, and every humiliation we have abroad is to remind us of the mess we have left behind.'

Subu hisses. 'Giving never cured poverty and Africans should stop begging for funds from developed countries. What is it? Isn't our continent the cradle of civilization? And this same Mandela that they keep using his name to raise funds, wasn't he the one they once branded a terrorist? No. They don't want us to be self-sufficient. They don't want us to be powerful. That's all. What you are seeing is the contempt they have for us.'

It is getting dark in the sitting room. Deola switches on her lamp and rubs her eyes until the framed batik on her wall and the photograph of her nephews and niece on her side table come into focus.

She couldn't care less if Africa is the cradle of civilization. What difference does it make to the state Africa is in? How could any reasonable person be comforted by the fact that long ago civilization began in Africa? Subu doesn't want to go back to Africa. Even black Americans, who champion the whole 'civilization began in Africa' business, don't want to go back. The Egyptians they credit with starting civilization barely identify with Africa.

'Naijas,' she says. 'That's the trouble with us, talk, talk, talk, no action.'

She curls up on the couch. She is too tired to argue. Why is she so tired?

'I hear our friend Dára says polygamy is a cure for AIDS,' she says.

Subu sighs. 'What do you expect? Someone who didn't finish his education. He is even in the Internet news this morning.'

'For what?'

'He was arrested for lewd and lascivious acts.'

'Hah?'

'They are deciding whether to charge him or not as we speak.'

'What's wrong with the *bobo*?'

'You're asking me?'

'Is he in jail?'

'He's out on bail. He says she was the one who violated him. You know how people dance nowadays. He met her at a nightclub and she either rubbed up against him or it was the other way around. The next thing you know, she was calling the police.'

'Swear?'

'Swear.'

'He is finished. They will bury him for this.'

'They've already started. They're putting pressure on his main sponsor to drop him.'

'It was a matter of time. I'm telling you. I didn't even know how to respond when I heard what he had to say about polygamy. I made excuses for him. My colleague called him "green", which was nice of her.'

'They saw fit to choose him to represent them.'

Deola yawns. She has already made up her mind. LINK's policy on Africa bothers her more than their public relations strategy, though she has no doubt the latest news about Dára will cause a stir in the office.

'That's their business,' she says. 'All I know is that I am going to work tomorrow to talk to them, and if they can't be open to an idea that involves a community of Africans being independent, then maybe I'm working for the wrong organization.'

'You will quit?'

'I might.'

'Just like that?'

'Just like that.'

'Why?'

'Aren't you the one who's against charity?'

She gets some satisfaction out of shocking Subu, but the thought of quitting her job scares her.

'Don't do that,' Subu says. 'You will meet the same attitude wherever you go. It's the Tarzan Complex. You have to make them feel useful to get ahead. If you ask for respect, they don't want to know. Forget about getting through to these people.'

After she hangs up, Deola checks her e-mail. Jaiye still hasn't replied. In her inbox, she has adverts for Viagra, male-enhancement drugs, Christian singles and a scam letter from a Mr Ahmed, who claims to be a managing director of a bank in Ouagadougou. She deletes them, resisting the temptation to look up more information about the morning-after pill. That would be like praying after the fact. Instead, she Googles Dára. There are several articles about his charges and a few that are critical of his comment on polygamy. She finds a blog where someone called 'TJ' refers to him as a 'punk ass African' and another called 'Nubian Queen' replies that he is a fine brother. Most of the postings are hostile to the woman who accused him.

She Googles Stone Riley afterward and finds an article where he says he has adopted Africa as his cause. Deola is not surprised. In the photograph, he looks as if he hasn't taken a bath in days, his hair is greasy and his belly bulges. Yet he has a smirk on his face, as if he thinks he is sexy.

How accurate is Subu? Deola asks herself after she logs off. Of course, her instinctive answer is 'very', but she wants to be rational. It is true she has to be careful about how her colleagues perceive her. Sometimes she acts a little reticent, as she did at Trust Bank, but for different reasons. She wasn't vulnerable in the same way she is here, working in London. Here she is anxious about being exposed. Everyone has an office persona. Everyone is subject to work norms and anyone who wishes to get ahead ought to learn how to keep their opinions to themselves. She can't for much longer.

This might just be the third job she'll resign from. Only once has she ever lost a job. That was when she was made redundant from the accountancy firm she trained in. She has since called the firm 'Stuckupsdale and Hoitytoityheim'. A Nigerian classmate from LSE who worked for Price Waterhouse referred to it as a Jewish firm. 'They probably don't open on Fridays,' he said, and she thought, What does he mean?

The only Jewish manager she was aware of at Stuckupsdale was never made a partner while she was there. He was married to a Filipina and Deola's fellow trainees said she had to be a mail-order bride, which Deola also found bizarre. How did they come to that conclusion?

Back then, bigotry was often cryptic, like a missed punch line in a joke. It always took her a moment to catch on. She was put off most by the gossipy culture in the audit department, the toadying and the fagging especially. Senior auditors ordering junior auditors, 'Get me these files.' 'Staple these papers together.' 'Empty this bin.' All trainees went through the same apprenticeship, so perhaps she was too proud, but she found her first year intolerable, walking around in skirt suits because female employees were not allowed to wear trousers. In the winter, her tights couldn't keep the cold out, and they laddered. She knew it couldn't possibly be her wool coats that gave her a constant feeling of being weighed down. Apart from the 'braids were unprofessional' business, she had a somewhat unpleasant encounter at a pension fund when a manager looked at her palms and said, 'You're two-toned,' another at a bank, when she arrived at the reception with audit files and said, 'I'm here for the audit,' and the receptionist replied, 'Deliveries are through the side entrance.' But those were not enough to say she was discriminated against. How would she explain Subu's rise in the management consultancy department otherwise?

In the audit department, she worked for a manager who was prematurely grey and all chin. He flirted with the department secretary, Trish. He went to pubs with senior managers and played golf with partners, so he was bound to make progress. He specialized in financial services and once invited her to a game of skirmish with clients, on a Sunday, and she didn't show up, so she lost favour with him. In retrospect, all she learned from him was how to make her audit files look tidy. She doubted her work had any impact. She was not surprised to hear about the Johnson Matthey Bankers, Barings Bank and other such scandals. She knew how easily they could happen and had to come to terms with the fact that the fat cats who ran financial corporations were doing the same work as her father.

The audit department had other trainees like her, except they were British born and their parents were immigrants. How did they fare during the redundancy? There was the Indian guy who complained that his jobs were outside London. He had a reputation for being difficult to work with. Management got rid of him. There was the Sri Lankan guy, who always pointed out that he wasn't Indian, but he seemed keen to explain the origin of his Portuguese surname. Management kept him. There was a girl from Grenada who would not make eye contact with other blacks. They kept her. There was another girl from Hong Kong. Management said she was 'good', which she really wasn't. They kept her, too. There was a Japanese guy, who *was* good, but he pissed management off with his Emporio Armani suits. They got rid of him and he didn't seem to care. Finally, there was a Polish guy who sat around in his socks in the summer months when the office was empty and listened to reggae music on his Walkman. Occasionally, he raised his hand and sang out loud: 'Africa unite!' He was rumoured to be selling marijuana in the men's toilets. Management kept him.

At Stuckupsdale, she was not alone on the lower rungs of the hierarchy. She couldn't care less about the preferences of the corporate clones on top, but she noticed whom they exempted from discrimination. Apart from Subu, there was a German-Ghanaian in the private investors department. She was exempted because of her complexion. There was a black American who came for a six-month exchange in the tax department. She was exempted because of her accent. Even the Nigerian security guard who sat in a cubicle by the door got a boost because people felt sorry for him. He was known as Jimmy. 'Hi, Jimmy,' they would say to him. 'All right, Jimmy?' He might have been Jimoh or Olujimi. His surname was Ojo. She called him Mr Ojo and greeted him with a 'Good morning', and he would answer, 'Good morning to you. How are you today?' His skin was darker than his navy uniform. She suspected he was working illegally in England. Without him, there were days she could have wept walking through that door. Whenever he saw her carrying audit files, he would offer to help her. She would protest and he would insist. He must have been in his sixties and he smelled of menthol. There was some talk among the managers that the smell was offensive enough to put clients off. She overheard Trish explaining to her manager, 'I think it's the ointment he uses for his arthritis.'

Trish was powerful within the department, omnipotent, as the department secretary. Trainees she didn't like ended up on the worst jobs outside London or they weren't booked on jobs, and they needed a minimum number of audit hours to qualify. Trish was asked to speak to Jimmy about the menthol smell, which she did in her mini skirt and patent stilettos, then she came back to say, 'Aw, he's ever so sweet, Jimmy, just like a big teddy bear. You just want to wrap your arms around him.'

Do that, Deola thought. When Jimmy grabs you, then you'll know who Jimmy is.

Everything she puts in her mouth in the morning tastes metallic, her toothpaste, the water she rinses her mouth with, even the orange juice she drinks with her breakfast. Her tongue tingles and she would describe her malaise as the onset of a cold, but she has had symptoms like this before, whenever she drinks too much or doesn't get enough sleep. This must be the case, she decides, the wine she had the previous night and her poor sleeping habits of late.

She gets ready for work. She is driven more by her obstinacy than a sense of duty. If she doesn't speak her mind to Kate, she will only become more and more dissatisfied, which might mean she will end up leaving. Kate is open to suggestions. Kate is flexible. She has just been distracted of late.

Kate comes to work with a list of illnesses and conditions afflicting her family: her husband and daughter still have stomach aches; her daughter can't keep her food down and is lactose intolerant; her husband had chills the night before and he almost blacked out. This morning, his pinched nerve is acting up and her nose is bunged up. She says she is not one hundred per cent well, but she came in because she has the whole weekend to recover.

Deola sits in Kate's office and pretends to have sympathy. She feels as if her flesh is on the verge of simmering. What a privilege to be sick without fear, to talk openly about being sick and wallow in sickness.

Kate blows her nose noisily and sits back in her chair. 'Can't breathe.'

Deola doesn't doubt that Kate is sick. Her eyes are puffy and her nose is red. She has brought in herbal tea in a flask. Her office smells pleasant and familiar. Is it lemon verbena?

'I hear Dára has been causing a stir,' Deola says.

Kate flops over her table, dangerously close to her mug. 'Dára! How could he? How did you hear?'

'I looked him up on the Internet yesterday.'

Kate raises her head. 'Anne sent me an e-mail. It's a disaster. He can't be our spokesperson now, not after this.'

'Whose idea was it to make him one?'

'Graham's,' Kate says, clearing her hair from her face.

'Has Graham heard?'

'I e-mailed him. He'll take care of it when he gets back from Mombasa. The tabloids have already got hold of the story.'

'They have? I didn't notice any.'

'It's not front-page news or anything, but once they get involved.' Kate shakes her head. 'We have to distance ourselves now. We can ignore his views on polygamy, but not this one.'

Deola thinks of the little she learned about Stone Riley online: the affairs he had during his marriage and his girlfriend, who is younger than his daughter. His son died of a drug overdose, which sent him into what he described as 'a downward spiral into hell', during which he was misusing alcohol and prescription pills. He has been clean since 1998. His story is so formulaic that Deola suspects it is made up, like Dára's.

'Stone Riley, too, has been making dubious statements,' she says.

Kate sips her tea. 'God. What's he on about now?'

Employees at LINK are in awe of celebrities or envious of them and Kate falls into the latter category. Whenever women in the office say Dára is gorgeous, she says, 'Yes, but he doesn't have much to say for himself, does he?'

'He says he has adopted Africa as his cause.'

'Hm, well worth ignoring.'

Deola agrees. Why worry about what celebrities have to say about Africa, so long as they can make themselves useful? It amuses her whenever she sees a photo op in an African village, where a celebrity meets with people who have obviously been prepped about how to welcome the important visitor from overseas. People who are probably grateful for the help they receive, but who are nevertheless thinking, Who the heck is this?

She brings up the issue of the microfinance scheme for WIN, explaining that she has to in order to finish her report.

'I realize that Rita Nwachukwu may not be interested in moving in that direction.'

'She's the CEO, though,' Kate says, holding her mug with both hands.

'But Elizabeth Okeke is from the community. Elizabeth was the one who talked about their needs, so I think I should at least suggest that to the board. I just want to be sure you are aware.'

'Did we talk about this when Graham was around?'

'Yes, after he left for Kenya.'

'We did? It must have skipped my mind. But I get e-mails from Rita and she has never brought this up.'

'Rita might have her own agenda.'

She resists telling Kate that she is an *oyinbo* to Rita, someone Rita can easily deceive. She will not repeat Elizabeth's allegations, but this ought to be the test. If indeed Rita is misdirecting funds, she will not favour a microfinance scheme that bypasses her as a middleman.

'It's getting too messy for me,' Kate says. 'I thought once we had Dára on board, we ought to contact a few NGOs in Nigeria. Now, I keep getting these e-mails.'

She shivers as if she has entered a sinister realm that involves Internet crime.

'I wouldn't worry about that,' Deola says, 'and it's just office politics at WIN. I was there. Rita is tenacious and Elizabeth wants control over what goes on in her community.'

'Look, Deola,' Kate says. 'You can make any recommendation you want. The board might take it into consideration, but it comes down to Graham's decision in the end and I doubt he will go for it, especially after this fiasco with Dára. You know what Graham is like. It was difficult to persuade him to get involved with Nigerian NGOs in the first place.'

Deola sits up. 'Why send me there, then? Why send me there when he knows he is not going to take my recommendations seriously? What was the point of my going?'

She shifts the blame to Graham, knowing that Kate has more clout than she admits to. What about Dr Sokoya, the malaria man? she thinks. Is this the end for him, too?

'I'm sure we can still work with Dr Sokoya,' she insists. 'I was very impressed with what I saw.'

Kate pouts. 'But you haven't done any fieldwork. That was just a financial review.'

'I know,' Deola says, 'and I know I have a lot to learn, but . . .'

The Tarzan Complex, she thinks.

'But?' Kate asks.

'Don't mind me,' Deola says, repelled by her own indolence.

Kate shuts her eyes. 'God, I can't wait for Graham to come back. I don't feel very well. I knew I shouldn't have come in today.'

'I'd better get started,' Deola says.

She can't suppress the idea that Kate may have pushed Graham to hire her because she is Nigerian – a Nigerian to match Dára. It is clear to her that Kate doesn't care what either of them thinks.

By lunchtime, she decides that her symptoms in the morning were due to one of two circumstances: either she caught the stomach virus from Kate or she is pregnant. She plays the gambling game again when a piece of paper slides off her table. She bends down to catch it before it touches the floor and bumps her head on the edge of the table. For a while she sits and rubs her sore spot. She has been afraid for too long. She is fed up of being afraid and soon a sense of calm overcomes her. She submits to it as she types her report on the malaria NGO and focuses on standard recommendations: one, clearly defined roles; two, separation of duties; three, dual signatories, while knowing her report won't make a bit of difference. She adds a paragraph about her disapproval of the way the Nigerian programmes were jettisoned.

She still feels guilty for letting down the women of WIN, but not enough to make a heroic effort on their part. A microfinance scheme might be useful to them, but there is no guarantee the scheme would work or even benefit them if indeed there is corruption at WIN.

She can't overlook Africa's self-sabotage. LINK has numerous beneficiaries in African countries that are in or recovering from dictatorships, civil wars and genocides. They account for the majority of LINK's developmental and rehabilitation programmes in Somalia, Sudan, Sierra Leone, Congo, Angola and Rwanda. Whose fault is that? she thinks, shrugging off the amputated sleeves of her summer jacket while imagining it as a one-armed child.

She has spent her career studying systems. People are surprisingly easy to categorize when they work within systems. There are Africans working for humanitarian and charity organizations, Africans in commerce and industry, Africans in education and in the arts. Africans everywhere, some causing mischief, and once in a while, they will be confronted with the notion that Africans are disposable and of as much consequence to humanity as waste material. This may not be personal; this does not even have to be part of a greater insidious design. This is exactly how systems serve people who are not party to conceiving and creating them. Their daily trauma is trying to survive systems that did not start off with their continuity in mind.

She checks the brochure for WIN to confirm that the average age of the widows is thirty-nine. How little the statistic tells her of them, and it is just as well. She is in the wrong business anyway. She has never wanted to save anyone but the people she loves. Isn't this enough? Don't organizations like LINK do the same when they decide whom to give what and for how long?

After work, she goes home by tube. This time, when she gets off at her stop, she stops at a chemist on the high street and buys a pregnancy test kit. She gets home and opens the box. Her bathroom is warm. She has to take her jacket off before she reads the instructions. They are easier to follow than she expected. When she is finished peeing, she checks her watch and goes to her bedroom to change out of her work clothes. Minutes later, she returns to her bathroom.

The blue cross is clear. She stands before her mirror in her sweatsuit marvelling at how ordinary the moment is. Is this all there is to it? Her face is the same, except for eye bags she has developed from recent nights. Her heart quivers like a chrysalis about to release wings. She has to tell someone, but she steps out of her bathroom and she is paralyzed. Tell who? Not Wale, who still hasn't called. Certainly not her family or her friends. The word 'unwanted' jolts her. Does she want to have this child? She plods down the steps to her sitting room, trying to interpret what it means to want a child: what does this mean for the child? Is it even a child yet? She has said 'absolutely not' before, while arguing with Subu. Abortion is not equal to the murder of a child. Now she sits on her couch as if the life inside her is too heavy to carry.

Tessa has left a message on her voicemail to remind her about getting measured for her bridesmaid dress tomorrow.

'It's me. Don't forget we're meeting on Saturday.'

Yes, this is all there is to it, the whisper of a beginning. Every moment someone learns she is going to be a mother. Whether or not she wishes to be one, even if she is able to share the news and her announcement is welcomed with fanfare, people are still making their everyday plans.

She goes through the motions and returns Tessa's call, surprised that she manages to sound normal.

'Tesco Supermarket,' she says.

'Don't call me that,' Tessa says.

'Why not?'

'I don't feel very super right now.'

She asks about Tessa's wedding plans. It is almost a relief to get caught up in someone else's ordeals.

'It's a nightmare,' Tessa says. 'Ever since Pete's dad found out the wedding is going to be here.'

'Wait. Since when?'

'We made up our minds. Pete's moving here.'

'Good for you, Tess.'

'Yes, but ever since he found out, that man has had something to say. "Oh, how come no one in Australia has heard of her if she takes her work so seriously?" "Oh, why England?" Honestly, I've had it with him. He's like a caveman. He raised Pete like a wild animal. He has no respect for women. He lives in the sticks and there's nothing for miles. Let's face it, there's nothing in that country, except kangaroos swinging in trees, koalas, kookaburras and Kiri Te Kanawa.'

'She's from New Zealand,' Deola says.

'What?'

'Kiri Te Kanawa is from New Zealand and kangaroos don't swing. They hop.'

'I don't give a toss.'

'Didn't you people watch Skippy the bush kangaroo in this country?' she asks.

Tessa manages a smile. 'Skippy.'

'I thought you loved Australia.'

She also thought Tessa wasn't nationalistic, but maybe all it takes is the experience of being discriminated against outside an audition, or an annoying in-law. The trouble is Tessa is not having the wedding for herself. She is having the wedding for her parents, to give them an occasion to celebrate, which is the worst reason to have a wedding.

'I'm fast changing my mind,' Tessa says.

'You've got what you want. You're going to live here. That's all that matters.'

'Pete's father hates me!'

'He's in Australia.'

It is retribution, Deola thinks. She suspects Peter might hate her on account of Tessa. Peter was interested in talking to her about safaris in South Africa, but Tessa told him Deola didn't care about animals or people who cared about them. What Deola actually said was that she couldn't understand why people cared more about African animals than they did about Africans.

'I'm too old for this rubbish,' Tessa says, 'and Pete won't put his foot down. They have this uncanny bond. They're very close. It's almost as if I've come between them and it's so obvious he wants Pete to be with a twenty-something-year-old Shirley.'

'Peter should stop telling you what his dad says.'

'I make him tell me.'

'You should stop making him tell you.'

'No, his dad should stop! I'm not putting up with this anymore! I'm not! He's not going to come from Down Under to ruin the day for my parents! Honestly, I've had it with him. I'd have cancelled the wedding, if I hadn't already paid the deposit on my dress.'

'How's that coming along?'

'Divine. You should see it. You will see it. Tomorrow. I'm having a fitting. Helen is a costume maker. Unbelievable. She's doing it as a favour. I'm paying her next to nothing. What time should we meet?'

'Where is Helen based?' Deola asks, wondering how she will ever fit into a bridesmaid's dress.

'Pimlico.'

She gives Deola the address and it is near the estate Bandele lives in.

'A friend of mine lives there. Not that I want to see him right now.'

'Why, what happened?'

'Nothing.' She thinks of an excuse. 'He is a writer, a bit of a grump.'

'Are you okay, darling?'

'Yes.'

'Sure it's not too much for you?'

'Of course not.'

'So when?'

'Let's say three o'clock at the station.'

'Smashing. See you tomorrow, then.'

Pimlico Station is within walking distance from her parents' flat. They bought the flat in the late seventies. At the time, there was a launderette on the street, a corner shop owned by an Indian family, a fruit and vegetable shop and a hair salon, where, for just five pounds, Deola could get her Afro trimmed. She would sit there with old ladies who were getting purple rinses. Her stylist thought her Afro was like a nice little hedge.

Now there is a BMW dealership where the salon and fruit and vegetable shop were. A Starbucks has opened on the next street, where there was once a shoe repair shop. Deola remembers going there with Lanre to duplicate the front door key of her parents' flat. The shopkeeper refused to serve them. 'Don't do that 'ere,' he said, though the sign on his door said he did. Lanre later explained that he must have thought they were a couple of thieves.

Westminster was her first neighbourhood in London. During her holidays, she would walk to the abbey, where tourists converged, cross St James's Park and end up at Buckingham Palace. Sometimes she went by bus with her mother to Victoria Street, to shop at Army and Navy, or to the Apollo to see a musical like *Fiddler on the Roof* or *Starlight Express*. There was that other theatre where *The Black and White Minstrel Show* ran for a while, but she didn't see that show. Her father was not in favour. He didn't care for musicals anyway. He only ever encouraged her to go to the Tate Gallery. 'Go to the Tate,' he would say, if ever she complained the neighbourhood was boring.

She couldn't be bothered with the Tate, and she rarely crossed over Vauxhall Bridge Road into Pimlico, except when she ran errands for her mother at the market on Warwick Way. Her mother would tell her, 'Ask them to cut the fish into steaks not filets, and they mustn't throw the head or tail away.' It was embarrassing to ask for fish heads and tails and other cuts that English people generally didn't eat. Her mother once sent her to a butcher to ask for ox tails and the butcher said, 'I'm afraid you'll have to go to Brixton Market for that.'

That was almost a quarter of a century ago, when she knew her milkman and postman. She has since been to more corners of London than she has of Lagos, yet she still thinks of herself as a Lagosian, not a Londoner.

As a student, she had an approximate sense of belonging while walking through Brixton Market or dancing to calypso music at the Notting Hill Carnival, or hanging around Speakers' Corner on a Sunday. She went to Hyde Park for Nelson Mandela's seventieth birthday and for the Pavarotti concert when she worked in the city. Afterward she walked to the tube station with other Londoners singing 'Free Nelson Mandela' the first time around and '*O Sole Mio*' the next. Now, she is not even part of the Nigerian community in London. It is too huge and fractured.

She parks her Peugeot on the other side of Vauxhall Bridge Road and walks across to the station. This morning she woke up with the same symptoms as the day before, which subsided before lunch, so she is sure she has been going through morning sickness. She is nervous about the side effects of the progestin pills. On Monday, she will make an appointment to see a doctor.

At Pimlico Station, she stops at the newsagent to check the tabloids for headlines on Dára. She can't find any. She walks downstairs and stands by the ticket machine, while looking out for Tessa. She hopes she will not bump into Bandele. She still can't get over the fact that he lives in Pimlico and the city pays for his rent and upkeep. Britain is great in a way, she thinks, but Bandele is not grateful. 'Pimlico,' he often says with derision, as though he has fallen in status.

She went to his parents' house in Belgravia only once. She had heard of Nigerians who lived lavishly in London, but to see their two storeys and a basement full of antique furniture was another matter. She later described the place to her parents, whose flat was crammed with faded velvety chairs and brocade curtains they hadn't changed since the seventies.

'They have an English butler and a Filipina maid,' she said. 'Your brother is our butler and you and your sister are our maids,' her father said. 'They have a Rolls Royce,' she said. 'We have the number eleven bus,' her father said.

He was so predictable. The Davises could have a jet plane parked in their basement if they wanted, he said. He would spend any exorbitant amount of money on school fees. Not so on other expenditures; they were not investments.

Her mother, who was an authority on the genealogy of Lagos society, said, 'That Davis fellow is a tricky fellow. He would not have this much money but for his position in government. He's from a good family, though. A very good family. He has impeccable breeding.'

By 'breeding', her mother meant a history of education, unlike the Bellos, who one generation back were hoeing on a farm.

—

Tessa arrives, her ponytail swinging. She wears jeans and a hooded jacket. The weather is cold and dull. They walk out arm in arm and cross the road.

'How've you been?' Tessa asks.

'Not so good.'

'I knew it. What's the matter?'

'I have the baby-in-the-baby-carriage sequence wrong.'

'Huh?'

'I'm knocked up.'

Tessa pulls away. 'What! How did that happen?'

Deola laughs nervously. People will ask for details? What will she say?

'How do you think?'

'How many months?' Tessa asks, looking at her stomach.

'About a week.'

'Why didn't you tell me yesterday?'

'I'd only just found out.'

'You should have told me, Deola.'

'I'm telling you now.'

They are walking in the direction of Bandele's block and she gets worried about seeing him.

'I knew something was wrong,' Tessa says, then she covers her mouth. 'Oh, what am I saying? It's not wrong. It's just that I can't believe this.'

'I can't either.'

'Who is . . .?'

'I don't know. Well, I do know who he is, but I don't know if he wants to be a father.'

'What does he mean he doesn't want to be a father?'

'It's not that, Millie Tant. I just haven't told him yet.'

'Are you thinking . . .?'

'No. I can't go through with that.'

'Gosh, darling. Well, at least your eggs are working.'

'I also can't be your bridesmaid.'

'Why not?'

'When are you getting married?'

'December.'

'By the time you walk down the aisle, I'll be rolling.'

'Gosh. Gosh. I didn't think about that.'

'I'll ruin the pictures.'

'Oh, please. My father-in-law has beaten you to that.'

'It won't work. I'll be adjusting my dress forever. It might end up looking like a tent.'

Tessa pulls a face. 'Well, that would be a first, moving a wedding forward because a bridesmaid is pregnant. But are you happy, darling?'

'I don't know.'

'Do you love him, I mean?'

'I could.'

'What d'you mean?'

'Remember when I said I wanted to be with a Nigerian? I've thought about that. I just have to be with someone who understands where I'm coming from. You understand?'

Tessa pats her arm. 'We can't control these things.'

'I can.'

'You're so careful. Too careful. How could this ever have happened to you? Or dare I ask why?'

'It was your brilliant idea. Live dangerously and all that.'

'You've never listened to me before.'

'He's all right, Tess. Not bad to look at.'

'That's it?'

'Isn't that enough for a night?'

'Not for me. I make them beg.' Tessa stops again. 'You're all right, though. I mean, you got checked out and all that.'

Deola nods. 'I'll get another one in six months, just to be sure.'

'I get one every year.'

'Isn't it terrible?'

'It's dreadful.'

'I feel so stupid and it's not like I'm in college or anything, but for the first time in years, I don't know what is going to happen to me next.'

'You'll be all right. I know you will. Come here.'

Deola shuts her eyes, knowing Tessa is thinking, What have you gone and done?

'It's a comedy of errors,' Tessa says. 'That's all it is, finding love. Wouldn't it be so much easier if we could see what the audience sees?'

Helen lives on the Vauxhall Bridge Road side. The houses on the estate are named after writers like George Eliot and Noël Coward. They walk to her flat as Tessa describes her dress. Deola would rather talk about that than listen to any belated advice.

Tessa once thought she was pregnant and she called Deola to say she was going to tell her parents. Deola advised her not to until she was sure. The French merchant wanker was the first man Tessa lived with. He was addicted to porn and she warned Deola not to make the same mistake. 'No moving in until you're engaged,' she said.

Tessa can be conservative, and it's not that Subu is completely intolerant, but telling her might mean that another Nigerian might get to know she is pregnant, and then another.

Helen is a bloody Nigerian. Deola knows as soon as she opens her door. Her hair is in two long braids and she is fair-skinned with dark gums. She has a British-born smile. Deola wouldn't know how to explain this if she had to, but she can tell that Helen was either born in England or raised here from a young age. Helen also has British-born skin. This Deola can describe. She observed as a student that Nigerians like Helen had drier skin. Her mother's reasoning was this: 'They don't use enough lotion.'

Helen's flat is similar to Bandele's, except that he has paper on the floor, whereas Helen has fabrics, thread, measuring tapes, scissors, needles and pins. Her flat smells like a haberdashery shop. Deola is nervous she might step on something as she walks carefully to the room where Tessa's dress is. It is white satin with a plunging back. She makes the mistake of calling the cut asymmetric.

'It's a bias cut,' Helen says.

'It's gorgeous,' Deola says.

'Isn't it?' Tessa says. 'I want to wear red satin shoes with it, but Helen won't let me.'

'Red?' Deola asks, wrinkling her nose.

'Don't look at her,' Tessa says, blocking Helen.

Helen laughs. She has a South London accent.

'So I'm not taking your measurements, then?' she asks, as Tessa undresses.

'No,' Deola says. 'Are you Nigerian by any chance?'

'My parents are,' Helen says.

'I didn't know your parents were Nigerian,' Tessa says.

Helen smiles. 'It never came up.'

'Nigerian,' Tessa says, lifting her hand. 'Look at that.'

'They came over in the sixties, during the civil war,' Helen says.

Tessa slips into her dress. 'Here, help me with this. Helen might know your writer friend then, the one who lives here.'

Deola pulls up the zip. 'We don't all know each other.'

Helen doesn't return her knowing look. In fact, she seems offended by it. Traitor, Deola thinks, jovially. She is excited to see Tessa in her wedding dress.

'I didn't say you did,' Tessa said, checking her armpits.

Tessa's back is freckly with a tan line from a bikini top.

'It's not Daily Davis, is it?' Helen asks.

Deola takes a step back. 'You know him?'

'I told you,' Tessa says. 'Don't tell him she was here, though. She's avoiding him.'

'I know Daily,' Helen says. 'And Charlie.'

'Charlie?' Deola says, assuming Bandele has found himself a Charlotte.

'Yes,' Helen says. 'His partner, Charles. We're good friends.'

Tessa smoothes her dress down. 'Small world. So how do I look? And please don't say I can't wear red shoes.'

Deola hopes her expression doesn't betray her. Her eyes sting. She doesn't hold back her tears. They are the audience and she is the dumb player.

After she says goodbye to Tessa, she walks to her Peugeot and sits in it for a while. She is familiar with the street. There is a school, which is closed for the weekend, and a small park surrounded by trees. The Thames is not too far away, looking like Darjeeling tea. It is cold inside her Peugeot. She could drive off and from now on pretend she doesn't know a damn thing. If Helen never mentions that they met, how would Bandele find out? But what good will come out of pretending? What kind of friendship would that be?

She decides to call Bandele on her mobile phone.

'He-llo,' he says, clearing his throat, as if he has just woken up.

'Hello, my love. Are you at home?'

'Yes.'

'I'm round the corner. I was thinking of dropping by.'

He yawns. 'Sure.'

'In five minutes?'

'No probs.'

She walks back to his block with her arms folded, twists her ankle as she crosses the road and catches a whiff of stale urine as she walks into the estate. Bandele's flat is on the other side of the courtyard, overlooking a green house. The smell of cigarettes assaults her when he opens his door. She is conscious of each swallow. He wears jeans that look as if he has slept in them and his shirt is unbuttoned. He doesn't have a single chest hair. His sitting room is tidier this time, but he still has paper on the floor, and a pile on his coffee table. He sits on a chair and puts his feet on the table as she tells him she was at Helen's flat and why.

'Wedding dresses,' he says, rubbing his uncombed head. 'Sounds like fun.'

'I was surprised she knows you.'

'She's all right, Helen.'

Deola heartbeat jumps. 'She also said she knows Charlie.'

'Who?'

'Charlie? Charles?'

'Oh, Charlie. Yeah, they both work in theatre.'

'She gave me the impression you're a couple.'

He laughs. 'What, Helen and I?'

'No, you and Charlie.'

He lowers his feet to the ground and reaches for a pack of cigarettes by the pile of papers. 'What, you think I'm bent or something?'

She thought she would know. In Nigeria, he sounded effeminate to her, but when she came to school in England, she discovered his accent was posh. He has a rude, boyish walk. It is hard to keep up with him because he moves too fast, unless he is feeling lethargic. He is not exactly well turned out. At home he can be a slob. He is spiteful in a way that most men are not. The last time she had spiteful friends, she was a teenager, but she attributes his spitefulness to frustration with his illness. She imagined his relationships didn't last long. He didn't talk about his relationships anyway. He was more guarded about them than he was about his writing. She thought he was embarrassed about his penchant for skinny blondes.

'I never thought you were.'

'What, a poofter?'

He lights up and the fumes nauseate her. He is being childish.

'You don't have to pretend with me. That's all I came to say.'

He studies his cigarette. 'Now that you've said it.'

'You said I could come over.'

'I didn't know you were coming here to recapitulate gossip.'

'You're in a good mood today.'

'Actually, I was, until a certain nosy cow wandered in. Come to think of it, you're more like a hen than a cow. It's nag, nag, nag from you, and I'm not sure why I'm hearing from you more than usual. What's happening to Ola, then? Missing him, are we?'

She gets up, snatches a piece of paper from the pile on the table and swipes at him.

'Miserable prick!'

He ducks. 'Ow!'

'Don't you ever speak to me like that!'

'You're fucking nuts!'

'Is getting knocked up by a man I slept with for one night self-righteous? Is having to get tested for diseases after a one-night stand self-fucking-righteous? I came here to tell you I'm sorry you had to pretend to me. I can't imagine . . .' Her voice trembles. 'I can't imagine having to pretend I'm not in love with someone. What is wrong with you?'

She wipes her tears with the back of her hand. Why can't she control her emotions? Are her hormones already acting up?

'Don't you start,' Bandele says, stubbing out his cigarette in a saucer. 'Don't you dare start. I should be the one bloody crying. Wish it were that easy for me. Wish it were so easy that all I have to do is pretend I'm not in love. It's my bloody secret I've held for years, not yours. You can't just barge in here and expect me to share it with you.'

'Try!'

'Fucking hell,' he says, rubbing his forehead. 'You have no idea how much this takes out of me. You said when I first met you, I mistook you for a housegirl.'

'Yes.'

'I don't remember that. I think of that holiday though, all the time. My parents, my sisters and Seyi. I fucking killed him, you know.'

She has never seen him this desolate and she examines his face, hoping she is mistaken. Surely, he could not have meant that literally.

'He caught me,' Bandele says. 'I was with our steward in the boys' quarters. We were not doing anything. He was laughing and I was laughing. You're surprised? Well, there it is, a steward. He was nice. Nice to me. Seyi beat him up. He wouldn't hit back. He just ran around trying to dodge Seyi, then Seyi cornered him by the barbed-wire fence. His uniform got caught in it. Seyi kept punching him. He ran away. My parents thought he had gone back to his village or something. Seyi threatened to tell my father, but he must have been scared of what my father would do to me. He was drinking a lot that summer. He was never a drinker. You really want to hear more?'

She cannot bear to hear about other people's pain, especially people she cares about. She cannot believe that Bandele, the biggest snob she knows, loved a steward because the steward was nice to him.

In her house they were called houseboys. She can count the number of times she went to the boys' quarters. It was in the back garden with the pawpaw tree and laundry lines. It had a communal kitchen, shower and latrine. The rooms had spring beds with thin mattresses. The staff that occupied them kept their transistor radios, plastic plates and aluminum cups on the cement floors. She either called out to them from the back door or pressed the electric bell in the dining room, which must have sounded like a death knell to them. Her mother had a silver bell that she tinkled until her wrists hurt.

She said they were impossible to train, but they were highly skilled at pretending they couldn't hear.

Most of her house help came from towns and villages outside Lagos. The houseboys, housegirls, nannies, cooks and drivers lived in the boys' quarters, and the gardeners, washermen and watchmen lived elsewhere. Deola cuddled her nannies when she was a child and played football with houseboys. They were a daily source of amusement and exasperation, with their love affairs, rivalries and accusations of juju. She grew up and she became Miss Adeola to them, not 'Aunty'. Her mother would not have any of that. 'Aunty' was too personal. Nor would she have her daughters sneaking their dirty underwear into the laundry for the washerman when they hit puberty. That might give him a false impression of intimacy.

No Nigerian employer she knew cared why boys' quarters were so called. They resented foreigners who came with their phony egalitarianism to mess up the order by being familiar with their houseboys and girls. It was normal to send them on errands and yell at them. Beating them was also acceptable, but sleeping with them was not. If ever she heard about a master sleeping with his housegirl, the question was not how he could do that to another human being, but why he would do that with someone who was not really considered human. What was worse for Seyi? The man was a steward, or the steward was a man?

'Was that why?' she asks. 'Was that why you had that trouble later?'

'Who knows?' Bandele says.

'Why didn't you just tell me you were gay?'

'You're Nigerian.'

'Helen is Nigerian!'

'She's not Nigerian like you!'

'I'm not Nigerian like that.'

'I wasn't taking any chances. Nigeria . . . It was such an emotionally brutal place to grow up in.'

'More than here?'

'For me it was, having to endure all those false divisions. But I'll tell you about that when I'm good and ready. Not before. Now, please, enough of this. It's too early in the day for a confessional.'

She would never describe the division between the haves and have-nots in Nigeria as false. They are bona fide barriers.

Bandele attempts to smile. 'Old Fanny. You should see the look on your face. So you're preggers. How did that happen?'

'How do you think?'

'What will you do now that you're damaged goods?'

'Go home.'

'For ever and ever?'

'Yes.'

'What about your job?'

'I'm going to resign. I'm beginning to have – what did Baldwin call it again? An intimate something or the other?'

'An intimate knowledge of its ugly side.'

She sits down again. He does this, changes the conversation whenever he is the subject.

'What about your novel?'

'I'm taking a break from it.'

'Why?'

'It's driving me mad, or should I say madder. I'm having trouble with my Paris scenes. I can't seem to get them right.'

His depiction of women in *Sidestep* was suspect: ballet flats and AA-cup bras. But he must like breasts. Why else does he keep making comments about hers?

'Take it easy,' she says. 'You don't want extra stress.'

'You should have thought of that before you charged at me. So you're having a baby and you're going back to Nigeria?'

'I made up my mind last night.'

'Knowing what the natives are like?'

'I'm not getting anywhere here and things are not so bad at home. At my age, my family will be happy for me, even my mother, once she's recovered. It might be difficult for her for a while, what with people talking. It will be worse for me if they think I was desperate enough to trap a man. I'm proud, you know, so proud I turned my back on a whole nationality of men. Is Charlie English?'

'How many gay Nigerian men do you know called Charlie?'

She doesn't know many gay Nigerian men, apart from a few who are supposed to have slept with a former dictator to get government contracts. She's heard about three others, two of whom are married. Her mother told her about one she grew up with. 'He was in the Boy Scouts,' her mother said. 'All of them in the Boy Scouts had problems settling down.' Her father called gays 'homosexualists'.

In a way, ignorance helps. Nigerians are not overly concerned so long as gays have the decency to marry and have children. The fundamentalists, both Christian and Muslim, are bound to consider homosexuality a heinous crime – she heard about a man up North who was sentenced to death by stoning under Sharia law and of course he was poor – but their attitudes are imported. It was the same when she was growing up. Once in a while at Ikoyi Club, she would hear that some guy or the other was a homo or a fag. Since she could not understand why anyone would say that unless they knew it was true, she believed the rumours. From then on the boy would be reduced to an orifice. Girls were more likely to be called nymphos than lesbos, but the only people who used words like that were in English boarding schools.

It is not as if Bandele can walk down a street in Pimlico holding Charlie's hand.

'It can't be easy here,' she says. 'As a Nigerian.'

He shrugs. 'Only when people aren't aware of my pedigree.'

Pedigree. He and her mother.

'You think that matters? We'd be foolish to buy into that rubbish.'

'Who does?'

'Don't you? Harrow this and Harrow that?'

'I hated Harrow! What are you talking about?'

'But you act as though going to a school like that gives you a leg up in life, and I'm not sure it does.'

'Well, I'm sure. I'll have you know I've been stopped by the police before.'

She imagines him in Soho or somewhere, the police mistaking him for a rent boy.

'Not that,' he says. 'I went for a walk in Belgravia. I'd not been there in a while. I just wanted to see the house. A policeman stopped me before I got there and questioned me. I said "I live here." He didn't believe me. I called home. My parents were around. I was so sure they would deny I was their son, but they didn't.'

Would his parents disown him if they knew he was gay or would they just pretend not to know?

He stretches. She wants to tell him he is brave and their friendship has not changed, but he will only accuse her of being trite.

'Are you tired?' she asks.

'A bit.'

He is crankier when he is tired. She walks to the back of his chair, puts her arm around him and holds her breath against his cigarette fumes. His stubble scratches her.

'You know, I quite liked the idea of having a grumpy writer friend, but I think having a gay grumpy writer friend is much cooler.'

'We won't be friends for much longer if you make fatuous pronouncements like that.'

She laughs. He is too mean-spirited to be attractive, but he was always there as a last resort, someone to flirt with.

'I'll leave you be,' she says.

He pats her hand. 'You treat me like an invalid. I just hope having this baby will cure you of your need to mother me.'

'Misanthrope.'

'Can you blame me?'

'No. I have been pissed off with people for years.'

'You? What for?'

She takes a moment to think. It is not a confession she is proud of.

'I can't live up to their expectations. Why should they live up to mine?'

Kate is more taken aback than Graham when she tells them she is leaving. They meet in Graham's office this time. She and Kate are seated opposite Graham and his desk separates him from them. This was exactly how they conducted her interview before they offered her the job. During the interview, Graham asked why she wanted the job. Deola said she was looking for a job that meant something to her, which was true, but she never expected them to hire her after an answer like that. Graham was impressed she went to boarding school. She lied that she was on a sports scholarship. He asked what sport and she said, 'Um, the javelin.' She would have added another sport, but she was not sure if it was the 'shot put' or 'short put'.

Graham's office is full of souvenirs like clay bowls and carvings. She couldn't stop looking at them during the interview and she was not sure if they calmed her down or put her off. Even back then, she knew Graham would prefer the most European of African countries, like South Africa and Kenya. She knew she would stand a better chance with him if she presented herself as an African in need. She also knew she did not want the job. Her hesitation over the 'shot put' clarified that. She'd spoken English all her life and she was still confused about basic words. What was the point of speaking English? What was the point of working for an organization that hired Africans like herself, who, in the process of being refined, could no longer think for themselves?

As an auditor, she can cope with her clients' habits. She doesn't have to be with them for long. It is not the same with the people she has to see every day at work. She never thought she would grow fond of Kate and Graham, and now that she has told them she is leaving, she realizes she is. She tells them how much her trip to Nigeria woke her up to the fact that she misses home and she ought to go back for good instead of contributing to the brain drain. Even to her own ears she sounds fake and she is tired of rounding her vowels. Rounding her vowels hurts her mouth. She wonders what would happen if Nigerians refused to speak phonetics for one day. Would their worlds fall apart? Would they realize that it would be just as absurd for them, as Nigerians, to speak in Chinese accents to keep up with the direction in which the world was going?

'Is there anything we can do to make you change your mind?' Kate asks.

'Thanks,' Deola says, 'I've thought long and hard about this and I'm so sorry to let you down, with the Africa Beat launch coming up and the business with Dára.'

Graham intends to drop Dára as a spokesperson. He predicts the charges against Dára will also be dropped and Kate is sure Dára's popularity will increase. To Deola, he's just another African who has been singled out for recognition and blown out of proportion. He may look as if he is being favoured, but he is being used. So long as he continues to make money for the people who discovered him, they will worship him.

'Do you have something lined up in Nigeria?' Kate asks.

'Not right now.'

'If there's anything we can do to support you, let us know. Graham? We may not be working with Dára any more, but we have worked with Deola and we still can. Yeth?'

Graham blushes. 'Well, let's not make commitments we can't keep. I'm sure Delia has the ways and means where she's going.'

He is suspicious, as he was when she said the javelin was

her sport. Does he sense that she is not to be trusted? Does he sense that she can sit comfortably with him, laugh with him, but what she has is an astounding indifference to his opinion that began when she first set eyes on him and heard the shutters of his mind click?

'I'd appreciate any help you can give,' she says.

She is within her six-month probation period, so she submits a letter of resignation giving two weeks' notice. Back in her office, she makes an appointment to see her GP and decides on her order of phone calls. She will call Ivie first, then Wale, then Aunty Bisi, who is the only one qualified to break the news to her mother. It crosses her mind that she could lie that she was artificially inseminated, which would be easier to explain. She would rather her mother doesn't think she is capable of having premarital sex, let alone around her father's memorial. She also has a superstitious moment when she blames Kate and Anne for jinxing her by talking about pregnancy, but that passes. She gets back to the practical considerations. What will Lanre and Jaiye think? She hopes Jaiye won't regard her as careless about sex and Lanre once said girls who got pregnant had the same dumb look about them. That was a while back and he may have just been trying to scare her, but as usual, his opinion stuck. It will be hard to tell Lanre and Jaiye. She is used to letting her mother down, but not her brother and sister.

Sidestep

She takes an afternoon flight from Gatwick Airport that arrives in Lagos in the evening. The time difference with London is only an hour, yet she has morning sickness after the plane lands. Murtala Muhammed International Airport is not a place to be with erratic hormones. The heat is followed by an obstacle race for Passport Control, by which time there is a delay at the luggage carousel.

The line at Customs is shorter and faster than the departure line at Gatwick Airport, but Deola approaches the only female customs officer and asks if she can move to the front. The officer continues to keep an eye on the other passengers.

'It doesn't mean,' she says. 'It doesn't mean because you are pregnant, madam. You know dat if you are in de UK, you cannot behave like dis. You see all dis people waiting? Ehen! So you must obey de rules in your own country. People don't obey de rules. Dat's what's spoiling Nigeria. *Oya*, pass.'

She ushers Deola through as a man protests. Deola ignores him and almost wheels her luggage over his shoes when he steps out of the line. The customs officer explains that she is pregnant.

'And so?' he says. 'Even if she is Mother Mary, what is my concern?'

Ivie is waiting on the other side of the doors. She is dressed in a *boubou* and towers above the crowd.

'Coz, coz,' she says.

Deola hugs her. 'I feel sick.'

'Don't worry, I'll get you out of here.'

Ivie navigates her through the crowd. It is dark outside. The usual touts approach them. Deola has never understood why they are called touts: they are unlicensed cab drivers. One reaches for her suitcase and Ivie calmly says, 'Get away from there. Who asked you to touch that?'

The tout retreats, smiling and scratching his head. His face is shiny and the heels of his shoes are worn down.

Ivie came to the airport in one of Omorege's cars. In the dark, all Deola notices about the car is that it is spacious and the air conditioner works. She settles in the backseat and unbuttons her trousers to relieve her nausea as Ivie gives the driver instructions. She is glad to be back home where she knows people, but her plans are more convoluted as a result. Her mother and Aunty Bisi think she is arriving tomorrow. Ivie will take her home in the morning, but tonight will drop her at Wale's hotel, so she can speak to him beforehand.

When she called to tell him she was pregnant, he said, 'Wow,' in the same way he might say 'Hell'. He asked, 'Are you sure?' and she said, 'Why would I call if I wasn't?' He offered to meet her at the airport and she told him it wasn't necessary. She called Aunty Bisi afterward. Aunty Bisi said, 'Don't worry, I will handle your mother. I won't tell her until the day before you arrive, otherwise she will get upset and start harassing you and you don't want that. Leave her to me. She will have to accept what has happened. There is nothing we can do about it anyway, and she has been very worried about you.

I think it is a blessing, but you know your mother, she likes her niceties.'

Aunty Bisi uses incorrect words that are somehow appropriate. By 'niceties', she means a civil marriage and children born in wedlock. She was a child of the sixties and they got divorced whenever they pleased. Polygamy worked in their favour. Whatever permissiveness they were up to, they could easily say, 'But we're African. One man, one wife is colonial.' Aunty Bisi once admitted she never got married because she didn't want a husband always around and irritating her. She doesn't live with Hakeem's father. She has her house and he and his wives have their compound. She calls him 'Sir' and refers to him as 'Daddy'. She is perfectly respectable. Still, she would expect Deola to go straight to her mother's house and arrange a family meeting involving Wale's family, but Deola is not ready for that.

'How now?' Ivie asks, patting her thigh.

Ivie's reaction was the funniest. 'Are you sure you didn't trap him?' she'd asked.

'Much better,' Deola says.

She focuses on the headrest in front of her. She cannot yet look out of the window, but she is aware of the shadows and lights they pass, the silhouettes of buildings and palm trees. Engines roar and horns go off. She can smell exhaust fumes and each bump on the way ends up in her temples.

'Did you hear about Jaiye?' she asks.

'I heard,' Ivie says.

Jaiye has gone to Jamaica with a couple of her girl friends, according to Aunty Bisi, and has left Lulu and Prof with her mother. Funsho is in Johannesburg again. He is threatening to move out when he returns. Jaiye is refusing to accept any phone calls meanwhile. She wants a separation without family interference. Deola was sad to hear the news, but she is pleased Jaiye is taking charge. Lanre would want her to do the same. 'You have to be tough,' Lanre used to say. 'You have to know how to defend yourself.' He meant physically.

'Have you heard from her?' Deola asks.

'I haven't,' Ivie says, 'but I think everyone should leave her alone. One has to draw the line with family. That's what I did and I advise you to do the same. Look at me. My mother was pressuring me to go overseas for infertility treatments. Before I knew it, everyone in the family was saying to me, "Go overseas for infertility treatments." I thought, these infertility treatments, are they free overseas? Do they think I can afford them? Or do they think Omorege, who has triplets – and you know how the triplets came about – wants to hear anything about infertility treatments?'

Deola raises her hand reluctantly to slap Ivie's. Ivie and her mother are alike once they get going.

'I've told my mother,' Ivie says, 'anyone who wants me to born *pikin* should volunteer her womb. None of them is paying my salary.'

'I have never been out of work for more than a month,' Deola says. 'I don't know what I'm going to do.'

'Don't worry,' Ivie says. 'You'll find something. This is Lagos.'

The driver slows down as they approach a traffic jam. The change in motion reminds Deola of the dreams she has had of late, where her car brakes fail or she misses trains at stations or she stumbles. She is able to look out of the window once the car is stationary. They are near Oshodi Market. Street hawkers are selling their wares by kerosene light. Some walk between cars, tooting horns. Bus conductors shout out destinations as people scramble to climb in. Taxi drivers stop to pick up and drop off passengers. It is past eight o'clock and thousands of commuters are still trying to get home. It could be daytime in Lagos, but for the indigo sky.

They get to the hotel and Ivie, who says she will tell Wale off when she meets him, can't open her mouth to talk when he appears at the reception. Her ability to exonerate men and elders is incredible. To show solidarity, she looks around as if she expects to see rats scurrying from corner to corner and gives Wale a limp handshake. He wears an *adire* tunic and trousers and has recently had a haircut. Despite her nausea, Deola still finds him attractive.

'Is the room ready?' he asks the receptionist, who confirms it is.

The receptionist seems to be aware that Deola is not a regular guest. Wale calls someone else to take her suitcase to her room.

'Would you like something to eat?' he asks. 'I'm sure you're hungry. You know what? I'll get the kitchen to prepare something for you.'

He turns to Ivie, who raises her hand as if he is offering her poison.

'No, thank you,' she says. 'I've already eaten.'

Deola sees her off. The driver is parked outside. The street is residential and barely illuminated by the security lights of neighbouring houses. Night watchmen guard their gates. The driver opens the door for Ivie.

'Maybe we can manage him,' she says. 'At least your child won't be ugly.'

'Look at you,' Deola says.

Ivie laughs and waves. The security guards padlock the gates after Deola walks back in.

Wale does not stay in the hotel: he has a bungalow behind it. There are a couple of wicker chairs on his veranda, which is covered with mosquito netting. Indoors, he has oil and acrylic paintings by Tola Wewe in startling primary colours and enough space in the room to study them closely. His sitting room is like an uncluttered gallery.

'How are you feeling?' he asks.

'Not bad.'

The air conditioner is too cold. She crosses her arms and comes to a stop at a computer table. He has one of those flat monitors she has been meaning to buy. On his table is a cigar box, bifocals, a Marvin Gaye CD and a framed close-up photograph of a teenaged girl who has eyes like his.

'Is this Moyo?'

'Yes.'

'She is a pretty girl. Do you smoke cigars?'

'Only for show.'

'Are the glasses also for show?'

'I can't read without them.'

'I see you like Marvin.'

The CD is *Let's Get It On*. She is not keen on the song. She prefers 'Distant Lover'. There is a pile of newspapers on the floor as high as the table. She is desperate for something else to say.

'You read a lot of newspapers.'

'That's all I read.'

'I haven't been following the news.'

'Why not?'

'I haven't had time.'

In London, she reads local newspapers online via Nigeriaworld.com and finds herself drawn to headlines like 'Vision of Mary Appears on Latrine Window' and 'Woman Gives Birth to Stone'.

'Have you heard that our president is seeking an extra term?' Wale asks.

'I've heard.'

'We might have a Mugabe on our hands. I just wish every Nigerian could read the newspapers so they can know what is happening in this country of ours.'

'What about computers?' she asks, trying to avoid the conversation they should be having.

'What about them?'

'Not every Nigerian can afford one.'

'We have radios. Radios connect us to the rest of the world.'

'But you turn on the radio these days and all you hear is "Yo, yo, yo."'

All that yo-ing was from disc jockeys putting on American accents. They copy American accents to the horror of those who copy British ones.

'That's in Lagos,' he says. 'There are good regional programmes outside Lagos, in Yoruba and other languages. People are always saying Africa needs to catch up with the computer age. I think it is the other way around.' He frowns. 'Have you seen your doctor?'

'Yes. She says I'm fine.'

'What does your family say?'

He sits and so does she, struggling to believe they are having this conversation. How should she speak to him? Formally? Casually? She relies on her hands.

'My mother is probably getting to know as we speak. I will see her tomorrow. I just want to find out where you stand.'

'Me? I'm prepared to do anything, anything you want. I know you would prefer to be married.'

'Married? Who said?'

'I just assumed, since that is how things are done.'

She laughs. 'Done where?'

'I'm just saying. I can imagine there will be pressure on you.'

'To do what? No one will force me to do anything. At my age, you're just a donor.'

'I hope I'm more than that.'

'Will you be a father?'

'Of course, but can't we be a little friendlier?'

'Sure . . .'

'Give me a moment, please. If I don't say this now, I may not be able to.'

She was about to agree with him, but she keeps quiet, hoping that his 'give me a moment' won't later develop into 'let me finish' or 'shut up'.

He presses his palms together. 'I don't pray. I haven't prayed in years. I know that may sound unusual to you because everyone here prays. God this, God that. You know how it is. I don't understand it. I think it's arrogant to believe you will be spared just by praying. The other day I read somewhere that we rank number one in a survey as the happiest country in the world and I thought, yes, that makes sense. Religion and oblivion go hand in hand. I used to pray. I prayed for Moyo's mum and that didn't turn out right. She was a doctor and she was advised not to have a child, but she did anyway. She joined a church. All that. I don't pray any more. But recently,

I was tempted to and I thought if there is a God, I have left Him to His own devices, the way I have left women to theirs. That was how I was able to sleep that night. Does this make sense?'

'I think so.'

She has the same attitude to God as she has to men. Sometimes, she gives her trust and other times, she can't. His grief gave him a clarity that she lacks. Her father's death simply left her bewildered. What if she never saw him again? What if the whole afterlife business was a lie? What if everyone was saying, 'Yes, it exists, it exists,' but thinking, Damned if I know it does. She hopes the dead don't miss their survivors. She hopes a lifespan is a mere blink for them. She would like to hear more about Moyo and her mother, Ronke. How did he feel when Moyo was born? Was he angry with Ronke when she died?

'What were you tempted to pray about?' she asks.

'That Moyo would have a family of her own before I die. Does that sound morbid?'

'It's practical.'

'Did I tell you she was with her cousins?' he asks.

'Yes.'

'The summer holidays can be rough for her. I'm between here and Abuja and she doesn't want to travel with me. I can't leave her unattended, so she stays with my sisters in Lagos. She says they have normal families.'

'It must have been hard to bring her up on your own.'

'I would have been finished without my sisters. My mother lives in Ibadan and she is in her eighties now, so I didn't want her running around.'

'How many sisters do you have?'

'Four. Moyo stays with my stepsisters. We grew up together. I also have two half-sisters, but we're not close.'

'Your parents were divorced?'

'No. My mother was not married to my father when I came along. His family didn't actually know I existed until he died. He left me this place. His family wasn't happy about that.'

'The Adeniran family?'

'Yes. My father is . . . was J. T. Adeniran. He was a lawyer. I'm his only son.'

'When were you tempted to pray, before or after we met?'

'The day you called from England. I was thinking how lucky we were to get over that hurdle, and the next time I heard from you, I was a father.'

'Seriously?'

'Seriously. It was like juju.'

She laughs. 'But it doesn't make sense chronologically. You were probably a father when I first called.'

'You think time is linear?'

'How else can time be?'

'I don't know, but I'll be older than my old man in a few years. Calendars are linear. I don't think time is linear. I believe in time, though.'

'In time? How?'

He shrugs. 'There I was thinking I was doing my child a favour by keeping our lives simple. I never let any woman get close to her because I didn't want anyone mistreating her. As it turns out, I have been selfish to her. I met you and at first I thought, what is going on? Now everything begins to make sense. Time provides all the answers.'

She is not sure he is right, but she nods.

'I don't think you were selfish. Nigerian families are too complex.'

'Would you like me to come with you to see yours tomorrow?'

'It's best I go alone. If you don't mind, I would rather not meet your family yet. Have you told them?'

'No. I haven't told anyone. It will be hard to tell Moyo, though.'

'You think she will take it badly?'

'I'm not sure, but it's not exactly what any girl wants to hear from her father, and we're in that phase. Don't get me wrong, she is a wonderful girl, brilliant and very smart, but she doesn't want to listen to anything I have to say. All she wants to do is get on the Internet, send texts and walk around in those low-cut jeans.'

'Low-rise.'

'They're very unhygienic.'

'Come on.'

'But they are. I asked her, "Can't you find jeans that fit?" She said they were the latest fashion so I'm not allowed to talk. Last weekend she wanted to wear them to a party and I told her she couldn't. When I was her age, boys were more civilized. Now, it's another story with hip-hop.'

Deola smiles. 'My sister is in her thirties and she loves hip-hop.'

'I don't mind hip-hop. I just don't want my child dancing in those jeans. She said if she was not allowed to wear her jeans, she was not going to the party.'

'She said that?'

'I couldn't believe it. The girl is headstrong. I felt so bad, but I don't remember my sisters being like that. My mother always worked and it was just her raising us. She had no time for nonsense. If she didn't approve of what you were wearing, it was coming off. These days, children will argue with you until they wear you out.'

She laughs. 'Or until you beat them.'

'Beat her?' he says. 'No way. What will that teach her?'

He takes her so literally. She imagines Moyo is testing him. She can't believe he hasn't figured out Moyo wants to be with his sisters so he can't keep tabs on her.

'What were you like as a teenager?' he asks.

'Awful. I didn't even get along with my brother and sister.'

His phone rings and he answers it. 'Excuse me. Hello? Yes, what is it? I said you should bring it here. No, I didn't say that. What is wrong with you people? Can't you follow simple instructions? No, bring it here. Yes, yes, she is here. Hurry up!'

'Who was that?' Deola asks, after he hangs up.

'My barman.'

'Why shout at him like that?'

'Don't mind the man. This place is like Fawlty Towers. If you don't shout, they don't listen. The next thing you know, he will be surfing the Internet and running up my bills. He can't remember anything. I told him to bring your food here.'

'Call him back. I'll go and eat there.'

'You don't want to eat here?'

'I want to take a shower and there is no guarantee I will keep my food down. I should go anyway.'

'Go where? You're always going. From the day I met you, you've been going. Where are you going? I was hoping to hear more about you.'

'You, who can't pick up your phone to call somebody?'

'I didn't want to get a damnation.'

'When did I damn you?'

'"Why did you sleep?" "Why would I call you if I am not sure?" It's not very encouraging. I'm used to a more . . .'

He stands up to accompany her and she begins to make light of her grievances. Perhaps she was rude and defensive. Perhaps he is just lousy on the phone.

'A more what?' she asks.

'It's like trying to get through barbed wire with you.'

'I'm not a cheap chick.'

'You didn't know that before?'

She pats his face. He has some nerve. First, he assumed she would be eager to get married and now he is assuming she will find him funny. He didn't even ask what she wanted to eat for dinner. He assumed that, too.

'You know I didn't do this on purpose,' she says.

'I know,' he says.

She realizes what it is about him that appeals to her. He makes no attempt to charm her.

Her mother is splendid in her disappointment the next morning, magnificent in her displeasure. Her face, bare of makeup, gives just the right touch of gravity to her appearance. Her *adire* scarf is tied high turban-style, like a crown of vindication, and her voice has an oratorical tremor. She stands in the sitting room and addresses Deola and Aunty Bisi in Yoruba.

'I ought to have been told, from the moment you knew. I ought not to have been kept in the dark for this long. I ought to have been given that respect, as a mother. Bisi, you should know better.'

'*Ma binu*, Sister,' Aunty Bisi says, motioning for her to sit. 'Don't be angry.'

'No, no, no. My child gets on a plane as you're telling me about her condition?'

'We didn't want you to be upset.'

'Upset? What is there to be upset about? Is this sickness or death we are talking about? This is not a matter to be upset about, and I will not have anyone making decisions on my behalf. Anyone at all. I decide what will or will not upset me. I ought to have been told. I ought not to have been kept in the dark, and that is my issue. I have nothing left to say. No. Let me speak. I have not finished. I have dealt with far worse situations than this and you of all people should know, Bisi.'

'*Ma binu*, Sister.'

'I am not angry. I am not.'

Deola is surprised by her own state of tranquillity. It is almost as if her womb has formed a protective shield around her. The chair she is sitting in is comfortable and the air conditioner hums. She is sleepy. She falls asleep easily these days and doesn't wake up until morning. After her nausea dissipates, she eats and drinks more than she used to. Her womb draws her energy. She observes the charade between her mother and Aunty Bisi. Her mother is angry with her, not with Aunty Bisi, and Aunty Bisi is not sorry. In fact, Aunty Bisi is overjoyed. It has been a while since she has been called upon to act as a mediator.

Ivie fled the scene. She walked into the house and Deola's mother said, 'I want to have a word with you.' Ivie said she had a meeting to attend. 'Go to your meeting,' Deola's mother said, 'but I will have a word with you in due course. It's enough now. You don't stay with a man for this long without securing yourself. That man has three children of his own. Triplets. You hear me? Their mother has no need to worry. She is well taken care of and it is high time you get yourself checked out.' Ivie hugged Deola's mother so tightly they looked as if they were wrestling. 'Aunty! I've got to go! I've got to go, otherwise I will get sacked!' She ran off.

Deola considers her mother fortunate to be in a position to hold sway at home, first as wife and now as a sort of dowager.

'As for you,' her mother says to her. 'I don't know what makes you think you can tell a man you are not interested in marrying him or meeting his family and expect him to be a father to your child.'

'I told her,' Aunty Bisi says. 'The families at least have to meet.'

'They live in Ibadan,' Deola says. 'I will meet them eventually.'

'Lest we digress,' her mother says, raising her hand. 'You don't give a man the impression he is not needed. I know you are very capable of doing just that and thinking you are a clever clogs.'

Aunty Bisi signals to Deola that she remain quiet.

Her mother sits. 'Ah! I have one daughter who tells a man he is not needed, and another who orders her husband out of their house, when she knows the sort of family he is coming from. That woman will not forgive Jaiye. Whatever one has to say about her, she is a Yoruba woman. She has her self-respect. Her husband was highly regarded in their circle. She may not be very modern in her thinking, but you cannot insult her family and get away with that. Now, you're telling me you don't want to speak to her and she is not allowed to see her own grandchildren because you're annoyed with your husband and I'm just supposed to agree with you? Why would I be a party to that?'

Deola's mother is still in touch with Funsho and his mother. She says she is doing this for the sake of the children, Lulu and Prof, who are upstairs. Comfort is getting them dressed. They are going to stay with Funsho's mother for a week. Deola is sure Jaiye will explode when she finds out.

'Don't worry, Mummy,' she says.

'Me?' her mother says. 'Worry? What for? I have lived my life. I had my own marriage and it was a successful one, to a man who treated me well. He never gave me any problems or cause for embarrassment. It's you and Jaiye who should be worried, not me. Jaiye knew what she was getting into with that marriage. You make your bed and you sleep in it.'

Again, Aunty Bisi signals to Deola that she should be quiet. Deola would like to tell her mother that any parent who expects their daughter to stay with a cheating husband should be prepared to bring their daughter back in a body bag, but 'clever clogs' is not how she feels, and for her mother, a family crisis is equivalent to a bank crash for her father.

'So,' her mother says. 'He is an Adeniran.'

'Yes,' Deola says and adds, in case her mother intends to summon him, 'he lives in Abuja.'

Her mother raises her hand. 'I don't care where he lives. His family has not come to ask for your hand and I have nothing to do with him until then. Which Adeniran is this, anyway? I hope it is not that troublesome politician who was always inciting riots in Ibadan with his "Power for the people".'

'His father is . . . was J. T. Adeniran.'

She can see her mother working out his family tree. 'J. T. Adeniran, the lawyer? I knew him. He was a quiet fellow. Well,

I'm glad he's the one. He was a gentleman. But he lived in Lagos and I didn't know he had a son.'

'His mother was not married to his father,' Deola says.

Her mother sighs. 'These men. Skeletons. Skeletons.'

Deola has to agree. She was relieved that no unknown siblings surfaced at her father's burial or at the reading of his will.

'Have you eaten?' her mother asks.

'I don't feel hungry.'

'You must eat something.'

'I won't keep it down.'

'Sit up straight, please. Pregnancy is not an illness.'

'If I'm sick, it means I'm doing well.'

Her mother raises her hand. 'I was a nurse before I became a mother.'

Deola agrees to eat toast and her mother calls Comfort to hurry up with the children. Comfort says she is 'oiling their legs'. She comes downstairs with Lulu and Prof. Their faces are polished and miserable. Lulu walks over to Deola with the emotional clarity that children sometimes have and hugs her.

'What's wrong?' Deola asks, smoothing her cheeks.

'Everyone in the world is sad,' Lulu says.

'Why?' Deola asks.

She is captivated by the honesty of Lulu's expression, although she has not always found Lulu to be honest.

'Because,' Lulu says, pouting, 'they haven't found Osama bin Laden.'

'He is hiding in a hut in Zamfara,' Prof says.

'Who told you that?' Aunty Bisi asks.

'My daddy,' Prof says.

'I'd better go and see what that girl is up to in the kitchen,' Deola's mother says.

Aunty Bisi signals to Deola to go to the kitchen with her mother. Deola is reluctant to, but she obeys. In the kitchen, her mother watches over Comfort, who takes a loaf of frozen bread out of the freezer.

'So you're coming home for good,' her mother says.

'Yes. I have to sort myself out first, get my checkups, ship my stuff and rent out my flat. Then I need to get a job here.'

Her mother points out the cutting board to Comfort. There is a microwave, but she expects Comfort to cut the frozen bread and return the rest of the bread to the freezer.

'You will be well taken care of,' her mother says. 'Your father made sure of that.'

Deola feels grateful, not belittled. She never turned down financial support from her father, and there are certain aspects of her life his estate cannot take care of.

'So how long are you staying this time?' her mother asks.

'A week.'

Her mother sighs again as if she has accommodated enough disappointment only to be presented with another. It occurs to Deola that her mother might assume she got pregnant on purpose, which, to her mother, might be the cleverest thing Deola has ever done.

'Ah well,' her mother says. 'Whenever you decide to bring yourself back home, we will be waiting for you.'

Her father inspired her with his leadership at Trust Bank. Whenever he visited the bank, he would walk through the corridors with employees following him. People who had cause to despise him got caught up in the procession. He always appeared distracted, patting his pockets as if he had lost his keys, but he knew exactly what was going on around him.

Deola was not in awe of his job as she was of her mother's. Her mother's job seemed like an impossible feat: to have food on the table, to be well groomed at all times and ready to play hostess. Her mother never had untidy hair, never burped or gave off any unpleasant smells – not once – nor would she tolerate unpleasant smells. How was that possible for a young girl to live up to?

Even when her mother drank too much, she became more graceful. Only in rare moments – for instance, when Deola noticed her mother's sanitary towels – did she regard her mother as a woman. How her mother met her father, why her mother did not get along with Brother Dotun's wife, all that remained unexamined because coming to terms with her mother's humanity would have been as cataclysmic as the earth losing gravity.

Her mother was a voice mostly, yelling from somewhere in the distance, 'Will you stop the caterwauling?' Or a spectre, appearing out of nowhere to mete out punishments. She was not the stricter parent; she was just always around.

Once when her grandfather, the only grandparent she knew, was ill, her mother left home to stay with him for a week, and for the first time, her father was left in charge at home. That week, her father would come back from work smelling of cigars and air conditioning. She and Jaiye would take off his shoes. He would watch the news and they would eat dinner together. He would say, 'That's enough,' if they laughed too hard or kicked each other under the table. After dinner, he would pour himself a glass of whisky. He never went to the kitchen. He would ask one of them to call the housegirl or the cook if he needed any help.

That week, Jaiye had a toothache. She woke Deola up at night. She was crying. Deola thought Jaiye had had a bad dream and all she needed was to say 'Get thee behind me Satan' three times, but Jaiye wouldn't stop crying. Deola went to their parents' room and knocked. She knocked about four times and her father never answered, so she opened the door and he was there, lying face up and snoring. The corridor light didn't wake him up. The room smelled of her mother's perfume. Her mother's negligee was hanging on the knob of the wardrobe.

For a moment, Deola watched her father. His face was narrower, dragged back. She shook his shoulders and said, 'Daddy, Jaiye has a toothache.' He grunted and rolled over, almost slapping her. 'Jaiye has a toothache, Daddy,' she said, but he continued to snore. 'Daddy,' she repeated.

Then he answered, 'For goodness' sake, what is it now?'

Now? she thought. She had not given him any trouble. That was her mother's final instruction. 'Don't give your father any trouble.' Even Lanre, who was asleep in his bedroom, was behaving himself. 'Jaiye has a toothache,' she said, tearfully. Her father was the one who bought Jaiye the chocolates that rotted her teeth.

He took a while to get up, then he scratched his shoulder. He was wearing navy pyjamas. 'Where is she?' he asked.

'In her bed,' Deola said.

'Bring her to me,' he said.

Jaiye was sobbing and holding her cheek, which felt hot. Deola led Jaiye to her father. His bedside lamp was on.

'What's wrong?' he asked Jaiye.

Jaiye leaned over. 'My mouth is paining me.'

'Do you brush well at night?' he asked.

Jaiye nodded, but Deola knew Jaiye didn't.

'Does she brush well at night?' he asked Deola.

'Yes,' Deola said.

Jaiye howled, 'Yow!'

'Don't weep,' her father said.

Don't weep? Deola thought. Her mother would never say that. Her mother would get a Panadol, cut it in half and go downstairs to get a cold Fanta so that Jaiye wouldn't throw up. Why couldn't her father do the same? She felt terrible for Jaiye and for him. In the morning he would come to realize what he had done. He would be sorry.

'It comes in spurts, Daddy,' she explained, and it was such a mature word to use, 'spurts'.

Jaiye started blubbering and her father stood up and asked, 'Where does your mother keep her medicine?' Deola went to the drawer. She was there all the time looking through her mother's Estée Lauder makeup, nail polishes, old letters, postcards, cards and photographs. The drawer was like a treasure chest.

She found the Panadol and a razor blade and told her father to cut the Panadol in half. Her father cut the Panadol on her mother's dressing table, not on a saucer, as her mother would. He cut a line in the table and muttered, 'Get me my glasses.'

Deola got his glasses and accompanied him downstairs as Jaiye sat on the bed, holding her cheek and rocking. Downstairs she took the kitchen key out of the silver teapot and opened the kitchen door. The kitchen was warm. There was no Fanta in the fridge and Jaiye was not allowed to drink

Coca-Cola, so she went to the storeroom, where the sacks of *garri* and crates of soft drinks were kept. Her mother's china plates, calabashes, steel pots and aluminium bowls were on the shelves. She could smell camphor balls, which kept cockroaches away. She got a bottle of Fanta from a crate.

Her father was waiting in the kitchen, holding half a Panadol. She opened the bottle of Fanta and he poured it into one of the glasses for grown-ups. Then he walked out without any ice. She locked the kitchen door and was returning the key to the teapot when she saw him pour whisky from a decanter into the Fanta.

Jaiye gagged when she drank the Fanta. 'This Fanta tastes funny,' she whispered.

Her father asked, 'What's funny about it?'

'It's bitter,' Jaiye said.

'It will help you sleep,' he said, patting Jaiye's head. 'That's a good girl. No more crying. Mummy will be back home soon.'

Jaiye kept heaving, but she drank it up.

There is a semblance of order at home that is deceptive. Nothing works. The taps in her bathroom are fixed on wrong: the hot water runs cold and the cold water runs hot. The mosquito netting on her window is ripped in several places and the window doesn't quite shut, so mosquitoes fly in and the air conditioner is not cool enough. Deola turns it to high and starts to keep a record of the anti-malarial pills she takes. Her doctor says the pills won't affect her baby, but she worries anyway. At night, before her mother switches off the electricity generator, she sprays her bedroom with mosquito repellent and sets a battery-operated lantern by her bedside table.

The church next door holds a spiritual clinic and their amplified singing keeps her up.

We are saying thank you, Jesus,
Thank you, my Lord.
We are saying thank you, Jesus,
Thank you, my Lord.

She is still not able to figure out if a man or a woman leads the congregation, but she looks out of her window and gets a back view of their legs and shoes. They *are* arrogant – to think that by raising their voices God will hear them above everyone else. Her mother seems to have accepted their singing, as she has other malfunctions in the house. After dinner, Deola opened the kitchen door and the doorknob dropped off. Deola asked for a screwdriver and her mother picked up the doorknob and whacked it back in with her hand.

In the morning it is the same. Her mother has two phone lines, which are both dead, so she uses a mobile phone. She still doesn't have a driver, so getting around will be tedious. Deola shows her mother how to turn on the cable television, a service for which her mother pays and forgets to use. The cable company is based in South Africa, and here in Nigeria, they can watch CNN and American sitcoms. Her mother enjoys *Everybody Loves Raymond*.

Lanre drops in at lunchtime. Deola has no idea when he found out she is pregnant or who told him, but he pats her shoulder and says, 'Hang in there.' For an awkward moment he looks as if he is contemplating doing the Ali shuffle around her and punching her, anything that might take her back to her asexual days.

They laugh about the doorknob and the frozen food. Lanre says her mother doesn't throw anything away and is reluctant to spend money on repairs. He spends practically all he earns on his house so he can live comfortably. He has a well on standby for water shortages, during which his houseboy pumps water to filter and boil. Diesel is his biggest expense because of his electricity generator.

'That's if you can find diesel to buy,' he says. 'That's if, when you buy the diesel, they haven't gone and mixed it with something that can ruin your generator.'

Deola panics, not at the idea of sending drivers on diesel explorations or making them queue overnight during petrol shortages, but ending up with that warped air of self-satisfaction people in Lagos have when they talk about their daily ordeals. Lanre advises her to sell her Peugeot 205 and buy a Peugeot 505, which can easily be serviced.

'Since you're a Peugeot person,' he says. 'But let me warn you, armed robbers like Peugeots.'

'How will I manage?' she asks.

'Small matter,' he says.

With relish, he tells her about the other difficulties she will face: traffic, poor quality repairs and servicing, stupid and devious house help. Mosquitoes. Good schools are expensive and so is pediatric food and medicine. Any serious illness and she would have to get on the next flight to London, if she wants to survive.

'I'm just warning you,' he says, when he notices her expression. 'There is so much frustration here. Too much. People will harass you, insult you and waste your time. They can't stand to see you happy or successful. They must bring you down somehow, and they're not the ones who are trying to rob you of your money, or your life. Every day, you're fighting to hold on to what you have and to stay alive. What you will go through here will make you want to run back to London. That is Lagos for you.'

'Why does everyone keep saying I should come home, then?' she asks.

'Because,' he says, 'abroad, you can have it all – money, good health and security – and it's as if someone is chipping away at your backbone every day with that racialism rubbish. I can't deal with that.'

On Saturday, Lanre visits her again, this time with Eno and the boys. They eat pounded yam and okra stew for lunch and afterward, instead of allowing the boys to watch a DVD, they entertain them with stories about the Lagos of their childhood. For the boys, this is like a history lesson. They have never played in their neighbourhood because it is too dangerous: armed robbers might attack. They are transported from an air-conditioned car to an air-conditioned room because of malaria.

'Remember when that sports car almost ran you over?' Deola asks.

'It was a Porsche,' Lanre says.

'He asked the driver if he could take a look inside afterwards. Can you imagine?'

'I was a bush boy. It was the first I'd ever seen in my life. What was I to do? Remember when I fell out of the pawpaw tree and I almost concussed myself?'

'Where was Mummy when this was happening?' Deola asks.

'Mrs Bello,' Lanre asks. 'Where were you when your children were roaming the streets aimlessly after school?'

Her mother is in the sitting room. She can't hear what they are saying because she is listening to a Pearl Bailey album. 'Takes Two to Tango' is playing.

'Taking a siesta,' Lanre says, 'and dreaming of Harry Belafonte. Day-O! Day-O!'

Eno laughs harder than the boys, who might not have not heard of Harry Belafonte. Eno might also be settling a grudge. Deola's mother has treated her the same way she treated Deola, ignoring her comments and accusing her of absenteeism.

'Remember Plaza Cinema?' Lanre asks.

'How can I forget?' Deola says. 'That's where we first saw a film in a cinema, *Born Free*, and those badly behaved American kids kept putting their feet up on our chairs. Remember how Jaiye told Mummy you bought cigarettes there when you just bought bubblegum cigarettes?'

'Jaiye was an Amebo.'

'Amebo!' Eno says. 'I remember her! Wasn't she the gossip on *Village Headmaster*? Now, I wish you boys could see that on DVD. Remember Doctor Bassey?'

'Dio, dio,' Deola sings.

'What?' Timi asks.

'Dr Bassey was a character on *Village Headmaster*,' Eno explains. 'He was Efik, like Grandpa. He sang like this: "dio, dio".'

'What is *Village Headmaster*?'

'It was a TV programme.'

'Come,' Lanre asks. 'Didn't you steal my Lorne Greene trading cards?'

Deola laughs. 'I never stole your Lorne Greene trading cards.'

'You did, and I beat you up.'

'Why were you always attacking your sisters?' Eno asks. 'Couldn't you find a little boy to pick on?'

'She deserved it.'

'Don't worry,' Deola says. 'My father beat the crap out of him.'

Lanre nods. 'Very abusive family, the Bellos.'

'What are Lorne Greene trading cards?' Timi asks.

'Like Pokémon cards, darling,' Eno explains. 'Yu-Gi-Oh and all that.'

'You had those?'

'They were only a penny,' Deola says.

'You had pennies?' Banwo asks.

'Pounds, shillings and pence before naira and kobo.'

'When we changed currency,' Lanre says, 'we couldn't go out to play for a while because of *gbomo gbomo*.'

'What is *gbomo gbomo*?' Timi asks.

'I know,' Banwo says, raising his hand. 'Kidnappers.'

The boys don't speak Efik or Yoruba. They only speak English. If asked they will say they are Nigerian.

'We were told they would cut off our heads and use us for juju,' Lanre says.

Timi holds his neck. 'Oh, Mummy, I feel sorry for you.'

'I was in England then,' Eno says, smiling. 'We didn't have juju over there.'

'Come on, clear off,' Lanre says. 'Calabar juju is the most potent.'

'We're talking about England now.'

'England has juju! What's the difference between psychics and *babalawo*?'

'We drove on the left side of the road,' Deola says to Banwo.

'Why?' Timi asks.

'Because Nigeria was a British colony.'

'What's a colony?'

Eno taps him. 'Stop asking questions. Just listen.'

'These children don't know a damn thing, man,' Lanre says. 'All they know how to do is to watch DVDs. That's why they all have ADD. Remember comics?'

'You read *Buster* and I read *Mandy*,' Deola says.

'And *Archie*,' Lanre says.

'I wanted a sea monkey,' Deola says.

'Your aunty and I used to ride from here to Ikoyi Club to buy comics,' Lanre says. 'Sometimes we walked. There was no traffic. Ikoyi was safe back then.'

He is still a member of Ikoyi Club, which has survived the dilapidation in Ikoyi. His driver takes the boys there. They compete in swimming competitions. Banwo is taking tennis lessons – he wants to be like Andre Agassi – and Timi wants to play golf like Tiger Woods.

'I met your mother there,' Lanre says. 'She was a heavy chick.'

Banwo pulls a face. 'Heavy?'

'You mean . . .' Timi says, widening his arms.

Eno pushes his shoulder. 'Who was fat? I was very skinny. It's because of you I put on weight.'

Timi hugs her. 'Sorry. I ruined everything.'

Eno pulls his nose. 'Look at you. Just sit still and listen for once.'

'When your mum was at Holy Child,' Deola says, 'and your dad was at Saint Greg's, he wrote her a letter saying she was the only flower in his desert.'

Banwo bangs the table. 'No! This cannot be!'

'He had an Afro, which he used to pat into shape like this. His shirts were always buttoned low, his collar stuck out and he wore a cross medallion.'

Timi covers his mouth. 'Ooh, Daddy.'

'I didn't have a medallion,' Lanre says.

'Seyi Davis had the medallion,' Eno says. 'But they both thought they were cool, with their sunshades and Old Spice.'

'Seyi D,' Lanre says. 'Are you still in touch with Bandele?'

'Yes.'

'What is he doing with himself these days?'

'Writing.'

Lanre shakes his head. 'He would be.'

'He's doing well,' Deola says.

Lanre taps his head. 'Is he still . . .?'

'That was long ago.'

'He was a strange *bobo*.'

'Too *oyinbo*,' Eno says. 'More *oyinbo* than my mum. Why was he like that?'

'Different schooling,' Deola says. 'Look at my father's family.'

Lanre gets up. 'My bottom is scratching me.'

'It must be all that pepper you keep adding to your food,' Eno says, laughing.

He goes to the toilet and she whispers, 'Or nerves. He says you and Jaiye have gone haywire and I shouldn't follow you.'

'Don't mind him. You are his whole life, you and the boys.'

'I keep reminding him.'

'You don't have to. He's not a fool. My old man made sure of that.'

Pearl Bailey is singing 'Let There Be Love' and her mother is snoring.

She and Eno share more of their childhood memories with the boys. Eno sings the jingles for Cortina shoes and Minta Supermints. The boys block their ears. Deola tells them about trips to UTC at Christmas. The store had a choo choo train, which would take her into a dark grotto. She would wave to her mother. Father Christmas was always fat and brown with cotton wool for hair. She would want to run away from him, but he would persuade her to sit on his lap and take a photograph. For what? A plastic yo-yo in a cellophane bag, every year.

After a while, they get tired of talking about when times were good for them. Lagos has changed.

Her mother is still asleep when Jaiye calls from Jamaica and wakes her. Surprisingly, Jaiye isn't upset that Lulu and Prof are with her mother-in-law. She speaks to Deola afterward.

'Let her have them,' she says. 'I'm free of that family. Don't be sad for me. Daddy is giving me strength and look, don't listen to Mummy. All she wants is for you to be married. Don't let her or Aunty Bisi push you into anything. No family meeting if you don't want one. Stand your ground.'

'I will,' Deola says, feeling tired.

'To think I cried over Funsho,' Jaiye says. 'How I abused him in front of his mother. I told him he had to leave, otherwise he would end up killing me. She said I was rude to him. Me, Jaiye. She said, "Just because your father gave you this house, you think you can treat my son like a woman." I told her to take her son. She said she would take her grandchildren, too, so I asked her, "How do you know they are yours?" She almost fainted. Funsho had to lift her up from the floor. I warned her, "Never, ever talk about my father again." She walked out, then Funsho said he would slap me if I ever insulted his mother again. Me, Jaiye. I told him that if he dared, just dared to lift his hand, he would never forget what I would do to him. He thinks I'm playing. He doesn't know me yet.'

'Princess Diana,' Deola hails her.

The closest any wife in Funsho's family came to challenging his mother was to suggest she was being unfair. Funsho had this to say about that incident, 'She was trying to do women's rights, until my brother gave her a dirty slap.'

Deola worries about repercussions. She blames Jaiye's attitude on the gangsta rap Jaiye listens to. Then it occurs to her that Jaiye is fighting for her life.

Princess Diana was gangsta, she thinks.

Wale seems to be the only sensible person around. Deola drives to his house on Sunday on the pretext that she is visiting Ivie. She would see more of him if she didn't have to give the impression that he is in Abuja. They sit on his veranda. His air conditioner is too cold. Outside the rain falls quietly and she can smell cut grass. He says he will tell his family about her after she returns to London. That way she will actually be in London when he says she is.

'You can't just lie to them?' she asks, impressed.

'It's not that,' he says. 'I like to keep my life simple.'

His life is no longer simple, thanks to her. She does most of the talking. He rests his elbow on the arm of his chair and cups one side of his face. His expression changes from dismay to amusement as she tells him about her family. Lanre will find him overly serious and will definitely think believing in time is pretentious. Jaiye would probably like him. Her mother will love him. Respectful is the exact word she will use to describe him. Calm and respectful, unlike her own children. Her father would have been disappointed. 'I don't care what the boy is like,' he would say.

'My family is crazy,' she says, after a while. 'I'm sure your family is more sane.'

'I don't know about that, but we are quieter.'

'You are quiet.'

'Me? I'm just listening.'

She wonders if she can live with a man who is this quiet, a man who was forthcoming only when the prospect of sex was imminent.

'You think my brother was right that men are incapable of monogamy?'

'You want an honest answer?'

'Yes.'

'Don't ask me, then.'

She pokes her tongue at him. She is not as anxious as she was in her twenties and is less vulnerable to being hurt.

Lanre once called her a manhater, but she genuinely liked men. Her friction with Lanre began when he sensed she no longer looked up to him, but it wasn't personal. It was only a part of Lanre's boyishness she stopped admiring. She never favoured girls. She just gave the impression she did. It was clear when she reached puberty that she had to choose what team she was on, his or hers. It wasn't that her team always played fair, but the older she got, the less tolerant she was of his team's unfair tactics. Was it simply their way? Or did the rules condone them? She didn't know, but she had to develop her own method of defence fast, especially as her team seemed less unified and prepared.

'Most men can't decide,' Wale says, unexpectedly. 'You have to decide to be with one woman, that's all.'

'It's the same for women,' she says. 'We just learn earlier on that there are consequences.'

'Hm.'

'I believe that love, trust and faith begin with a choice.'

'Is that why you're still single?' he asks.

'Why? Something must be wrong with me?'

'That's not what I said.'

'I should be asking you the same question, since you have more choices.'

'Actually,' he says, 'it's not that great to have more choices. You meet a woman and you want to get to know her, and already she's planning a wedding. Even your family is planning a wedding. No one thinks you should be single as a man because you have more choices.'

'Aw,' she says, unsympathetically.

'It's true. And it's worse when you're a widower. Six months after I lost my wife and my family was trying to get me married. My mother suggested I get married just to have someone to take care of Moyo. I was the one changing her nappies and feeding her, but I wasn't supposed to. To this day, I can't be with someone without people saying how relieved they are that she will have a mother.'

She rethinks the idea that his dating life as a single man is better than hers.

He says Moyo wants to go to boarding school in England next year because her cousin is going. The school she attends in Abuja is a Jesuit school. Students perform well on foreign examinations like O and A levels, SATs and the Baccalaureate. They end up going to universities abroad. He went to International School Ibadan and the University of Ibadan before Columbia University, but education in Nigeria is not as it used to be.

'Boarding school in England,' she says, uncertainly.

She remembers arriving at Heathrow Airport and being questioned over the validity of her student visa, walking through Nothing to Declare and hoping that customs officers wouldn't search her luggage. She was always nervous about having enough taxi fare and it was disconcerting to see so many black people in London sporting dreadlocks and walking fast. Back home, walking fast and dreadlocks were signs of madness.

'Things have changed,' he says. 'It's not like before. There are so many Nigerian kids in school there now. They have mobile phones and they can text and call home whenever they want.'

'It's a new millennium,' she says.

Nigerian students in England are definitely more integrated now. Whenever she sees them in one group or another, they look like Benetton adverts. She watches them with admiration.

'She's excited,' he says. 'It will prepare her for universities overseas. Universities here are a mess. I hire graduates who can't construct a basic letter. I spend half my time training them and the worst part is, you finish training them and they leave. We're always recruiting new staff. It's never-ending.'

'That's one area I could go into,' she says.

'Recruiting?'

'No, training. I have been around enough businesses and organizations to know how they should work.'

'Good idea,' he says. 'You will have competition, but in this place, even trainers need training.'

He tells her about his staff's incompetence and lack of professionalism. She is convinced he is exaggerating to amuse her. Recently, he had to sack a waiter for pestering his guests for tips, and he once caught a housekeeper sleeping in the room she was meant to be cleaning.

Deola feels more relaxed with him, but later, as he walks her to her car, she gets self-conscious again. She makes a move to hug him and their ears collide.

'Listen,' he says, stepping back. 'I'm glad about this. At first I was a bit . . . but I'm glad now.'

'Glad?' she asks.

'Aren't you?'

'Glad isn't the word,' she says.

'Can you think of another?'

She searches the sky, which has since cleared, as if it might collapse on them.

'Terrified,' she says.

'Of what?'

'Can I do it on my own? How will I cope?'

She doesn't know where she stands with him, other than being the accidental mother of his child.

'You're not on your own,' he says.

'I know married couples,' she says. 'They're not compatible.'

'Don't worry. We will be fine.'

He holds her face as if he is tired of talking and she chooses to believe him.

For Good

The rainy season is almost over. She calls Wale before she leaves, to say goodbye. He flies back to Abuja on the day of her return flight. As usual, she is eager to leave Lagos at the end of her stay, but the moment she arrives in London, she begins to miss Lagos.

It is autumn and her flat is cold. She wraps herself up in her duvet, contemplating the coming months. At least she won't have to answer intimate questions. At least her mother will be spared the embarrassment of having to tell family friends she is pregnant. At least she will be able to turn her attention to becoming a mother. It is a voluntary exile, after which she will return to Lagos. She will not miss London, but she will miss her flat.

As her sitting room heats up she calls Tessa and Bandele. She expects Tessa's reaction when she tells Tessa how she managed to deflect calls for a family meeting.

'Gosh, why don't they all just sod off?' Tessa asks.

'It's family,' Deola says. 'What can one do?'

'I suppose.'

Tessa has given up control over her wedding plans. She says Peter has asked his father to be his best man.

'All I need now is for him to say his dad's organizing his buck's night,' she says.

'With strippers,' Deola says.

'I can't believe you're going back to Nigeria.'

'I'm going home!'

'But you've been here so long.'

'I'm not getting anywhere, Tess.'

'But you never said.'

'Because you wouldn't understand.'

'Why wouldn't I understand?'

'You just wouldn't.'

'But you never gave me a chance to.'

'It's not about you, Tessa.'

'I didn't say it was.'

'Just admit you wouldn't understand.'

'There are good and bad people everywhere!'

'There's also "your people" and "my people", and if you choose to ignore that, there's no point in us getting into an argument.'

'Fine. I give up, then.'

'Thanks. That's all I ask.'

'I tell you what,' Tessa says. 'If you do end up marrying this man, think very carefully before you commit yourself to a wedding. It's rubbish, the white dress and everything. It's completely commercialized now. You should see how much the flowers are costing us. What a nightmare. I can't believe people do this in Nigeria as well.'

Deola can't believe anyone would want to be married after the acrimony she has witnessed, but she wouldn't mind a civil ceremony. Her lack of imagination is inexplicable, coming from a country where she has seen so many ways of cohabiting, a country where she could have been handed over to a man at the age of twelve, under the guise of respectability.

She describes the traditional engagement ceremony Jaiye went through a week before her church wedding. Funsho's family wore red *aso ebi* and hers were in blue. They sat on opposite sides of the garden under canopies. Funsho arrived with his relatives and they were given the usual snub and made to wait outside the gate for almost an hour. When her father consented, Funsho and his entourage were finally allowed in. Funsho prostrated himself on the grass in his white lace *agbada* and everyone cheered. Jaiye was indoors for most of the ceremony, which alternated between prayers and sexual innuendo, then Jaiye came outside, led by her own entourage. She knelt before Funsho, chose the Bible over the bag of money and everyone cheered again.

The ceremony went on for over four hours. Their house was packed with guests. Relatives Deola had never seen in her life wandered into her bedroom to ask for safety pins and extra plates. Jaiye changed outfits for the night party. She must have worn about ten outfits that week. After her church wedding and reception, there was another night party at home, then she was taken to Funsho's house, where Funsho's people removed her shoes and poured water from a calabash on her feet. That was followed by more prayers and yet another night party that went on until after midnight.

'I'd hang myself if I had to go through that,' Tessa says.

Tessa's father will walk her down the aisle. He will not remember her wedding and is beginning to forget who she is. He might eventually have to go into a home, but her mother is refusing to consider that option.

'It's getting harder on her,' Tessa says. 'And there's only so much I can do. It's awful, Alzheimer's. It's everywhere, and it will only get worse as people live longer and longer. There's no support here. I'm sure you have a lot more support in Nigeria, with extended families.'

Deola isn't sure. She is loath to idealize Nigerian culture. Her family is not typical, but is hardly unique. She imagines that if people are incapacitated in their old age, and they have the means, they are treated better. If they don't have the means, they are likely to be seen as burdens. But she can't think of many Nigerians her age who have both parents alive and she can't name one Nigerian her age who has a grandparent alive.

'People don't live that long back home,' she says. 'Our lifespan is getting shorter and shorter.'

'We can't win,' Tessa says, 'either way.'

Bandele has never been interested in her womanly problems. He grunts as she tells him about her trip to Lagos and when she is through asks, 'Hey, you know when you got tested, how long was it before you found out the result?'

'The same day.'

'Yeah?'

'Yes. Why?'

'I'm thinking of having one. I haven't had one in ages – what with everything else I've had to deal with. But it's been bothering me ever since you said it. I should do something about it, shouldn't I?'

She is more protective of him. She wants to tell him off for being irresponsible, but she imagines what it is like to have to be tactical about the most ordinary conversations. Perhaps he has even lost friends. It still bothers her that he deceived her, but perhaps she knew all along that he was keeping a secret. She was aware of his manner of steering the focus away from himself. His charades of being prickly were marvelously timed.

'Anytime you're ready,' she says. 'I'll take you there.'

'Thanks. I couldn't handle it otherwise. You know how you can be close to someone, but they don't understand why things are different for you because you're Nigerian.'

'I know,' she says.

She can't promise he will be fine. She couldn't even predict the outcome of his literary competition. She won't mention prayer. He might take offence. He thinks only thick people pray.

'We'll go to Paris,' she says. 'After it's over.'

Paris, she thinks. How ridiculous, but he doesn't have a retort.

'How's Ola?' he asks.

'His name is not Ola.'

'You haven't said much about him.'

'I've mentioned his name.'

'When?'

'Think!'

'It's confusing! You keep going on about all these inconsequential people! Ola, Bola, Fola!'

'What is his name, Bandele?'

'I'm just saying.'

'I knew you weren't listening.'

He laughs. 'I can always tell when you've been to Nigeria.'

'How?'

'The hostility quotient goes right up.'

All she remembers is that she was loved there and surrounded by people she knew, Olas, Bolas and Folas.

She reads him the telephone number of the clinic and

after she hangs up begins to research business training on the Internet.

An e-mail comes from Kate, who has seen her report on the malaria NGO. Kate considers her criticism of LINK's vetting policies 'a gross betrayal', to Deola's surprise. She says it makes her and Graham look bad. Deola never thought Kate was capable of being confrontational. She skims the rest of the e-mail, her eyes resting on phrases like 'I fought for those programmes', 'Graham was reluctant to offer you the position' and 'We were both concerned that you were so eager to accept a salary that was clearly not commensurate with your experience.'

To Deola, the e-mail reads like, 'Deliveries are through the side entrance.'

She types: *You stupid cow.*

She hits delete.

She types: *Evidently, I did not know you as well as I thought I did.*

She hits delete.

She types: *Perhaps you were not listening when I told you.*

Then she trashes Kate's e-mail. Why bother to reply? She is going home, where she will have a lot to deal with, but not this rubbish any more.

On Thursday evening she drives Bandele to the clinic. He smells of cigarettes and Thai food. It is too cold to have her window down and she is gambling again, speeding through traffic lights after Vauxhall Bridge.

'Will you slow down?' he asks.

She gambles the other way around when she gets to Camberwell, waiting for traffic lights to change to red.

'Um, could you go a little faster?' he asks.

She turns on her car CD player and they listen to 'Love All the Hurt Away'. The song makes her want to cry. Her legs are shaking. The symptoms she had when she first went to the clinic are back.

'Who's this?' Bandele asks.

'Aretha and George Benson.'

'Is it an old one?'

'Eighties.'

He huffs. 'I hate eighties music. I hate duets.'

Bandele listens to black music so old it's gone white. He bites his bottom lip. She would give him a pat on the shoulder, but that might mean he has something to worry about. She ejects the CD. It is a relic she recorded, labelled *Ballads*.

They get to the clinic and Bandele, who normally refuses to identify himself as Nigerian, begins to show signs of the most common Nigerian phobia – of situations that remind him of his mortality. He is so petrified that he huddles over as he walks from the car park to the clinic. It is not that cold this evening.

'Are you all right?' she asks.

'Yeah,' he mumbles.

He waits for her to speak to the receptionist. She has to fill out his registration form. He can't think of a suitable fake name other than 'J. M. Coetzee'.

'No one will be able to pronounce that,' she says. 'What about James Baldwin?'

He nods. The waiting room is full. She wonders how many of them will know who James Baldwin is. The receptionist calls out his name and Bandele, who once called Nigerians a bunch of backward religious fanatics, lets out a cry, 'Christ!'

He doubles over. The receptionist comes to his aid. 'Are you all right? Does he speak English?'

Everyone watches as Deola helps him up. She assures the receptionist that he is fine and speaks English. She leads him to the doctor's office and prods him in. She prays as she waits, begging, whining, accusing and bargaining, conscious that she has prayed harder here than she has in any church. If only she could go to clinics every Sunday.

Bandele comes out still huddled over. Instead of stopping in the waiting room, he walks out of the clinic and she follows him to her car.

'Open the door,' he says.

He sits in her car. She knocks on the window several times, but he won't wind it down. She gets into the car. What should she do now? Drive off? Call the police?

She, too, has another common Nigerian phobia – of mental illness. She makes some attempt to rub his back. When it looks as if he is unlikely to budge she ends up going back to the clinic to get his results.

The receptionist is pleasant as usual. 'I'll send you in when Dr Srinivasan is free.'

'Thanks,' Deola says.

She hoped she would never see Dr Srinivasan again in her life. She waits another ten minutes for the doctor, whose expression has not changed. Nor have her clothes. She wears the same black shirt under her white coat and the same ornamental gold earrings. It is almost as if she has been waiting for Deola's return.

'He's had a breakdown before,' Deola says. 'I didn't think this would trigger another one. I just want you to tell me if he's okay. I'll tell him if you want. There is no guarantee how he will take it.'

'I can't do that,' Dr Srinivasan says.

Her demeanour suggests she may not have encouraging news, but Deola is unsure: perhaps she is just irritated.

'Please,' Deola says. 'All I need is a hint. I won't say anything to him.'

She rubs her leg, which has since gone numb. Why Bandele? After everything he has been through. The traffic lights were not in his favour.

'We'd better get out there,' Dr Srinivasan says.

As they approach her car, they don't see Bandele and Deola hurries over. He is still there, but his forehead is practically on his knees. She knocks on his window again. What has she caused? Is he in shock? Dr Srinivasan motions to her to wait and gets into the driver's seat. Bandele sits up obediently and Deola leans on her car, unable to watch. She stands up straight when Dr Srinivasan comes out.

'He's fine,' Dr Srinivasan says.

Deola shakes her hand. 'Thank you.'

Dr Srinivasan smiles. 'He might want to go to somewhere else next time. Somewhere he can get the care he needs.'

Dr Srinivasan returns to the clinic with a heroic strut. Deola gets into the driver's seat and Bandele is now slumped against the window.

'Are you all right?' she asks.

'Yeah.'

'Sorry I brought you here.'

'It was my fault.'

'I'm glad your test was okay.'

'Me too. I didn't mean to give you a scare.'

His contrition doesn't last. On the way back, she is driving past Kennington Park when her phone rings and she asks him to answer it. The lights of the tennis courts are already on. The call has to be from someone at home, her family or Wale calling to check up on her. Wale never speaks for long, but he writes her e-mails asking if she is keeping well and getting sufficient rest. She laughs out loud at his accounts of the daily events in his hotel he calls 'Fawlty Towers'. He always ends with a 'Looking forward to your safe return. Yours, Wale.'

'Wally who?' Bandele asks.

Deola signals to him to hand her the phone.

'No, you haven't got the wrong number,' he says. 'No, she can't take your call right now.'

'Give me the phone,' Deola says.

Bandele dodges her. 'I'm her friend. Pardon? I said I'm her friend. Yes. We're off to Paris. Pardon? Yes, I'm sure she'll call you when we get back.'

He cuts Wale off. Deola keeps her eye on a cyclist ahead.

'Why did you do that?'

'He'll get over it.'

'Bloody hell, that was so childish of you. We're finally beginning to talk.'

'He'd better do more than talk.'

'I can't believe this. I don't play games. Give me that phone.'

'God, I feel as if I've taken a sleeping pill after speaking to him.'

'Give me my phone back!'

'No.'

'Bandele!'

'No! And I'll tell you this, this isn't another job in Wolverhampton!'

'Wembley!'

'Wherever. You'd better get more demanding. He'd better

know what you're worth. This might be your last chance out of spinsterhood.'

'Oh, shut up.'

'No! The least he can do while you're getting fat is call you!'

'Give me back my phone.'

'Go on, then. Call him, if you must.'

She doesn't, but she has had enough of Bandele. She decides she won't see him for a while.

'I can't go to Paris with you,' she says.

'Why not?' he asks.

'I'm not allowed to travel in my first trimester.'

He looks her up and down. 'You little liar.'

She doesn't admit to lying and she resists pushing him out of her car when she drops him off. He takes too long to say goodbye.

'I just don't want to see you acting so feeble any more,' he says. 'No, really. I don't think you get it. I don't think you get it yet. You need to be more demanding. I know I may go on at you about this or that, but you're a good friend. A really good friend, and I'll miss you when you're gone. No, really, I will. Don't look at me in that way. I'm being serious here, for once, and I just . . . I just don't want anyone taking advantage of you. Why do you keep looking at me like that?'

She wants to go. Wale might be calling her at home.

'I'm serious. He'd better be nice to you. That's all I'm saying. I don't know what he's like, but if he's anything like the others, then don't do that to yourself.'

'I won't,' she says, to hurry him.

'Good, because you're better than that. You are, Old Fanny, and it's time you start demanding more. You can't be too timid. "There are casualties, but there is nothing to fear." Those were your words.'

'When did I say that?'

He smiles. 'Well, to paraphrase.'

She is exhausted. Bandele exhausts her like no one else.

'Say hello to Charlie,' she says.

He raises a brow, then seems to remember he is having a kind moment.

'I will.'

'Does your family ever ask why you're not married?'

'No.'

'That's good. It's good you're a man.'

'It's good that I am mad. It has its advantages.'

'Is your novel about you and Charlie?'

He eyes her. 'Why?'

'You've done autobiographical before. Is it about two men?'

'I think I have enough imagination to write about an unsuited hetero couple. If I don't, I have you and Wally What's-it to use as muses.'

She would like to ask if his characters save their relationship in Paris, but that would be gambling yet again.

He imitates her cheerless expression as she drives off. He is not mad; he is extremely annoying. Her oblivion still astonishes her. It is odd to imagine him with a man. She would like to think he is faithful. She hopes he will finish his novel.

When she gets home, Wale hasn't called back or left a message on her phone. The least he can do and he hasn't even done that. Why would she expect more from him? She eats dinner and still no phone call from him.

Tonight she watches a Hollywood film that takes place

during a genocide in an imaginary African country. The usual elements are in the film: the benevolent missionary priest; the hopeful expatriate and cynical foreign journalist who has a change of conscience; the sidekick African intellectual and the corrupt local politician. Red-eyed African military men drive around in trucks brandishing machine guns. Arrogant UN troops are unsympathetic to the hungry refugees and barefoot children. The children run after their trucks. A token pet dog gets slaughtered. There is much drumming and singing and panoramic shots of green hills. Normally, she allows herself to be seduced, but not today. It is painful to watch, almost as if a mass sacrifice has taken place so the journalist and the expatriate can fall in love.

She has never recognized this Africa. She is increasingly dissatisfied with what she sees on television about Africa, most especially on the news. Not the barrage of news clips on wars and poverty-stricken villages – after all, they are not made up – but the lack of perspective and continued absence of her experiences.

What she would give to see a boring old banker going on about capital growth, as they do in Nigeria, just for once. Why not? Don't they exist? Don't they count? Or are they so well assimilated into the rest of the world that they are no longer visible? Or – and this would be a conspiracy of the most tragic consequence – are Westerners, now that Africans readily process themselves for Western consumption, developing a preference for Africans who are pure and unadulterated?

Morning sickness is meant to prepare her womb for her child. She is beginning to believe it is also preparing her as well because it is becoming more and more trying to get up and eat breakfast, yet she does. She has to get enough nutrients and stay active. She thinks of her growing child as a friend, a friend she is getting acquainted with. She must have grown up to some extent because she is able to put her fears aside, and what might have been a sense of failure is now a determination to be worthy of being a mother.

On Saturday afternoon she is recovering from her breakfast of cereal and banana when her doorbell rings. She thinks it is Subu again, but looking out of her window, she can't see Subu's Audi. She takes off her dressing gown and changes into sweatpants. It is a cold day. She opens the door of her flat and Wale is walking up the stairs.

'What are you doing here?'

'I came to see you.'

'Who let you in?'

'Your neighbour. She was on her way out.'

She hugs him out of shock, but he doesn't hold her.

'What's wrong?' she asks.

'Can we?' he asks, pointing indoors.

'What for?'

'I want to talk to you.'

'About?'

'You want to talk out here?'

She crosses her arms. 'It depends what you have to say.'

'Paris.'

'That's why you came?'

He shuts her door after he walks in and looks around as if he expects to find an orgy.

'I don't know what is going on,' he says, 'but I have just told my family about you. You don't want to meet them? Fine. You have other men in your life? Fine with me. All I need to know is if you are pregnant or not. I also have the right to know if you have jeopardized my health. Now, I'm sure you have evidence of the tests you've had and I want to see them.'

Jeopardize. She is still a little nauseous. She will always associate her love for him with nausea. She goes to her bedroom and retrieves her tests from the drawer by her bed and hands them to him.

'Are you satisfied?' she asks, as he reads.

'What was the phone call I had with that man about?'

'I've known him longer than I've known you.'

'You didn't mention you were going to Paris.'

Typical, she thinks. The moment he opens up, he is given to acts of heroism, flying across the Sahara to stand on her head and stick a flag in her arse.

'He's gay,' she says.

'He sounded gay.'

'He sounded English.'

'Is he Nigerian?'

'Why? Are you interested?'

He smiles. 'Sorry.'

'It's all right,' she says, shaking her head. 'When did you arrive?'

'This morning.'

'Where are you staying?'

'A hotel.'

'A hotel where?'

'In Bayswater.'

She never thought she would have to humble herself.

'You could have stayed with us.'

'Us?' he asks.

Again, that quick inspection of her flat. Where does he

think these men are hiding? On her ceiling? His puzzlement turns to remorse when he realizes what she means. He reaches for her, but she lifts her hand as if his might burn her.

'What?' he says. 'I can't hold your hand?'

'No.'

'Why not?'

'Because it belongs to me.'

'African woman,' he says, 'your trouble is too much.'

He presses his hand to her belly. She has forgotten how sensual he is and she doesn't stop him. He traces the dark line from her navel down. Her desire for him overwhelms her. Now he holds her and she abandons her misgivings for his warmth.

'Is there a pharmacy around?' he asks.

'Why?'

'I don't have anything on me.'

'No more pharmacies.'

'After all you've been through?'

'You're as paranoid as I am. I can safely say that.'

He ruffles her hair. In her bedroom, she turns on her CD player. She still owns one and Bandele may not appreciate her *Ballads* CD, but she is sure Wale will. It has other songs, like Womack and Womack's 'Baby, I'm Scared of You', Patti Labelle and Grover Washington, Jr's 'The Best Is Yet to Come', Brenda Russell's 'It's Something' and Luther Vandross's version of 'If Only for One Night'.

Wale sits on her bed and he tries to disguise his impatience as she makes him sit opposite her, but she has no remorse. Where did it get her when he led? He shifts closer, looking unsure about this manoeuvre until he is inside her. His hands stray to her thighs and she pats his stomach.

'You have no meat on you.'

'People keep telling me I need a wife to make me fatter.'

'You need someone. Your crotch is going grey.'

'From experience.'

'I have questions for you.'

'What questions?'

'Has anyone ever told you you look Hausa?'

'I am Hausa.'

'What!'

'My grandfather was. My mother's maiden name is Sanusi. Why?'

'Oh God, don't tell me you're a bloody mullah.'

'Please, don't ruin this.'

She claps. 'I should have known. A Muslim terrorist. I want immediate answers.'

'Using torture tactics?'

'If necessary.'

He winces. 'Go on then, ask.'

He is not ideal. She has to coax him to talk, and he snores in the early hours, but the next morning, he follows her to the bathroom when she throws up and watches her wash her face and brush her teeth. As she pees, he hurries out, covering his nose. She laughs, though her pee hurts. He makes her toast and burns it. She has to go back to bed after eating the toast. He leaves the flat to buy newspapers and shaving paraphernalia. She falls asleep and wakes up when she hears her radio. She doesn't listen to the radio and she can't believe the number of newspapers he has bought. After he takes a shower, he lies on her couch in his boxer shorts and reads them. She sits on the carpet beside him wrapped in her dressing gown.

His mother is a Muslim. He was raised as a Christian because his father was. He went to church and to the mosque, celebrated Muslim and Christian holidays, as she did. He speaks Yoruba and Hausa. He thinks her mother was lenient. His mother was strict: Nigerian strict. Nigerian strict meant that you didn't dare misbehave in the first place. He never resented his mother's strictness, and he is thankful for it now. He was eight when a boy called him a bastard. The boy didn't mean it literally but he beat the boy up. He took a trip with his father only once, when he was about eleven. They travelled from Lagos to Sokoto and he began to see how small Nigeria really is. He wants a son. He will be a present father, not like his. Moyo will testify what a pain he is. She is the only reason he was (he changes 'am' to 'was') afraid to die.

She says if they have a son, she will call him Babajide, to honour his father and hers. He agrees that Jide is a solid traditional name.

On the front cover of the newspaper he is reading is a headline about soldiers who were killed in Iraq by friendly fire. Deola has not thought about the war in a while and all she wants is to see Wale's face again. Her skin smells of his sandalwood. There isn't a part of her body his hands and tongue have not touched. She tasted herself on his lips and fell asleep with him inside her. He told her she is beautiful. No man has ever described her as beautiful. They might say she is attractive.

'You don't read books?' she asks, still looking at the newspaper headline.

'Hardly ever.'

'How come?'

'I just don't.'

'I can't be with someone who doesn't read books.'

'Do manuals count?'

'No.'

'I can't be with an Apple-user, then,' he says.

She tosses the newspaper and lies on top of him. He shouts as his glasses topple off and holds her differently, with less urgency. He pats her when he becomes uncomfortable. She gets up and moons him when he continues to read. She, too, is used to being alone. She goes to her bathroom and sees he has left her toilet seat up. She will let him off, just this once. She lowers her toilet seat and removes his shaving cream from her sink.

He will be in London for ten days. He doesn't want to go to Paris for a weekend. He prefers to go to Barcelona. She agrees to go. She has never been there. In the afternoon, when her nausea subsides, she drives to his hotel, the Hilton in Hyde Park, which is nearer Queensway than Bayswater tube station. She parks in a pay-and-display on a street parallel to Bayswater and they walk there. She can't think of anywhere else in the world where a five-minute walk can lead her past Chinese, Japanese, Italian, Lebanese, Indian and Persian restaurants. There are people smoking hookahs, Russian shops, Thai and Swedish massage parlors, newsagents with Arabic newspapers. Why did she think she would not miss London?

They eat at a Chinese restaurant and through the window look like one of those annoying couples, leaning close to each other. He insists on keeping his room. He says he will overstay his welcome, sensing this about her, but he promises to come back tomorrow. She promises not to interrogate him again and drives back to her flat fighting her loneliness.

Passing Maida Vale, she decides to stop at Subu's place to tell her what has happened. She has not seen Subu in a while and she regrets their past frictions. When did that begin? Not when Subu gave her life to Christ, surely. She was happy that Subu could. So when exactly did that change? When her father died, she remembers. When the idea that her father deserved to be in Hell became repulsive to her. Her father never talked about holy books or prophets, but he was a believer. She is a believer and she has looked to traffic lights for assurance, paper floating on air and the endless possibilities of creation, billions of people on earth and no two are exactly alike or share the same experience.

In Maida Vale, the streets are wider and cleaner. The dry cleaners, real estate agents, hair salons, restaurants and bars are more up-market than Willesden Green's.

Subu's Audi is parked outside her block, which means she is back from church. Her flat is on the first floor of a two-storey building with a basement. High steps lead up to the front door and an intercom system. The front garden is paved. Deola parks across the road near a telephone box and calls from her mobile phone.

She is nervous. Subu will not judge her directly, but she might say everyone is a sinner.

'Shoe Boo.'

'Deola?'

'Are you at home?'

'Yes.'

'I'm outside. Can I come in?'

Subu pauses. 'Okay.'

Deola wonders why there was a delay in Subu's response. Perhaps Subu has a new boyfriend in her church family. She gets out of her car and runs across the road. It is too cold to walk. She does not ring the bell and she hears Subu's footsteps on the staircase before Subu opens her door. Subu's hair weave is pulled back. She is in a black suit, which she must have worn to church.

'How now?' Deola asks. 'When did you get back from Shanghai?'

'I've been back for a while,' Subu says.

Subu's flat smells of incense and candles. It is full of electronic gadgets Deola can't identify, except the surround sound system. Subu has nothing hanging on her walls because she doesn't want to damage them and devalue her property. She only reads Christian books and there is a wooden shelf of them, by Joel Osteen and T. D. Jakes. Her shelf, her tables and the steel surfaces of her gadgets are crammed with saint candles, novena cards, holy water bottles and incense sticks.

'Is it Lent?' Deola asks.

'Lent is next year. My mother is here.'

'Your mother is in town?'

'She came in last week. She's in the kitchen.'

They go there as Deola tries to recall if Subu mentioned her mother was coming to London. No, Subu's mother was meant to come at Christmastime. That was the last she heard.

Not until she sees Subu's mother standing at the kitchen sink does she remember that this is exactly the scene Subu described to her: her mother coming to pray for her. Deola's legs give way and it looks as if she is kneeling.

'Adeola,' Subu's mother says. 'Is this you?'

Subu's mother is frail with copper-coloured skin. Her

hands are arthritic. She hugs Deola and asks about her family and work. She has been steaming *moin moin*. Subu begins to peel them out of wrapped foil paper.

'Come and eat,' Subu's mother says.

'Thank you, ma,' Deola says, though she is full.

'I was just asking Subu about you. If you are married and have any children.'

'No, ma.'

'You, too?'

Subu arranges the *moin moin* on a plate. Deola keeps glancing at her. Could Subu have been tested? Could Subu have tested positive?

'You young women,' Subu's mother is saying. 'You work too hard.'

'You worked hard in your day,' Subu says.

'It was different,' her mother says. 'Now, you are overseas on your own with no family to guide you. But God will guide you. You will have all you want, a good husband and children.'

'It is well,' Subu says.

Deola rubs her hands together as if she is washing them. She could be panicking unnecessarily. She can't even remember what she came for. The smell of the incense and candles is overpowering. The table hides her trembling. In time, she repeats to herself, in time, but it is unbearable to believe.

'What happened with your flat in Shanghai?' she asks.

Subu smiles. 'Man proposes, God disposes.'

Deola has always thought the saying should be the other way around. She picks up the used foil wraps and empties them in the bin as she regains her sense of calm and shoos her fears away. She is familiar with breaking bread. She can always rely on that.

'How are you?' she asks Subu.

'We're fine,' Subu says. 'We're here.'

Acknowledgements

Many thanks to my husband Gboyega Ransome-Kuti, our daughter Temi, my publisher Michel Moushabeck and my editors and proofreaders Hilary Plum, Pam Fontes-May, Markeda Wade, Miranda Dennis, Tade Ipadeola, Sarah Seewoester Cain, Stephen Guise and Mark Richards.